DARKVOID DEATHSHIP

DARKVOID DEATHSHIP

Victor, New York

For Jess, my starlight in the vast dark.

1.

Living corpses shambled across sands glazed red by the blood of conscripts and fools. Amber waves of a hungry sea lapped at the shore, grasping for bodies untouched by necromantic miasma. The tide would have its tithe of souls.

Ser Áine Kard, knight sworn in service to a lord who led thousands to pointless death on Gorgon's Head, lay buried among the human wreckage, her wounded body held together by her armor. Magical sigils—concentric circles, half-moons, and circuit-board-pattern lines—glowed blue against teal plates affixed to a black chain mesh bodysuit. The armor's aether levels remained strong, as Áine had expended very little in the preceding battle.

For half a day's time, she lay unconscious among the bodies of her shattered infantry column and foes alike. The armor had spent its energies encouraging her fractured skull to reset itself and the blood pooling in her brain to return to the vessels in which it belonged.

Her helm had saved her life by absorbing pounding blows from a foe who towered over her. The red, transparent eye lenses had cracked under the concussive force of the giant's warhammer. The holographic blue raven crest projected above her helmet had sputtered out with a coughing fit of sparks. Áine had dropped her sword and shield and fell to a knee as the world went dark around the edges. Her column had saved her by filling the giant's body with holes, drawing its attention and hammer away. It was all black after that.

The armor could create conditions to heal, but it could not call her consciousness out of the darkvoid into which her soul tumbled. Whether she survived was not a matter of the armor's magic, but of another kind entirely.

In pockets of internal illumination of death and dream:

Swirling red and purple lights and tendrils of stellar darkvoid energies emerging from the total blackness of space through an aperture in reality. A crack leading from one dream to another. A portal. Something drifting through. Metal and pulsing light, carried on waves of invisible radiation borne from the birth of the heavens. It emerges, one strut of metal and sparkling energy at a time, at a deliberate pace. Inevitable.

A flame fluttering on the edge of darkness, of smoke and nothingness.

Burning candle smell. A holy chamber of stone and mirror, solemn and at peace. An altar: a helm, a statue. A candle, the flame reaching back to her, through time, through death. Through the darkvoid, which was of her and in her, and would be forevermore.

A choice made. A prayer formed. A flame rekindled.

Áine awoke with blood dripping down her face and the mournful cries of ghosts in her ears. She had survived her first battle. The levymen of her column had not.

There was pain and there was relief. There was shame.

The light of sunset, reflected off the anxious sea, touched limbs and shattered shields, armor, and broken swords. Her helm had reformed the transparent red lenses, protecting her eyes from the sharp edges of weapon fragments, radiation, and the stinging sand and misting seawater. She reached for the light.

Her right arm was stuck. Trapped under the body of the giant. She shifted her right leg, her foot finding purchase on the shoulder of a corpse. With a grunt, she pushed. Her left leg had some freedom of movement and gained footing on the body of an armored warrior—whether hers or the enemy's, she could not say. In death, all were united.

She pushed and repositioned, and the bodies around her shifted. Already they had begun to stiffen, while others released noxious expulsions of gas or fluids that splattered against her armor. Through grue and grume she climbed for the surface, one inch, one limb, one destroyed person at a time. Corpses shifted and a great weight pressed down upon her, threatening to halt her movement, to hold her in place and keep her as one of their own. She held off panic by trusting in her armor, which vastly multiplied her own considerable physical strength. Áine focused on the *now*, as if it were the only thing that was and would ever be. Her father had imparted that lesson when she embarked on her journey to become a soldier and knight in service to her lord. His face was smoke in her memory but the wisdom lingered.

A warrior moves through each moment with perfect focus, as if it were her last. She focuses on the task— cleaning her armor, sharpening her blade, pulling her boots on, bringing her sword down upon the enemy, taking a piss—with reverence and determination. Perhaps you cannot swing a sword properly or possess the stamina to hold your shield. But you can focus on the moment, this moment, in all of its immediacy and pain.

A teal, gore-soaked gauntlet emerged from the rat king of corpses, balled into a fist in triumph. Áine roared as she pulled herself up and through the final layer of bodies, emerging waist deep from the human wreckage. She ignored the burning in her arms and pulled herself the rest of the way out, completing this ritual of gruesome rebirth with an ignoble tumble to bloody sands below.

The light of the setting sun was fire along the rolling waves. Every advance and retreat of the tide drew more of the dead out to sea. Shields glistened in the sun and bobbed on the waves. All was amber and pink. The sky was cut with slashes of alien purple. The tide baptized her in seawater, cleansing the blood from the teal plates of her armor. She breathed, feeling relief, letting her body release the near-panic that had threatened to consume her when she was trapped with the dead. Everything hurt.

A sound other than her own labored breathing and the roll of the tide caught her attention. Footsteps. Unsteady, uneven. One step, two—a drag of a foot. Another. A groan.

The dead approached: faces ruined by fire and the slash of weapons or the crush of warhammers; limbs mangled by battle but held upward, toward her, grasping and covetous. Bloody slop and guts immodestly poured out of torsos opened by spear and sword. Padded armor or chainmail shirts smeared with blood or shredded by the eldritch fires of aether. The dead of war, bent to undeath, and coming for her. A dozen of them, more, soldiers bearing the raven insignia and protective runes of her lord's house upon their breastplates and helmets. Others wore strange light armor and the now-familiar centipede banner of their enemy. Necromancy had united these factions in death with a hunger for living flesh.

Her pain forgotten in the presence of new threats, Áine pushed herself upright, spreading her armored legs apart in combat stance, balanced for maneuver. She balled her fists and felt incomplete.

My sword!

The fear that her weapon was missing was greater than that inspired by the presence of the undead. It was a primal fear, drilled and beaten into every levyman, every squire, every knight.

I am my sword.

A refrain from the training grounds in which she had lived, worked, and fought throughout her formative years. It was one of the first things they taught young aspirants entering knightly service as squires. She had recited it endlessly, even before possessing one of her own. It was the only prayer that mattered.

I am my sword.

The trainees' mantra was elemental in its simplicity, and a reminder of her first priority, now that she was back on her feet. The undead did not run, but they made for her at a steady gait. She turned back to the corpse pile and pulled bodies out with the augmented strength of her armor. She skirted the edges of the mound, her gauntlets searching for steel as the sigils in their surface glowed iridescent. The armor's glow confirmed the presence of malign magic.

She understood that she was otherwise alone on this battlefield, with no indication of victory or defeat for her side. Regardless, she would not allow herself to be caught and put to the chain or cage as a hostage or worse. No, if the enemy had prevailed, she would refuse to be a bargaining chip, as officers often were. Her rank was too lowly to be of real value, but her armor was sacred and powerful. They would peel it from her, plate by plate, piece by piece, and the flesh beneath would be made to suffer and labor for the enemy's pleasure or industry.

"I will die as a *warrior*," she said, meaning only to think it. But the words came out anyway, as they often did when her choler was up.

Now, the corpse mound bore better fruit. She pulled out and tossed aside short swords of mass-produced quality, and spears broken or too lightweight. She was considering a poleaxe when the glimmer of familiar, malign metal caught her eye. The giant's warhammer.

Its massive slab of a head was as a rock in the sediment of the dead. She reached in, mindful that the blood spattered across the head and handle was that of the levymen who had died defending her in the opening moments of the melee. She found a solid handhold on the handle and pulled with a shout. The dead released their claim. Freeing the hammer from the mound, she held it aloft, then let its weight fall against her right pauldron. It was as tall as she was, and perhaps just as heavy, but she was strong and her armor made her stronger. She raised the warhammer with a cry and turned to face the approaching horde.

They were upon her. Their hands, bent into claws, raked at her armor. Fingernails chipped and broke; mouths split open and teeth cracked against her armored limbs. Áine fell back into the corpse pile. She used the long handle of the hammer as a crossbar, shoving her foes away. More came forward, stumbling into and past their brethren, mindful only of her, of her desirable flesh, reaching, grasping.

With a flourish of strength, she raised the hammer high, then brought it down on a slouching half-creature who was all torn flesh and jagged, red-slick bone. The hammer struck squarely on its head, splitting its skull apart like a melon. The others hissed and groaned through lipless mouths and advanced with awkward stumbles, undeterred. Áine raised the hammer to her shoulder, shouting with effort, arms burning in protest, and swung again. Her blow was clumsy but the hammer and her power armor did their mean work, knocking a pointed metal helmet off one of the living corpses and collapsing its face like a pumpkin gone to rot. An explosion of blood and grey-blue brains was her reward.

Áine brought the hammer's bulky slab back up to chest level. She bent her knees and leaned forward, then charged at full strength. She smashed through a levyman's thin metal chest piece to crush ribs and burst the organs guarded within. Pink liquid sloshed from the fresh cavity and the creature tumbled back into the arms of its comrades. They let it fall to the sand and advanced again, ignoring its wheezing protests and marching through the trail of gore it had left behind.

With each exertion, the pain grew behind Áine's eyes. Her arms, even assisted by the magic and mechanisms of her armor, were already fatigued from the few swings she had managed. She tried to lift the giant's weapon again, straining and releasing a cry of frustration, before letting it fall to the sand between her and the approaching revenants. Eyeless faces, shredded flesh, clawing corpse-hands, and short swords caked in the blood of conscripts came forward. The procession of nightmares approached.

Áine scrambled backward, finding the mound of stiffening corpses suitable for climbing. The dead supported her weight. Her breathing was loud and it pounded in her helmet's enclosure, but the rushing of the waves was louder and constant. Time was against her.

The poleaxe graciously remained where she had first seen it, lying across the bodies of two women in the inexpensive footpad armor of the centipede lord's forces. Their faces, pale and beautiful in death, were spattered with dried mud and crimson slashes set in deep chasms of ruined flesh. Their faces were Áine's.

The poleaxe was fashioned in stout wood braced by steel and inscribed with the runes of the blacksmith who had bound metal to wood and magic to arm. Áine intended to honor their work, and it did not much matter for which lord's army the weapon had been crafted, for all weapons are blind to their allegiance, but eager to their purpose.

In her gauntlets it felt as nothing compared to the giant's hammer, which was now buried under sand beneath the feet of the eager horde clambering up the mound after her. She spun the poleaxe blade outward in a wide arc, slicing the skull caps off two revenants. The blacksmith's work was true after all. The dead paused, as if confused by a command issued by their line sergeant, and reached flaying fingers to probe the exposed reaches of their brains.

Áine drew upon her training with spear and pole among the fresh-cut grass and cool clay of the fighting grounds and swung again, letting the blade's sharp edge clear her foes from reach. The momentum of her swing carried the blade through pliable grey flesh and brittle bone. Heads tumbled and blood erupted in orgasmic geysers, spraying crimson across the advancing tide of water and dead alike. Decapitated corpses fell into a growing pile. She let the adrenaline and elation of violence bring a crazed smile to the face hidden behind her menacing helm. What honor she had failed to achieve in the battle proper, she might be able to recover, here.

The runes on her armor glowed hot and bright. She brought the poleaxe back for a swing at three undead levymen, who were mere steps away from the mound. Her attack was interrupted by grasping, grey hands finding her pointed metal boots. The very platform that had given her an advantage now conspired against her.

Desperate, low moans of the recently resurrected drowned out the roar of the hungry sea. The poleaxe fell from her grip and disappeared in a tangle of limbs and grey hands. Her right leg was held in place. She howled in fury and pulled free, then crouched and leapt forward, hoping her armor's strength amplification would get her airborne and free.

The armor did not fail. She landed on her chest, her head thudding into the impacted sand and sending up spikes of pain behind her eyes. Movement in the periphery signaled danger. She scrambled onto her back and into shallow water, the waves crashing against her shoulders.

The corpse mound writhed and *stood up.*

Bodies clasped together in amalgam-limbs of arms, legs, and feral visages of gnashing teeth and rending fingers. The flesh golem's emerging physiognomy defied comprehension as its dimensions assumed the contours of a humanoid giant, with feet made up of arms and hands for toes, legs of blood-soaked bodies bound together, a torso of split-open ribcages in stacked columns, and shoulders, arms, and hands of grotesque configurations of despoiled flesh. Its head was coils of entrails, stretches of leg musculature, and tiers of skulls impossibly assembled into the vague impression of a slack-jawed face. Sharp, broken bones were teeth, suddenly arrayed for mastication. There were recesses of flesh and shadows for eyes.

The mountain of the dead walked. It reached for her.

Áine rose to her feet, ignoring the pain that rippled across her skull and neck. Water lapped against her armored feet and ankles in gentle reminder of its patience. She considered turning toward the sea and trying to swim away, hoping the creature would fail to find buoyancy among the waves. Instead, she charged the giant corpse-golem, falling head first into a roll past its malformed left foot as it clumsily swung its arms toward her like twin battering rams. Áine allowed the momentum of her roll to carry her forward into a stand and then into a run. The creature made no sound other than those heavy footfalls on sand and the creaking and cracking of bones twisted into unnatural configurations. It followed in pursuit.

She had no plan other than immediate survival. While her armor was strong, she did not want to test its limits against the blows or grasp of the golem. As the creature closed the distance between them, the heat of panic threatened to set in.

I am my sword.

The trainee's prayer. The knight's assurance to herself.

And then, another voice. The words of her father, and later of the yardmaster who set her to training all those many years ago, on the verge of womanhood and the life of a soldier. Words she had never spoken herself, because she did not understand them. Not yet.

A sword is a burden.

The creature reached for her, missing its grab but knocking her forward. Áine's wind fled her lungs and she tumbled side over side until she was lying on her back, the corpse-giant above her, its head canted like a confused dog. It hesitated in its reach, its clumsy aggregate body and simple magic-logic mind giving Áine the time she needed to shove herself out of the way.

The flesh golem swung its grasping arms toward her in clumsy, mechanical fashion, anticipating another retreat. Instead, she clambered closer, grabbed its leg, and shuffled herself around to its backside. She held on tight as the creature struggled to angle its blundering limbs back toward its own misshapen legs. The horror was not designed by a mind but was borne of the opportunism of sorcery and plentiful dead, and thus greatly imperfect for all its strength. Dead hands slapped and grasped at Áine. A smashed face pressed against her boxy chest plate from within the folds of the leg-thing, teeth gnawing at magic-infused metal. Áine leveraged her armor's power and punched straight into the golem's back thigh, slamming through overstretched human meat and misaligned bone substructure. Her gauntlet found metal and she seized it, holding on for her life as the creature shuddered in pain and fury. It lifted its leg and stomped down twice, rattling her teeth and triggering new waves of pain inside her skull. But her grip was true, and the effort had shaken the object loose from its hiding place embedded in human ruin.

Both creature and knight roared as the sword came free. Áine stumbled back and, with her hands on the hilt, easily kept her balance with the familiar weight and heft of a power sword in her grip.

It was a greatsword, meant for a two-handed grip, with a wide blade with a diagonal tip leading down to a straight, sharp front edge of impeccable quality. Its back side was flat, meant for parrying attacks that might otherwise chip the sharp front edge. Thin channels of crystal ran the length along either side of the oily black blade, marking the signature ley lines of a power sword crafted by a master blacksmith. The hand guard ran crosswise over the hilt, which was long and heavy, designed for a two-handed stance. Held in her armored hands, the sword sprang to life, those crystalline rows running hot with glowing blue aetheric energy transmitted from reserves within her armor. The plate and helm likewise assumed a soothing glow.

This was not her sword—it belonged to some other poor knight, their meat now serving as muscle for the monstrous form that bore down on her—but holding it felt right. It felt like home.

2.

The blade's pulsing energy and weight led Áine into a familiar combat stance: legs wide for balance, shoulders and head upright, the wide sword standing upward at her right shoulder, elbows tight.

The flesh golem's mangled corpse-leg sprayed blood and black ichor. It turned clumsily, favoring its wounded limb. Áine charged and swung the unfamiliar sword, testing its weight and power by bringing it down and across her body in an all-or-nothing attack. The weapon and her armor hummed energy in harmony. Blue aether light trailed the path of the strike. Twisted flesh burst into wilting flowers of ash along the blade's course.

The golem could not scream, and whatever pain it felt was dull, but it staggered all the same. Its trunk of a left arm pushed against the sand to try to keep its grotesque bulk upright as it collapsed on its wounded leg. Áine was a dancer, spinning off the momentum of her first strike to bring the hunk of dark metal back up again for seconds. Targeting its other leg of amalgamized bone and flesh, her attack cleaved off the tops of a bundle of skulls serving as collective kneecap, releasing a rush of grey-pink matter. Dark aether bled into the air, turning blood into mist. The runes on her armor glowed a soothing blue.

The golem swung its free arm clumsily in defense, swatting Áine just as her sword finished its second bloody strike. The blow knocked her down onto her side. Black void fluttered around the periphery of her vision. The pain in her head and body sloughed off with a merciful dose of aether released by her armor directly into her bloodstream. Then she was back on her feet, sword held aloft, light as a feather with the magical energy that arced through her circulatory and nervous systems. The golem charged, its ruined legs permitting one final assault.

The aether gave Áine clarity. She let the sword drift downward, tip pointing out. There was no escape, but perhaps she could split the creature open before it ended her.

If she were to die—or die again—she would die as a knight, on her feet.

The tide rolled in, eager for her.

She was denied her hero's death by a spray of purple lightning, jagged and searing across the red and pink sky. The air was ozone and sharp and the boom that followed knocked her back a dozen feet, her armored feet dragging straight lines through the wet sand before she tumbled backwards into the water. The great golem, its charge interrupted and frozen in place, heaved as if struggling to catch its breath. Charred shoulder and face sloughed off in smoking piles of ruined flesh, diminishing the creature, forcing it to spend its energy to reform a new arm, a new upper torso, a new face from its inner reserves of flesh.

A second blast of spiderweb purple light followed the first, halting the creature's efforts to recover, sending up a spray of gore and effluvium greater than the first.

Áine, emboldened by the euphoric effects of the aether and this unexpected boon, saw her chance. She stood upright, then charged, letting her momentum and armor power her into a leap, the sword held high overhead, the humming between the weapon and her plate a soothing song. The blade split the creature's assembled corpse-head into two distinct, blood-erupting halves. The sword sliced into neck and upper torso next, and Áine landed with her feet pressing against the creature's shuddering chest. She could not dislodge the power sword, but she angled its blade down, and pushed, *pushed* with all the strength she could summon. The golem fell to its knees, or what passed for them, and its clumsy hands reached and found her, but fell limp as its carcass shuddered into stillness. Whatever vile spirit once animated it fled out into the sea.

The power sword came loose and Áine fell backwards into the sand as the abomination collapsed before her. The waves rolled up to wash away the bloody grit and grime spattered across her armor. The roar of the sea drowned out her heartbeat. It drowned out her aether-sharpened thoughts. It drowned out the soft footsteps in the wet sand as a dark figure approached, waves of post-aether release radiating off his shoulders and arms, distorting the air—time and space—around them both.

He said something, his words coming to her from within the folds of a dark hood. Áine supposed she said something back, or meant to, but the void overtook her once more.

3.

The weary knight found herself propped up against hexagonal stones stacked together in errant grass overlooking the beach. The distant sun had diminished over the watery horizon, radiating pink and purple light in darkening splendor. Dried blood and salt were on her lips, and the air was cool and pleasant, kissing away the sweat in her close-cropped blond hair.

The dark figure sat opposite her, hunched over and working a driftwood branch in a young fire. The fresh smoke and the pop of burning wood were old friends, soothing and familiar. His face was in shadow, but eyes reflected the licks of flame and cinder.

She made no sudden movement. She half-lidded her eyes, then moved her hands around herself, slowly, exploring. Her left gauntlet clinked softly against her helm. Her right found nothing but grass and dirt. Her eyes, however, found her sword—she was already thinking of it as hers—in the near distance behind the man in the cloak. It stood tall, handle up, blade down in the earth, like a grave marker for a fallen warrior. A sudden rise into a run, a burst of adrenaline, and she could have it in seconds.

"Have you passed through the doorway of death?"

Áine kept still. Her body was awash in the nervous vigor of the moments before a sudden, violent action. The man pushed the driftwood stick across the fire. A burst of ash and cinder heralded rising flame.

"Has death or injury robbed of you the ability to speak? You may nod if so. I can see you quite clearly in this dusky splendor." As if reading her thoughts, the man turned back to the sword posted behind him. "I moved it because it made me nervous." He paused, considering that this might not be enough. "It had traces of necromantic energy about it. I thought it best you both had a little time to let your choler settle. After the killing."

"A sword doesn't have humours."

The man turned back to her. His reflective eyes opened wide and red. Inhuman.

"You wear a knight's armor and yet you believe otherwise? You must be younger than you look."

Áine pushed herself up to stand. A wave of dizziness and a cloud of dark passed over her vision, but then her balance was sure. She walked a cautious, respectful arc around the man and reached her sword. A low hum surrounded the weapon, growing steadily as she reached for its handle, and then falling silent as her gauntlet closed around it. The weapon pulled easily from the earth. She wiped away the dirt from its edge and its point. Bloodstains were more persistent.

"You did not answer my question."

He was standing, back to the fire, framed by the growing flames he had tended so carefully. The wind lifted sparks and embers up, spiraling them into a question mark.

Áine gripped the sword with both hands, then lifted it over her shoulder. The aetheric energies at the center of her back alighted, generating magnetic force to hold the sword in invisible scabbard. It clicked into place. Her armor compensated for the weight, distributing it evenly across her shoulders. She held up her hands in a show of peace.

"Was it a riddle?" she asked. "If I were dead, I would not be speaking with you."

For a moment, the man said nothing. Her neck hairs stood up in the cool of the salty breeze. The sun dipped lower, and the man's eyes shined crimson. Blue sparks passed between the tips of the fingers of his left hand.

Are you not filled with questions after facing horrors on the sand?

A voice. *His* voice, not coming *from* him or muffled by the wind, but coming from close by. From all around her. Within the privacy of her own mind.

"Survival comes first. Questions can come later." Áine lowered her gauntlets and turned away from the man who had become a shadow. She would show no fear to whatever this creature was. She had faced battle and impossible horrors since arriving on Gorgon's Head. This one would not frighten her so easily with tricks of shadow and sound.

She nodded toward the beach, to the south, where the armor of fallen soldiers glimmered in the sunset.

"Where are the armies? The victors, or the defeated? Who won?"

"We are all that remains," the man said. Shadows coalesced around him. "Nobody 'won.' Save for the hungry dead, as you saw, and the crabs and gulls. It seems you have some boon to remain among the living when so many others have passed into the darkvoid."

"Just luck. And the bravery of my column. They bought my life with theirs."

"They must have been quite loyal to their lieutenant."

"I barely knew them. But they fought for me all the same."

The man nodded.

"A concentration of necromantic energies is responsible for the revenants, who made short work of us," he said. He took a careful step over a log set near the fire and joined her to look upon the battlefield. He smelled of the fire—no, of something deeper. Ancient ash. Brimstone, even. He did not seem a danger to her—few men would be, especially when she wore her plate—but something about him, within, put her on edge. Strange that she had not gotten a good look at his face yet.

"What does that mean?"

"Sorcery. Our side or theirs. A desperate conjuring to turn the tide of the battle. Raise the enemy's fallen—and our own—to fight once more."

Áine raised a light eyebrow. "Our lord would never resort to war crime."

"Our lord resorted to a great many things in this vainglorious campaign."

"Careful," Áine said. "Your tongue strays toward mutiny."

"One cannot mutiny against a dead man. At least, assuming our lord has *stayed* dead."

"How are you so sure we were on the same side, you

and I?"

"Your armor is of our smithy's manufacture," he said. "Of the sword's provenance, I am uncertain, but I assume you found that in the chaos of the battle. Your plate—yes, you are one of my lord's knights."

"And you? How did you serve my lord?"

"*Our* lord." A pointed correction. "I was of his college."

"A wizard."

"I prefer 'scholar,'" he said, a weary refrain. "But sorcerer is also accurate. 'Wizard' is something of a low insult, implying a hostility and degeneracy that learned men and women have come to resent."

Áine turned to get a good look at her companion for the first time. The man's waxen face showed no sign of emotion, no scars, hardly any wrinkles around the eyes or mouth, for that matter. Young, or affecting youth. His robe was dark, but upon closer inspection it was simply a deep purple, interwoven with threads darker still, punctuated by teal trim at the wrists, waist, and hems. That green-blue bright color was the underside cloth, providing a false illumination in contrast to the purple. He wore a leather belt adorned with pouches for field work. Glass bottles of neon-bright liquid sloshed about silently as he moved. Strange stones sparkled from the faces of objects she could neither recognize nor guess at.

He sensed her eyes on him and shifted his face away from hers, ever so slightly.

"Why won't you look at me?"

"You are a knight, and therefore a noble, and above this one's station. It is impolite."

"Your words care not for station. Look at me, wizard."

"*Sorcerer.*"

Áine grabbed his chin and pulled his face back to hers. He grimaced in discomfort. His red eyes went colorless in the light of sunset, as if drained of a glamour. They were odd, weren't they, in how they seemed to vibrate to some unheard frequency, almost as if the pupils were attempting to split apart?

Áine felt revulsion. She pulled the sorcerer's hood off, and some of his strawlike hair fell away with it. He was balding, as if from an irradiation sickness. The waxy skin was stretched too taut over his forehead, where twin points pressed up from the front of his skull plate.

"What is this? What are you?"

He stepped away, swiftly pulling his hood back up.

"What am I *becoming*, you mean," he said.

Áine's eyes grew wide. "You're sprouting *horns*."

Face safely within his hood once more, the man's confidence returned. His robes flowed like shadow.

"Yes. Among other things."

Something stirred within his robes, where only his belly should be.

Áine stepped back and reached over her shoulder for her sword's grip.

"I assure you, I am no threat to you, ser knight. I saved you from that abomination that we might work together, and perhaps find our way off this wretched moon."

"What is happening to you? Can it happen to me?"

"Not unless you are a journeyman in the darkvoid arts," he said. "My transformation is my own doing. A price I am paying. The benefit will outweigh the costs. A benefit for you, as I suspect you may come to rely upon my abilities as I will soon rely upon yours."

Áine considered this. She surveyed the beach. The dead wandered about in the distance. The tide rolled ominously.

"Sorcerers use aether," Áine said. "One cannot wield the darkvoid, without…"

"Without being twisted by it, mutated," the sorcerer said. "It was aether that we used in battle, but it was darkvoid energy that kept me alive when the others fell. It was darkvoid and aether both that felled that great slouching beast and saved your life."

"You are a heretic, and have involved me in your heresy," Áine said. "You should have let me die."

"Those words—*heretic, heresy*—are most often spoken by madmen and killers. I pray that you are not the former, and if you be the latter, that you use your talents for our survival. Now, we should not linger. When have you last eaten? We should find what supplies we might. Two armies wasting themselves against one another—there is bound to be food, water, weaponry, agents for aetheric practice."

"Survivors," Áine said.

"You are the only other I have seen thus far. Besides those who have…returned."

"I was struck down in battle," Áine said, finding that her words lacked shame. "How did you survive?"

"The dead broke our circle, but not before we could incinerate the lot of them. We scattered and helped the battle as we could. Eventually, with our soldiery diminished and the dead rising, I hid, reverting to casting darkvoid spells to fell the enemy en masse. There was no sense in hiding my knowledge of the art, as all of my comrades fell, and the enemy burned faster and brighter in the lightning than the aether flame. Does my heresy, used to survive, shame you, ser knight?"

"It doesn't matter. The battle is over. If it is as you say and our lord is dead, the war is over, too. All there is now is to find others, to regroup. Perhaps we can signal the fleet and call for retrieval."

"I do not believe the fleet remains in orbit."

"I am not interested in your beliefs, sorcerer. I am interested in surviving. You saved me from that fiend, so you have bought my thanks, at least while your tattered humanity remains, before it is shed completely. So let us find supplies, or survivors, while we yet live."

Áine retrieved her helmet, then kicked dirt over the fire. She walked off—south, she reckoned, keeping the beach to her left. The sun was almost gone.

"Can your magic make a light?"

"It may attract the revenants."

"Let us do without for now, then." The sorcerer followed at a respectful distance, perhaps wary of his new companion, or merely allowing her armored form to take the lead.

"What is your name, sorcerer?"

"Grimlar," he said. "Soon to be the Goat-Headed."

"Gods save me," Áine spat.

4.

The dark allowed them to move along the edge of the beach quickly with little chance of being seen by hostile eyes. They encountered a handful of the living dead, who shambled aimlessly in their ruined armor and tattered uniforms, some clinging to their weapons, others missing arms and armaments both. But the majority of the dead kept still. Thousands of bodies arrayed in rest, ruined by sword or ignoble burn of sorcerous weapons and caustic spells. The smell challenged the natural rot-stench of the sea.

Grimlar muttered to himself about a "concentration of energies." He often consulted a handful of crystals—scattering them on the ground, leaning over to discern their pattern and brightness, then scooping them back up before indicating a slight correction in course. In the growing darkness, it would have been foolish to loot the bodies for supplies—one might animate suddenly while being stripped of its worldly possessions—so they made for what they hoped was the rear of the dead's lines, where an encampment might be found.

Áine knew that her battalion had more than enough food, fresh water, and materiel for an extended campaign on Gorgon's Head. In the weeks leading up to their departure for the moon in the Outremer, she had spent many sleepless nights and long days procuring and organizing the supplies. She had even led sorties into the countryside around their muster camp to draw final tithes of horses, straw, and foodstuffs from the poor people who had the privilege of living so close to the noble crusaders. There was talk that some had taken much more than necessary, and laughter around the fires for those foolish enough to beg or fight back against theft, rape, or worse. Áine had told her sergeants that she would have none of that in her section, under penalty of death. She heard no more of it when she walked among the levymen's fires.

In the early hours of the night, they crested a low hill overlooking the bloody beach and found a ring of tents below. As they descended, Grimlar risked a light. A small stone levitated from the palm of his outstretched hand. It emitted a pulsing, steady blue glow, just enough to splash illumination for several meters in each direction, but not so bright as a torch. The tents likely belonged to some minor lord, as neither Áine nor Grimlar recognized their stooping banners, which flapped weakly in the breeze that blew in from the water.

"Ships," Áine said, pointing at looming shadows just off shore beyond the tents.

"Boats," Grimlar corrected. "Landing craft for infantry and cavalry. Perhaps the very ones we made moonfall within. Let us find food and water before we try for them."

Stacks of crates among the tents sat unopened, and the ash piles in the firepits were still warm. Áine drew her sword and carried it pressed against her shoulder. Grimlar seemed unbothered by the possibility of encounter, fearlessly entering tent after tent, emerging once with a pair of canvas infantry packs, from another with cylinders of water, and once with bags full of dried meat and pack bread. Áine, for her trouble, found metal pieces to machinery that she did not recognize, racks of cheap wooden shields and light spears, and plastic-wrapped bedrolls. The bedrolls had been spilling out of an opened crate, but had been shielded from wet and were serviceable. She grabbed two.

They were going to explore further, emboldened by their initial discoveries, when hushed voices and fluttering light emanated from a nearby tent. Grimlar froze, his strange eyes going wide. Áine put a finger to her lips and pulled her helmet on. She crept ahead, her armor lithe and quiet, the heavy sword upright and ready for a deadly slash. She stepped through the tent flaps.

A wooden chair broke against her left shoulder and a glass bottle shattered against her helmet, leaving its metal humming. Rather than counterattacking with her sword, Áine reached up and grabbed the low-hanging tent fabric and pulled. The tent came crashing down in a jumble of snapping wood, flapping canvas, and the clang of metal poles. Men shouted. Áine stood upright in the chaos, pulling the canvas away until she stood under open sky. At her feet, two forms struggled to free themselves from the collapsed tent, cursing and flailing.

"Are you quite done?" she asked, placing a boot on one and applying pressure. She poked the tip of the greatsword against the other writhing mass, freezing it in place.

Muffled words floated up through the fabric.

"What was that?"

"We surrender!" This from the form shuddering under her boot.

"Speak for yourself!" This from the other man trapped in the remains of the tent. A swift poke from Áine's sword helped change his song. "Oof! Yes, surrender! Mercy, ser!"

"If you have weapons, I suggest you leave them be when we pull you out of this mess," Áine said.

"If we had weapons, ser, we would not have hit you with a chair."

"Fair point," Áine said.

"Sorry about the chair, ser. And the bottle."

"Yes, sorry about that."

Áine pulled the canvas back, freeing the two men in a flurry of flapping fabric and jangling metal poles. They were curled up on the ground to protect their heads, their eyes inching open, afraid to look upon their captors.

"Stand up. Slowly." Áine placed both hands on her sword's grip for emphasis. The men complied, standing with their hands behind their heads.

The man on the left was older, wrinkled and with a weariness beneath the layer of sand and dirt that encrusted his face. He wore a simple chainmail shirt and plated shoulder pads not unlike those of Áine's company.

"Name, rank, position, and company," Áine demanded of him.

"Arturo Synod, mum, ser," he said, spitting out a lipful of sand. "Corporal, levyman piker. Sans pike, as you can see. Fourth company, second battalion."

"What happened to your weapon?"

"I stuck it in a living corpse and could not convince it to return it, ser," Corporal Arturo Synod said. "Right about when things went to shit." He lifted his chin to the beach beyond the camp. "My company was about a kilometer up the beach, that way, when the dead started to rise. Thought we had the battle in hand until that moment."

"Fourth company was on our left flank," Áine said, softening her modulated voice from within her helmet. "We are countrymen."

"Aye, ser," the man said. "Does that mean you forgive me for the chair?"

"A uniform is easily found and a side assumed when the dead lie unburied," Grimlar said. "Let us not be too trusting. This man lacks a weapon and was looting."

"As did I, and as are we," Áine said. "You are a corporal. You have some sense in you to make rank and survive this long."

"I am a corporal merely because of my age, ser," Synod said. "I was a levyman like most of the rest, but I am older and had sons. I know how to deal with boys, so they gave me rank. Not much of a privilege. Lots of headaches keeping the boys—and girls, especially the pretty ones—from killing one another, and even more trouble keeping the sergeant happy."

"Are your sons on Gorgon's Head?"

"I saw to it that the levy did not fall on them," he said.

"How did you manage that?"

Synod said nothing. He looked away from the knight—not in shame, but with resolve. Áine knew there was no point in pressing, especially when a woman of her station might construe any explanation as something approaching treason. She had more immediate concerns.

She turned her attention to the other man. He wore no armor, but was wrapped in the green field cloak typical of the servants in the supply train that followed the army in the field. He wore a chef's turban on his head and a thin scarf wrapped around his face, over which his piercing blue eyes stared at her, unblinking and unafraid.

"Private Lam Leftworth, mum, of the headquarters company," he said. "Mess staff. No pike nor sword to my name. I wielded knives meant for cutting potatoes, not the enemy."

Áine smiled inside her helmet.

"A cook survived all this?"

"Aye. An enemy patrol had found our camp and put most of us to the blade. Some of us lived again, and set the enemy to tooth and claw, as you may have seen. That broke them."

"And did it break you, Lam?"

"I hid, mum, among my charges."

"Charges? I thought you said you were kitchen labor."

"My potatoes, I mean." He pointed to a sack set against a nearby crate, full of brown root vegetables.

Áine laughed, then removed her helmet. She made her choice—the same choice she had made with Grimlar. If she were to survive, she would need help, and help required trust. The same could be said for them.

"Do you know how to prepare your 'charges,' Cook Leftworth? I could use a hot meal."

5.

By torchlight they filled bags and small crates with the potatoes, carrots, dried meats, hardbread, and whatever foodstuffs they thought might last more than a couple of days. Crates of unopened wine were an unexpected spoil, another gift from the absent lord of the camp. Áine hoped they would not need to come back for more, and left plenty for other survivors. The officer's voice inside her head reminded her that "survivors" could include the enemy, but she was increasingly beyond such concerns, save those tied to her own immediate needs and that of her new party, formed in haste and now looking to her to lead them out of this hell.

Near the staging and supply area lay more of the fallen. Navy blue coats and painted shields of the enemy force outnumbered their own dead. Corporal Synod found a power pike and a short sword on the stilled body of a fallen comrade. The pike had nearly a full charge of aether. The poor sod from whom he had taken it was missing most of her head. From the looks of the carnage, she'd had little opportunity to use the weapon, but he silently thanked her for keeping it sharp, all the same.

Cook Leftworth searched among the dead for some time, returning to the group with a pair of daggers in his belt and carrying an ornate crossbow. The cruciform weapon was hand-carved and plated with a shining metal that appeared liquid in the right light.

"You have no case or quiver," Áine remarked. "But it is an impressive weapon all the same."

Leftworth smirked at Áine and held it up for Grimlar's inspection. The sorcerer squinted in the dark, then held up a hand to reveal a faint, green light in his palm.

"I suppose you'll be wanting this," the scholar said, holding up the cylinder of light for Leftworth to take. The cook settled the green bolt into the groove atop the crossbow. "How did you recognize what this was?"

"Not all aetherwork is taught in academies and libraries," Leftworth said.

"You are a cook."

"And you are a man turning into a goat-demon. It did not seem to matter to our lord who or what I was when the recruitment gangs came a-calling. They needed cooks for their campaign, so that is what I was to become." He turned away from them and pointed the crossbow out into the darkness of the sea beyond.

"What is he doing?" Áine asked.

"Demonstrating his usefulness beyond the kitchen," Grimlar said.

A satisfying, reverberating *ka-thock* signaled the release of the bolt, which fired a straight line out over the water, chased by the reflection of its illumination. Another bolt immediately appeared in the groove, and the crossbow's limbs bent back automatically on an invisible string, ready to fire again.

"Aetherial crossbow," Grimlar explained as Leftworth turned back to give them a toothy grin. "A good find."

"Fortuitous," Áine said.

"Yes. Quite." Grimlar's voice was flat, and his strange eyes fell on Leftworth in suspicion.

"Boats ahead, mum," Corporal Synod said, some ways down the beach. "Still right where we made moonfall."

"Let us hope the dead do not infest them. Be ready to move."

The landing craft that had ferried their army from orbit stood at strange angles, pockmarked with black wounds from enemy ballista fire. Revenants wandered through the shallows, aimless, clinging to their spears, pikes, and swords.

"Shit," Grimlar said simply.

"Those look more dangerous than the others we fought through," Áine said. "They look capable of using their weapons properly."

"They are, ser," Corporal Synod said. "I've seen them hack men to bits. I thought mutiny or betrayal had broken out among our ranks. But it was the dead who raised arm against their living brethren, and soon made more of their own kind."

"Perhaps there is another escape for us. Might this moon have a gate, Grimlar?"

The sorcerer put a hand to his chin and considered the question.

"I would have to scry. The boats have spirit chambers, which would aid that work. These craft are tougher than they look and likely remain sealed. Our objective remains the same."

"If we are careful, we can reach the boats before being overwhelmed," Synod said.

Áine did not like the feel of this. But she saw no alternative.

"Then careful we shall be. I will take the lead. Follow on at a distance of five meters. The water will slow us down. Watch your footing."

6.

They were not careful enough.

The party sneaked from the low, mudridden cliff overhanging the beach down to the sand, then moved in single file toward a row of landing craft moored within the shallows. Metal profiles shined silver and blue in the moonlight.

An undead footman in blue uniform rose from the cold waters in the shadow of the landing craft. The creature was missing half of its face and its shield was a shattered ruin, but its sword still held its sharpness as it dripped with acrid saltwater. It did not moan or point or otherwise raise an alarm. It waded through the low tide, slow, determined to intercept the line of survivors scurrying toward the boats in the dark.

Others rose to join its deliberate pursuit. A pikeman, missing a left arm, saltwater pouring out of the wound. A knight, sans sword or shield, but reaching with briny gauntlets. A woman wrapped in clothes of foreign color and threaded design, perhaps a scholar or senior officer. They shuffled along in the watery shadows of the boats until they were upon the survivors.

Leftworth spotted them first. He shouted a curse in

surprise and stumbled back.

"*Quiet*," Áine hissed, right behind him, her eyes on the middle landing craft, eagerly searching its hull for mortal wounds. "We are almost there—"

"The dead! They wait for us!"

A scouring blue light flared up from Grimlar's hand, revealing the grim faces of living corpses reaching, shambling up out of the sea to drag them all down.

Synod lowered his pike and stepped forward to skewer the footman above his leather armor at the base of the neck. Blood poured out of the hole, dark and watery, spattering against the low tide.

Áine stepped up and brought her heavy sword down at the undead pikeman's shoulder, collapsing much of his upper torso with a crunch of metal on bone.

Grimlar's fingers emitted a cascade of blue-green light that caught along the outline of another revenant, silhouetting it in rolling, pleasant illumination. Crisscross patterns of green aether energy appeared briefly across its face, neck, chest, and arms, before a sound like the fluttering of wet pages heralded subatomic collapse. The creature was gone, though its stink remained.

Leftworth readied his crossbow. He looked over his shoulder and despair crossed his face. Shadows descended the small cliffs overhanging the water from which they had made their approach.

"There is no going back," Áine said. She turned away from the slow approach of death. Grimlar, illuminated at irregular intervals from green aetherbursts, sent spiking energy toward the briny corpses that rose up endlessly. His robes flashed dark and light, growing heavy with wet and exertion.

Áine squeezed Leftworth's shoulder, then turned him toward Synod, dozens of feet away and much closer to the nearest boat's glistening hull.

"There. Synod is on the left, his foe is on the right," Áine said. That was clear to her in the moonlight, but she had learned that what was clear to one soldier in a heated moment was not necessarily so for another.

"We will never reach him before the ghoul has him."

"*Shoot* the bastard. The *corpse*. On the *right. Our right!*"

Confusion passed from Leftworth's face, replaced with resolve. He raised the aetherial crossbow to his right shoulder.

"Left foot forward for balance, especially in this muck. Look lively." Áine thrust her sword tip into the shallow water to convince a soldier to reconsider her resurrection. Blood and vile liquids bubbled up.

The cook fired once, twice. Green bolts of energy snapped out in succession more rapidly than a normal crossbow could manage. The first shot went wide to the right, glancing off the hull of the landing craft. The second found its mark, tearing into the torso of Synod's opponent in a brilliant flash of green.

"Get to the boat!" Áine shouted. The water around them splashed in cacophony. Tenebrous pillars of living shadow slipped into the tide. Heads and helmets wrapped in seaweed emerged from the surface of the water, followed by stiff bodies granted renewed life by necromancy.

Áine encouraged Leftworth forward as she turned to make sure Grimlar followed. The sorcerer's body appeared in negative. Water hissed into steam where he walked. Shards of purple icicle-light fired from his outstretched fingers. In desperation, he had switched from aether-magic to summoning darkvoid energies. But still the dead came. He turned toward Áine and ran.

When the three of them reached Synod, the levyman was slapping his hand against a square control panel of runic lights and glyphs mounted at shoulder-level on the hull.

"How do we open the gods-damned thing?"

"Scholar!" Áine shouted. Grimlar was busy weaving dreams of verdant fire to incinerate the tide of the dead. He failed to hear her cry over the roar of the sea and the explosive power that emanated from his own hands.

"Sorcerer!" Still nothing. "*Wizard!*" That got his attention. He turned to her, his face twisted and elongated into goatish countenance. Áine banged a gauntlet against the boat's hull. Grimlar floated through the water toward them, steam rising from his path. He placed a hand—a hand losing its physical consistency, and covered in a skein of pixelated segmentation that reflected the shifting possibilities of darkvoid mutation—onto the boat's cold hull. Red wisps of energy were tears dribbling up into the sky.

He was interrupted by a forceful pull on his right leg from below. Áine found the source: another levyman who, denied the full length of his life by his lord's desire to play at crusade, now sought to end theirs. Mangled hands tried to drag Grimlar down into the water, as if the sorcerer were responsible for the double curse of conscription and undeath as an unthinking ghoul. The knight delivered an aether-powered stomp to his chest, crushing thin armor and bursting his ribcage open. Water flooded into the corpse's interior, and whatever magic that animated it was soon gone.

Speaking words that brought back Áine's headache, Grimlar focused on finding just the right command to get the boat's landing ramp to yield. The *ka-thwhack* of Leftworth's aetherial crossbow, the grunting of Synod's pike thrusts and parries, and the harmonic hum of Áine's armor as they fought a battle of helpless attrition were insistent reminders of the stakes.

"I have it."

Within the boat, metal clanged and gears and mechanisms turned; at their feet, water churned in fury. Grimlar and Áine backed away as creases in the metal hull appeared and the landing ramp laboriously unfurled itself from the curved profile of the hold. The smell of hay and crystal-scrubbed air joined the brine and blood smell of their melee in the shallows.

Áine pushed Synod and Leftworth out of the ramp's path, then raised her sword in a crosswise slash that felled two zombies at once. The pikeman thrust his weapon with a burst of crackling blue energy, exploding the lower torso of his target. It jettisoned its roiling guts into the impatient tide, blackening the water.

"Get on board, now!" Áine shouted. Leftworth hesitated. He pointed beyond the half-dozen dead that ambled toward them. There, where the water met the rise of the beach, the shadows loomed, their bodies darkest black and their teeth and eyes wide and white. Áine's stomach went cold with a near-panic she had not felt since childhood nightmares. A bolt of green energy from Leftworth's crossbow went out and passed through the gaunt forms floating inexorably toward them, cutting a hole in shimmering black fabric, but doing nothing to slow their advance.

Áine and Synod turned and bounded up onto the ramp. Grimlar and Leftworth followed and stood within the relative darkness of the hold, firing out at the tide of the dead and undead. When the knight and the levyman reached the far bulkhead, the sorcerer pointed and shouted words that bent the physical forces of the world. The ramp rose back up, sealing them inside just before the shadows reached the boat.

7.

The landing craft was the same design as the one that had ferried Áine's battalion to Gorgon's Head. As an officer, she had been afforded some privilege in walking its decks, one she took advantage of to snatch the occasional break from the constant, close proximity to the bodies, smells, and voices of the levy troops during her battalion's weeks-long voyage through the heavens. Memory served to deliver her now to the command pod, a snoutlike appendage that overlooked the beach through clear viewports. There were cushioned, hand-carved wooden chairs for the navigation crew and boat commander, installed facing lacquered consoles inlaid with faintly glowing runes and inset jewels. Aether power still flowed throughout the vessel.

"What were those things, ser?" Synod asked, keeping to her heels. Instinct and training told him he was safer in the shadow of a knight in full plate. "Not the dead. The shadows."

"Do not speak of them," Grimlar said. He appeared at the entrance to the command bay. "We will be safe here, for a time." With the use of darkvoid energies in the skirmish in the shallows, his physical form further degraded. His eyes were fully bisected, and his chin was distended and sprouted inhuman hairs. The others did not want to look at him.

"There is a gunpod, aft, dorsal-side," Áine said. "I could operate it."

"That would require a spirit to power it," Synod said. "We ran through a gunpod range shortly before mustering for campaign. They had a spirit crystal in a localized node. Took a lot out of the poor ghost by the end of the day, running a hundred fighting men and women through the range."

"We need to rise," Leftworth said from the hall. "Our priority should be to leave this moon, and as fast as possible."

"Might you know how to fly a boat, cook? Or any of us?" Áine said.

"A simple application of the shipboard spirits' energies and concentration should get us out of the water and into the air," Grimlar said. "They are likely experienced navigators."

"Simple," Áine said. "Right. Right?"

Grimlar held his chin in thought with two hands, while a third, emerging from between the folds of his robe, tapped a polished wooden console, where jewels glittered in the low light.

"Perhaps some of the crew remain," Grimlar said.

The boat's metal passages were narrow, allowing room for two people to pass at a time if they pressed themselves against the walls. Dim blue and white emergency lighting ran along the plated grate floor and just above eye level along the walls. They moved in a staggered line, Leftworth leading with his aetherial crossbow pointed forward, Áine behind him. Grimlar and Synod made up the rear, with the levyman frequently looking back after the echoes that dogged their movement through the boat's tight corridors.

They did not have to search long before finding the crew. In a small chamber strung with rope and hammocks to serve as quarters, they found the remains of a game of cards and coins, half-played and unfinished. Bottles of wine and rum sat open or emptied nearby, some spilled over onto the floor. The air smelled sickly sweet.

"Where is everyone?" Synod asked. He picked up one of the small bottles, sniffed, and took a swig. "Crew do not leave their drinks unfinished," he said.

Áine moved about the room, her powered armor making her comically oversized for the cramped chamber. Before her were cots, small lockers, and tables—enough for ten men to berth here, maybe more if they relaxed protocol. She picked up a coin and examined it between the forefinger and thumb of her gauntlet. The faded face of a distant emperor was in profile, his features blurred by the endless passing of common thumbs over royal countenance.

A shuddering, groaning sound came to them from the passageway. They froze.

A *crash*—the collapse or tumbling of something metal and glass—came next, making them jump. Silence followed.

Áine moved to the door and pressed herself to the right side. She gestured for Synod to stand a few feet back from the center of the door, pike at the ready. Grimlar look troubled but made no move to join them. Leftworth kept his crossbow aimed at the portal.

The knight donned her helmet, knelt, and peered out into the passageway. She looked left, then right, seeing only the stretch of narrow metal hallway, haunted by shadows in the low light. Her heart beat loud and her breathing was amplified in the helmet's enclosure.

Moments were minutes in adrenaline-time. But no further sounds emerged from the passage, and the tension began to unwind in each of them.

"It could have been anything," Áine said. "Something stacked up in a hold that fell over. A mechanical system kicking on or off."

"It could have been anything," Grimlar said, meaning precisely that, but in warning.

Áine stepped out into the hall, her armor dominating the passage. No sounds. No approaching footsteps. No whispering of interlopers or crew. Just a distant, persistent banging on the outer hull, by hands bloated by seawater, by inhuman appendages from those vile shadow-things.

Leftworth screamed. An honest-to-gods scream. Synod cursed. His pike whirred to life. Grimlar whispered something, words rapid and reverberating. Áine tensed for action.

Three gaunt men now stood among the hanging hammocks. Pale, eyes wide and bloodshot, lips and skin split open by the decay of seawater. A sudden stench of mouldering soil. The air was sharp with the crack of hot light, strobing in rapid succession. Ozone.

Grimlar tried to shout, but his words caught in his throat, turning from warning into a violent coughing fit. He doubled over, blood leaping from his lips to spatter against the deck. A low, percussive ringing grew louder and louder, complementing the distant, deep banging of undead hands against the outer hull of the boat. The rhythmic approach of death.

The dead men let their heads fall back to stare upwards at the ceiling, as if in ritual prayer. A grotesque *hum* reverberated through the core of the living, low at first, but soon wrenching and nauseating. Grimlar, on his knees and hands, vomited blood and seawater, croaking like a dying frog. Áine's mind drifted from this scene, back to a moment from her childhood. She wandered alone, away from the familial manor into the nearby wood, where the trees grew close and thin. The babbling brook—her companion in those lonely years—led her away. It led her deep. It led her to the low rise of the fairy mound. Stone markers, surfaces faded and unreadable. Graves, ancient and untended, overrun with roots and weeds. A peaceful place. A place she might never leave...

Synod buried his pike in the throat of one of the revenants. Blue-green light flashed from the tip of the curved blade and the *whir* of his weapon's power system drowned out the low hum in their guts. This sudden act of brave violence broke the spell. The dead man's head snapped off at the neck, releasing a geyser of malignant blood that splattered against the low ceiling and deck.

The pikeman, well-drilled and committed to the movement, pulled his pike back, held it parallel to the deck, then sent it thrusting forward once more. It struck a second undead, lodging deep into his belly. Green and black sludge bubbled out of the wound. Another *whir* of power and the blade pulled itself in deeper for the kill. Synod angled for the spine. The creature collapsed.

Áine pulled her helmet off to vomit. The expulsion tasted of moss and old stew. Grimlar was struggling to get back to his feet, his hand outstretched toward the third dead man in the room, purple sparks flickering weakly between his fingertips.

The revenant's pale eyes flicked from the sorcerer to Synod and back again, leveraging a psychic weight from one to the other. The crystal light fixtures along the wall dimmed and sparked out. Leftworth collapsed against the wall, his crossbow falling from his hands. He pressed his palms against his eyes, but still the blood came.

"Shadow, shadow, grave," he whispered.

Synod had his pike free, but the final revenant's gaze fell upon him in full. A nose bleed, then a bruising of skin beneath the eyes. He staggered back a step, tears streaming down his cheeks.

Áine's arms were limp, but her legs retained their strength. She summoned a burst of aether energy from her armor. She stepped carefully around Grimlar, lowered her shoulder, and charged. She rammed the dead man at full force, his decaying body held to her shoulder through sheer speed and momentum. They blurred across the room in a flash of metal and green aether discharge.

The dead man came apart upon impact with the far wall. The left shoulder pauldron absorbed and refracted the collision throughout the armor, giving Áine a shuddering, not unpleasant sensation along her left side.

The humming ceased and the ozone dissipated. The lights flickered back on. The rhythmic slap of dead hands—and worse—on the outer hull ceased for a blessed moment, then resumed in time.

8.

The threat was gone, but the crew's quarters felt unsafe. Fouled.

Áine dragged Grimlar into the passageway. Synod helped Leftworth through the door and let the man lean against him until his strength returned.

"Get me to the spirit chamber," Grimlar said, blood dried around his lips. "The radiation is fostering malignancies. We have little time."

"You are in no shape for communion," Áine said, real concern in her voice. "I thought you were dead."

"We were all dead, if not for our brave pikeman and for you."

"You need to recover."

"We need to leave this moon," Grimlar said, his voice weak but his words firm. "That was the crew, dead, twisted into things that meant to feed on our spirit. I think they were drawn to me, first. Aether-eaters from the darkvoid. More will come."

Synod, eyes wide, looked between sorcerer and knight, trying to find some measure of hope or direction. Tears glistened around Leftworth's bloodshot eyes.

"As you wish." She pulled the sorcerer to his feet.

Áine and Grimlar navigated the narrow passageways of the boat as they descended, deck by deck. The light was lower here, the shadows darker. The air tasted coppery and the smell of burning candles guided them to the spirit chamber.

They came upon it suddenly, having turned down a passage to find the space opened up and home to a sphere of hexagonal tiles carved from shining stone. Wires and ductwork lanced the imperfect sphere from above, an interconnected network of mysterious purpose and function. Seeing the chamber, Grimlar's strength returned.

"I will not be long," he said. He placed a hand—fingers elongated, webbing a thin membrane between digits—against the azure stone plating of the door. "You may hear things, smell things. Do not enter the chamber. Under no circumstances must you enter. Should you see spirits or energy of any kind emerge, the chamber has cracked, and you must leave this vessel. Put it to the flame. The dangers outside may be preferable to a breach with my body and abilities under their control."

The door swung open on silent hinges. The space inside was dark. Mist drifted out, pooling at Grimlar's feet.

"How long should we wait?" Áine asked.

Grimlar paused at the threshold.

"If I do not return to you within an hour's time, do not come after me. Get away from the battlefield. Take your chances in the forest and swamplands beyond. There may be a stoneway gate, somewhere."

"Gods be with you," Áine said.

The sorcerer disappeared into the gloom of the spirit chamber. The door sealed him in without a sound.

51

9.

The air was cool and dry, tasting of burnt candle wick and incense. The sphere was composed of interlocking hexagonal supports in outline, filled in by a foamlike stone. Light strips ran along the hexagonal patterns, casting a warm and hazy glow. A pair of chairs stood affixed to the center the chamber's open floor, facing a small altar, where the accoutrements of communion waited. Bronze dishes for the burning of offerings were stacked, and candles, long since melted low, stood crooked and idle.

Grimlar took a seat. He leaned forward to put his elbows on the altar. From within the folds of his robe, a third arm emerged, carrying with it a small, ornate red and gold box, which it placed on the altar. Popping it open, he removed a pair of sealed glass jars and a pipe. Opening the jars released the smell of cannabis. The air around him stirred and shifted, and the light strips glowed synthetic reds and purples.

He set a bit of plant matter in the brass dish, then, pointing two fingers at each low candle, willed them to alight. By their illumination, he placed flower in the glass pipe's chamber, then brought the implement to his lips. He snapped the fingers on his left hand and a blue spark floated down before his face, then split to descend upon both offering and his pipe.

The flower was aflame instantly, blue smoke rolling and roiling in the air and in his mouth, throat, and lungs. His body heaved with welcome. It had been a stressful few days since making moonfall. There were greater trials ahead. But for now, in this brief moment, there was a peace. His body unclenched and his mind released its tight grip of hypervigilance. The ridiculous and foolish demands of the command staff; the idle threats and bullying of the officers who saw the members of the college as hangers-on and effete servant-class riffraff; the physical and spiritual demands of their rituals and monotonous preparatory work before the battle—it was all too much.

Then came the humiliation of their wasteful deployment near the lord's retinue so the scholars could conjure entertainments and phantasms of erotic fantasy instead of laying defensive barriers for the army or granting the levymen and honorable knights among them boons of occult power. But that was the way it always was, and always had been, as long as he had been a scholar in service to this lord: the wealthy and powerful got everything at the expense of those on whom they depended. The command staff were fools for wasting the scholars' limited aetheric power so, and had paid for their pleasure with their lives.

Of course, the common folk had paid for it first, and in greater numbers. Grimlar often wondered why a god or gods would build such a world or, seeing its sad, diseased cycles of evil and stupidity play out over and over again, why they would tolerate it without radical intervention. Such thoughts were anathema to the state sorcerer-priests of the church who enforced moral discipline through a gospel of fear, but Grimlar's orthodoxy, body, and spirit had long ago been tainted by greater heresies. His darkvoid mutations were growing, and no amount of glamour-magic could hide further degradation. In a way, he was thankful his colleagues and lords were all dead. He would not have to hide anymore.

Smoke rolled up from the offering dish and his lips, filling the sphere with a haze that, working with the pulsing synthetic red and purple lights, had the effect of transporting the chamber's occupant to another world entirely. The foamlike stone appeared to Grimlar suddenly as the material of ritual-site totems, the top of the chamber pulling back to melt away into the dark of heaven. Stars twinkled down at him and celestial phenomena tumbled across the glimmering darkness of deep space and his mind, between which now stood no barrier, if there ever had been.

Grimlar set the pipe down, knowing he had to walk a fine line between opening himself to the spirit world and remaining capable for the trial to come. They would sense his anxieties and inner feelings, though they could never know his thoughts precisely and, should they feel bold, could use the disorientation of the sacred flower's kiss against him.

10.

The smoke, pulsing light, and celestial projections made for a potent, relaxing combination, successfully decoupling his sense of self from a fixed position in space-time. What he felt of his body was no longer the trembling stress of the campaign and his need to deceive those around him, but now a low, pleasant warmth, an absolute lack of bodily pain and need, wherein all of his unnamed aches and needs were washed away. The universe—the whole of existence— flowed back in. Grimlar was not a being, but *being*, decoupled from the petty concerns of flesh, and that awareness floated toward a wooden door set in a stone hall, where torches flickered and the low, underlying hum of *all things* was the soundtrack to his sojourn.

Some believed that the spirits of the dead flowed up and out of the atmosphere to journey among the stars. Others theorized that they left our world and went to another. Neither explanation was quite right, as every stellar astrologer, amateur or otherwise, eventually learned. The souls of the dead are always nearby, or could be, through a subatomic, divine uncertainty—a yes/no, zero/one proposition, largely determined by an observing consciousness. The darkvoid was not merely another energy field comparable to aether, albeit more dangerous. It was *the* dividing line, a permeable portal. It was a doorway, one that swings both ways, through which both life and death flowed, if one could make a distinction between the two.

That door had long ago been breached by brilliant or foolish scholars—the difference meaningless—and the bridge was established. Chambers like this one had been built to corral those dead who might perform miracles like interstellar travel. But the dead were fickle. Most scholars made for poor social company and were unsuited for such work. But Grimlar was no mere scholar of aether-magic. He was a secret student of the darkvoid.

The door opened. Beyond it, swirling darkness, deeper and darker than that of the space between the dying stars dancing in the upper reaches of the chamber above his slack body. He wanted to drift upward into those heavens, to explore the ship's myriad systems at a subatomic level, and to gain a deeper understanding of the interlocking metasystems of his companions, who now stood out in his mind as luminous pillars of light. From within the smoke-filled spirit chamber, Grimlar could see that they could not be considered *individuals* except by the most myopic of perspectives. They were energy fields bound to matter, matter in turn producing energy fields, systems atop systems, particles and waves of energy and vibrating matter-states aligned and in concert with everything around them.

The knight, the pikeman, the cook—what was it about the cook that so darkened his perception of sign/signified in varying quantum states?—they were not what they thought themselves to be. Grimlar suddenly found them to be very funny in their self-seriousness. Did they not know that they were actors on a stage? So invested in their performance, they had forgotten their true nature. Was that a necessary element of the performance? *Forgetting?* If so, could one remember, while in performance, that one was a performer? What strange secrets might such gnosis unlock? What greater good?

Gods, he was high.

Why should we listen to you?

The voice was lightweight and cold, chasing away the vibrational warmth he had so enjoyed on this journey of communion. Turning his attention back to the metaphysical door, he was surprised—afraid, even—to discover four vertical plumes of cold, shimmering blue flame, standing on his side of the portal. The side of the living. Grimlar gathered his awareness back in slow, careful handfuls, pulling it all back in.

"Because I command it."

Spoken by his slack body, his words lacked the conviction and confidence he needed to bend these spirits to his will.

Laughter, cold as metal in deep space. Washes of blue light, drifting closer. Hands outstretched on preternaturally long limbs, dripping with ectoplasm and static.

"I *command* it."

What are your commands to us?

Fingers, ethereal and indistinct, pressing bolts of ice through Grimlar. It became harder to speak. Those fingers moved up, searching, probing for *mind.*

They found it.

Ahh, of course. You are lonely. The ones who try to command us usually are.

A wrenching sensation. A light taste of blood. The first release of gum around a loose tooth.

Would you like us to keep you company? Would you like us to give you the pleasure that the living deny you?

A searing anger and shame flooded him. Of course they could see through him, into him. He should have been prepared for this. The spirits were emboldened by his silence.

We will take that pretty mind and spirit and join it with ours, and we will make ourselves the mistress of your body. We offer to play your nervous system like an instrument. We offer possession, and in that possession, something like love. Something that...she...never reciprocated. At least not in the way that you wanted.

Grimlar pushed away thoughts of his past. He willed his consciousness to remain steadfast in its position. To show fear or to waver would embolden the spirits further. It was all in the books and scrolls he had read, in the lectures he had attended on the subject of astrological navigation. But that had been *theory,* and now, faced with four shipboard spirits bound to its systems, he realized the iron will he fancied of himself was only as strong as his weakest, innermost insecurities and desires. Such a contest would not end well for him. Grimlar decided another approach would make him master of these spirits.

"Yes, I am lonely," he said, words reverberating throughout the spirit chamber. "I have been so lonely for so long."

He opened his mind wide, all the tension of effort released.

The spirits flowed forward, one into another, into him, gentle but possessive. They found his mind, his deepest core of subconsciousness, and searched hungrily for the mechanisms by which his body might be compelled to their will. There, they found his secrets.

You poor, misunderstood thing!

Their words were tender but with an edge of manipulative cruelty.

"Yes. Perhaps you will understand me."

Oh, we will, and very intimately, our dear scholar. We see, ah…we see that not only does your scholarship keep you from others, but you have…

Wait.

What is this here?

Silence, where before there was confidence and seduction.

The sorcerer smiled. The trap was sprung.

You…you have traded your humanity for power. You have made a pact with forces beyond the aetheric plane?

You…He belongs to the darkvoid!

It pollutes your soul!

Where before Grimlar had vainly focused on keeping the spirits *out*, he suddenly focused his energies on keeping them *in*. The fingers in his mind pulled back, but the spirits were held tight. The blue plumes of light wavered and blinked.

"Like a cancer that does not rot the body—but it gives it new, awful *life*. See now the face of me, the one you would hope to possess, whose body and spirit alike are slick with the black oil of the darkvoid. See now the face of your master!"

The shipboard spirits cried out in terror, their seductive confidence stripped away at fleeting glimpses of the darkvoid flowing through the inner reaches of his mind and spirit, of the darkness that churned and grew and expanded, that gave him power and strength even as it warped his will and mutated his body.

"I am fearful to spirits," Grimlar proclaimed, standing up, the spirits still trapped in his mind, their plumes of light unable to retreat. "I am a scholar, a sorcerer, and a heretic of the highest order. I have seen and touched the darkvoid, and it is within me and of me. And now, so are you!"

No, scholar, o great sorcerer, we beg of thee, release us!

We will do as you ask!

We ask only to be spared the wrath of one who wields the flowing power of death itself.

Please. Please.

"Doing as I ask is not sufficient. You must be mine, as you sought to make me yours. You must swear an oath of service. To me."

The pillars of whispering light shuddered, but no longer struggled against him.

"I command thee to make this vessel fly. You make me no offers of pleasure or temptation. You merely serve."

But one such as you, tainted and corrupted—

"You *serve*."

We fear the darkvoid, for it is the tear, the veil, the holy curtain—

"Serve, and deliver me and mine crew to safety, and

I assure you that this corruption shall not spread over your precious luminosity."

Their silence was the beginning of their assent.

"Fulfill your purpose, and lift this vessel into the heavens. Ferry us to safe harbor."

We have tired of our purpose, o great sorcerer.

We have been held here so long, toiling for the living. We are tired.

Grimlar was stunned into momentary silence. He expected more pleading, bargaining, or perhaps acquiescence. But this?

"How can the dead grow weary?"

Monotony. This vessel is ancient.

We have moved it from one rock to another, delivering young men and women to their deaths for centuries. We have seen enough.

We wish to leave this home that has become a prison. We remember not our old lives, but instead yearn for something new. To be renewed, perhaps, on the wheel of life and death, to face what judgment the dead may pass, and to continue on, or become nothing.

You are a master of the darkvoid. You could deliver us through that door.

"To become nothing is to become everything," Grimlar whispered.

We shall see if that is true.

Grimlar felt pity for these spirits. He had never heard of something like this happening before. But what consciousness would not grow weary in toil? The implications gnawed at his comfort: how many spirits were locked away in prisons like this one, spread across the stars, their only reward rest and the occasional dalliance with the minds and bodies of lonely astrologers and scholars? What if *he* were trapped aboard a vessel much like this one, made to serve the petty whims of lords for generations, until the ship's destruction or the degradations of its systems allowed for his escape?

"Then fulfill your purpose once more," Grimlar said. "This boat is in danger. There are enemies seeking to gain entry, even now, and destroy us. They seek flesh, not machine, and your imprisonment within this vessel may be indefinite, should we fall to them."

The spirits considered this.

"I have seen shadows moving about the ranks of the undead. Some foul necrotic work swirls upon this moon, and it may seek your harm as well as ours. Launch this boat into the heavens, and I will spare you that fate. I will keep my corruption far from your pristine spirits. When our journey is complete, I will release you from this chamber, and you may complete the journey unto true death which was denied you so long ago. I will guide you unto the darkvoid if I am so able."

Do not lie to us.

"I would ask the same of you. Perhaps we should choose to trust one another."

A passage of time. Uncertainty. Voices whispering among themselves. The mood in the chamber shifted. A consensus had been reached. A sensation of weariness, yes, but also of peace.

We shall prepare the vessel for flight. Tell your crew you command us, and that they should prepare to leave this damned moon.

Grimlar smiled—his physical body smiled. The smoke-filled chamber hummed with power and light.

He had done it—and it was the darkvoid within him that had brought him success. It was not merely pride at having brought these spirits to heel–it was confidence, slow and sure, building within his strange and mutating body.

11.

The chamber door drifted open on a cloud of sweet-smelling cannabis smoke, which tickled out a cough from Áine's throat. The knight understood little about the ways and techniques of sorcerers and shipbound spirits, and had never understood the appeal of the wizard's weed, although others enjoyed its narcotizing effects and swore by its medicinal value in calming the mind and soothing the body.

Grimlar suddenly emerged from the fog, glassy eyed but sure.

"Is something amiss?" Áine asked.

"No," Grimlar said, smoke pouring out of his nostrils and mouth. "We should get to the command bay. We will be ascending soon."

"But you need to talk to the spirits," Áine said, angling her head to peek within the chamber. She saw only smoke and pulsing light.

"Yes."

"But you haven't begun."

"What?"

"The door just closed, and now you re-emerge."

Grimlar gently closed the door to the spirit chamber,

sealing the roiling smoke and light within. Áine's questions and the soft ministrations of the cannabis befuddled him.

"They have agreed to honor my commands, for a time."

"For a time? How long do we have?"

"I made them a bargain."

"That seems like bad practice for a shipboard astrologer."

"I am not that, and we are under certain duress," Grimlar said. "The undead seek entry to our vessel, and the spirits here are weary, nearly spent."

"Much like us," Synod said, eyes on the closed door. Leftworth leaned against a bulkhead that was grey like stone.

"We have little time," Grimlar said, and strode out of the chamber.

With an expenditure of will, Grimlar's hands reverted to soft, light flesh and fully separated fingers, rather than the cloven-hoofed mutations he had become used to in recent weeks. They easily accepted his commands, dancing over the runes and jewels inlaid along the lacquered wooden control console. Ahead of him, the command bay's main viewport was a wide, clear expanse of glass that revealed much of the battlefield they sought to flee.

Sunlight peeked over distant hills, the first signs of morning. Day and night seemed to have no discernable effect on the masses of the dead that stalked the beach. If anything, the rhythmic pounding of flesh against the landing craft's hull had summoned more of the fallen. Grimlar cursed the fool who had ordered the use of necromancy and double-cursed whoever carried out the order. There were limits to what soldiers should do, even and especially in war.

Screens in the bay displayed various camera feeds. One cycled perspectives on a loop, starting with the beach, where a tide of shadows slithered off from the sand and plunged into the shallow waters. They moved like inky stains through the waves, but with flashes of humanoid physicality. The shadows were not simply amalgams of dead flesh, but born from the raw material of nightmare. Grimlar had no idea what they were.

"What is happening to this place?" Áine asked, eyes on the screen.

"That is no longer our concern." Grimlar hoped he sounded more confident than he felt. "The undead will continue to rise, and reform, until the magic is spent."

"Those shadows do not look undead."

"I know."

"How long will this curse persist?"

"I do not know."

"Is this not your domain?"

Grimlar grew impatient. He was trying to focus. But this idle line of questioning was typical of those of Áine's noble rank. It did not matter if they were interrupting the work of a commoner. The commoner could simply be blamed later when the task was not completed on time.

"I know enough to know what I do not understand," he snapped. "I have made an agreement with the spirits in the chamber. What they do next is up to them. I hope that means escape from this cursed moon."

Áine opened her mouth to respond, but the rhythmic pounding on the boat's hull increased suddenly, doubling in intensity.

The message was clear. Let us in.

Let us in.

Grimlar closed his eyes and willed his human fingers to dance over the runes, spelling out his command to the spirits and the systems they empowered and managed: *take flight.*

"What if the spirits will not or cannot fly this vessel?" Áine asked.

Let us in.

Grimlar's fingers hovered over the console, the commands sent, the buttons glowing, the display monitors showing all the appropriate data, or near enough as he could tell. He was no pilot or astrologer.

LET US IN.

The assault boat shuddered and rose out of the water. Something within Grimlar unclenched, and relief washed over him. Synod and Leftworth appeared in the command bay door, entering to take seats to watch liftoff.

The main viewport offered a clear view of the battlefield as it rose. The dead were numerous— stumbling, marching, a tide that would not go out.

"We could not have survived that," Áine said, with some finality. Grimlar put his hands over his face. He did not want to see the scale of the horror from which they had escaped.

The sky, cloudy but bright, overtook everything as the boat hummed and lights glowed from the console's jeweled buttons, casting soft, calming illumination on the faces of the survivors. Soon, the darkness of the heavens replaced the early morning sky.

The boat swung around to face the moon, revealing it as a great blue and green orb of impossible beauty amidst a vast sea of black nothing. Beyond it was an even greater sphere, a massive, primordial planet cloaked in swirling red gases. The sight inspired awe in the four who survived the Battle of Gorgon's Head, and for a delicate moment, their fear was washed away on a tide of wonder.

12.

We are far from home and our vessel is small and vulnerable," Leftworth said, adding a dash of salt to the pot of boiling potatoes. The small mess chamber was alive with the smells of cooking and the humidity of the boiling pot. The large oven emitted warmth and a most pleasurable aroma, a testament to the roast crisping and dripping fat within. The beef had been a happy discovery, something squirreled away by the boat's captain or crew, found in a crate in the back of the cold chamber, unspoiled. A good omen.

Synod and Áine had taken over a counter Leftworth had not needed for his preparations. There they wiped down and oiled their weapons, checking their mechanisms and testing their power levels. Áine had removed her plate armor, remaining in her thin black mesh bodysuit. Grimlar sat alone at one of the tables beyond the kitchen in the mess chamber, a pair of scrolls laid out before him and held open by plates. The figures and images on the parchment were nonsense to the others, but the scholar considered them in deep contemplation, or appeared to for confidence's sake. He absently puffed on his pipe, the tobacco and cannabis mix a pleasant complement to the aroma of Leftworth's culinary efforts.

"What are you suggesting, cook?" Áine asked. She finished wiping down the power sword. She heaved the weapon upright with her own strength to view it in the light, then set it down against the wall. She took her helm—scarred and battered as it was from battle—and set it on the metal table. Markers of battle damage should have filled her with pride. Instead, she felt empty. She set to work scrubbing blood and salt from its metal surface with a brush. It must have been days since she had removed her armor. Her body was exhausted, her shoulders tired and weak. While the suit's aetheric systems drastically improved her strength and extended her stamina, she had grown weary nonetheless, and was glad to be free of it.

But she did not know these men. Free of her armor for the first time before them, she did not want their eyes lingering. Áine was muscular, but not particularly tall outside of her armor. Her shape was nothing to gawk at—gods knew the other girls had made sure she never forgot *that*—but she was a woman alone among strangers all the same. She had little doubt that she could kill any one of them if it came to that. She hoped it would not. They had worked well together thus far, and they had each proven their utility in the fight to reach the landing boat, yes, but that did not mean that they were what they seemed. Men and women had served together in their army for countless generations, and the shared hardships of training and campaigning in the Outremer regions brought a certain respect and intimacy among one another. But she would remain cautious. The first sign of real trouble would mean killing.

"Our army is defeated, our lord is dead, or fled without us." Leftworth's words hung in the air, suspended among the vapor from the boiling potatoes. "We are the only survivors, or the only ones who matter, now."

Blood and sand fell away from Áine's helm. The raven skull symbol on the upper part of the visor was scratched, but it remained, black and impassive. The left eye lens, red as blood, was framed by a scratch on the visor in which it was embedded, but was itself free of damage after it had reconstituted. The helm had saved her life, and now it would bear the marks of her combat experience. She felt both proud and ashamed, knowing that she had survived the Battle of Gorgon's Head not on her skills as a combatant but because of the selfless bravery of her column and good fortune. Success in war was often decided by time, place, and chance. No amount of discipline or parade ground preparation would have saved her fighters from the enemy's lances and bolts, nor the undead plague that consumed those who lived through the initial melees. Her helm's battle scars were a reminder of that lesson.

"We should make for home," Synod said. "I do not care how long the journey would be. I have no place elsewhere."

"The spirits do not know the way," Grimlar said.

"They brought us here, didn't they?"

Grimlar shook his head.

"This landing craft was deployed from one of the troop carriers. These spirits only navigated the flight during moonfall. We should consider that returning to our homeworld is not an option, at least for now."

"What the hell are you talking about?" Áine said. "We should make all effort to that end."

Grimlar let the question hang for a moment, then spoke slowly, as if explaining the principles of advanced alchemy to a drunk.

"We cannot, ser. We would be returning in dishonor. In defeat."

The room was silent, save for the soft sizzle of the meat in the oven and the bubbling of the potato pot.

"Every battle has a winner and a loser," Áine said. "Why should our campaign have been any different?"

"We would return as a reminder of our lord's failure," Grimlar said. "We have failed to die honorably. We have failed to give everything in his glorious crusade and are therefore accountable for its failure. Further, our survival would invite suspicion, and eventually accusations of heresy. Tales of necromancy spoken by cowards or traitors would not go over well with our lord's heirs."

Synod raised his eyebrows, considering the implications.

"If our lord is dead, we would be at the mercy of his court, whether senior survivors of Gorgon's Head or those who stayed home during the crusade," Grimlar said.

"A succession will occur," Áine said, flatly, all the hope drained out of her voice. "It will be bloody business." The wealthy and powerful were crude and capricious beings, prone to following their baser instincts and sacrificing others for petty reward.

"So you start to understand my view," Grimlar said,

tapping out the ashes of his pipe on the edge of the table and sweeping them to the floor with a hand once again covered in unpleasant, strange fur. "Let us assume we are not executed outright as traitors or heretics. What role in the new government might soldiers of the former lord play? Hmm? What real value could we bring our new lord or lady, who would be anxious to forget the failures of their predecessor? Now, think beyond that moment of crisis to the next: rivals will look to our territories with hunger and confidence, knowing that the army and fleet are shattered or lost. We would be in service from one failed lord to another. More death and war await."

"You speak of courts and intrigue," Synod said. "I am a conscript with a simple life, and family yet. I have a wife, children, a loyal hound. I intend to see them again. No lords or ladies will care about me. I can make up whatever story I want about how I returned home, or no story at all, and shall speak to—and of—none of you."

Áine thought of such a fate for herself. Could she avoid the castle and manor houses where she would be familiar? How could a knight fall back into labor among the common folk? Could the deception take? Was that even what she wanted, to work in the fields or forests in isolation and anonymity? And what of her power armor? Would she be content to become some farmer's wife and pump out children, only to have her descendants discover the plate as some great mystery in the years after her death?

I would rather die, she thought, the idea darkly funny to her.

"Our master is dead and our army is broken," Leftworth said, restating his point as if his betters had not heard him. He heaved the pot of potatoes over to the basin, then carefully poured the contents into a strainer. Hot vapor flowed up to obscure him in a white mist. "That world will soon fall into ruin, either through civil war or by the predations of vulturous foes. What do we do? We do what soldiers always do when they are left behind. We fight for bread and coin. We pay our way by sword and spear arm." He set the empty pot to the side and watched the steam rise from the potatoes. "Once we have enough resources to travel, we can go our separate ways. You can risk returning to your family, or to your court of vipers, or wherever you wish. As for me, there is nothing there that I consider *home*. I would invite you to join me in accepting this fate, rather than struggle against it."

"I am not ready to give up so easily," Áine said.

"I do not speak of giving up," Leftworth said. He turned to face her, the steam a rising curtain behind him. "We are ronin now, ser. Masterless warriors. We invite suffering and death if we do not fight for ourselves. Hot food, a warm bed, strong drink, treasure—these are the things that should concern us now."

"Ronin? I am a knight, not some petty mercenary—" Áine started, incensed, but Grimlar hissed and held up a finger.

"Do you hear that?" he asked. He stood, pushing his chair back and making for the door. Áine, fearing more of the undead or some new threat, heaved her sword onto her shoulder and followed Grimlar. Synod took up his pike and followed the knight. Leftworth sighed, glanced back at the potatoes, then followed.

They made their way through the twisting passages of the landing craft, back to the command bay. As they walked, the noise that had roused Grimlar grew apparent to the rest. A shrill, persistent beeping, emanating from one of the consoles in the command bay. It called them forward, until the four stood staring out of the great viewport at the horizon of endless darkness and glimmering stars.

"Proximity alert," Grimlar said, reading the runes that flashed on one of the console's screens. "Imminent translation. Something is coming through."

"Another vessel?" Áine asked.

"Ours or theirs?" Synod asked grimly. "Should we man the gunpod?"

A blinking red light appeared deep within a taut stretch of pitch-black space. It grew in size and was soon joined by a billowing gas cloud of royal purple expanding outwards. Áine smelled candlewax and felt the cool humidity of a stone chamber. She remembered her dream, when she lay wounded and unconscious on the beach. She remembered and witnessed, the events one and the same.

Swirling pink and purple lights—tendrils of stellar darkvoid energies—emerged from the blackness of space through an aperture in reality, a crack leading from one dream to another. A portal.

Something drifted through.

Metal and pulsing light, carried on waves of invisible radiation borne from the birth of the heavens. It emerged, one strut of metal and sparkling energy at a time, at a deliberate, confident pace.

"That is no mere vessel," Grimlar said as the hulking fortress translated from the spinning chaos of the darkvoid into material reality.

His voice slipped into reverent whisper.
"That is a deathship."

13.

Darkvoid irradiated the space between the hulking darkvoid deathship and the small landing boat. The radiation's writhing touch suffused each deck of the dwarfed vessel, surrounding and flowing through the survivors. It marked them. Changed them. It altered the course of their mortal lives, and the lives they might live beyond.

Grimlar fell to a knee, not in pain, but in pleasure. The part of him already bound up in darkvoid rejoiced. Warmth bubbled through his core. His brain's pleasure centers lit up in erotic delight. The sorcerer held his balance on one of the command bay's consoles, breathing heavily, trying to maintain his sense of self in the presence of such power. The darkvoid deep within him resonated with the overpowering wash of radiation, growing, spilling outwards. The cost would be great. The rewards would be undreamed of.

Áine, enchanted by the sight of the darkvoid deathship and consciously unaware of the changes occuring with her own body but feeling relaxed and pleasurable all the same, finally noticed Grimlar on one knee. She moved to her companion and placed a hand on his shoulder.

"Are you alright?"

"The darkvoid is upon us, on every deck of this vessel," the sorcerer whispered, his strength in no way diminished but his body shuddering with the pleasures of the radiation's touch. "We should perform rites of cleansing." He pushed himself back to his feet, invigorated.

Leftworth and Synod, their own flesh likewise enraptured, were in awe of the floating star fortress before them. They moved closer to the bay's viewport, their eyes locked upon the titanic wonder of alchemical engineering.

"It is beautiful," Synod said. "Like a cathedral. A painting of a holy site, come to life."

"A synthetic god," Leftworth said. "A machine-god."

"Built by the powerful and ancient races that preceded our own, the darkvoid deathships were castles of the skies and heavens," Grimlar said. "War chariots of the gods. Fortresses of vast, inscrutable intelligences. The most treasured possessions of void-mad emperors and philosopher-queens for a thousand-thousand generations."

"They are haunted, and cursed thirteen times over," Leftworth said, his voice a worried hiss. "If what the scholar says is true, then we are already touched by it, and our danger multiplies as we linger. We should flee."

Áine approached the viewport. The ship was a mass of cylinders and cubes, held together by connecting rods of glimmering diamondlike material and a metal superstructure of interconnected lines. In aggregate, it resembled the rough shape of a castle with pointed towers and rows of battlements. Purple and red energy sparked across the endless landscape of the deathship's wondrous architecture, an illuminating beacon of wonder and awe in the deep dark of nightmare.

Áine turned back to Grimlar, her face and figure framed in the viewport by the dancing light of the deathship's arcing energies.

"It must hold treasure worth the value of a whole ship many times over," she said. "A whole fleet, even."

"No, ser, no way," Leftworth said shaking his head. "That's a fortress of the damned. It will be our doom."

"I am not afraid of stories told to scare children," Áine said. "I see a chance here, translating into real space before our very eyes, and instead of hope, you lot retreat into fairy tales."

"It is much worse than fairy tales," Grimlar said. "We might each know snippets of story or legend, but we will be groping blindly in the dark through such a place. Whatever awaits us aboard is unknowable, save the potential for great danger."

Áine crossed back to Grimlar, standing opposite him across the glittering surface of a control console, her face illuminated from below by green light.

"A ship of magic and legend, is it?" Áine asked. "Seems to me that magic is what we need. Our spirits cannot make much of a journey." Áine turned back to the ship, her face flowing from display readout green to darkvoid purples and reds. "Perhaps we can find new spirits aboard. Or aetheric crystals for power and trade."

"Or treasure," Synod said.

"Or treasure," Áine said, nodding. Here, now, was a

true opportunity. An opportunity for her to lead her men to some fate better than starvation in deep space. "I intend to try my luck onboard that vessel. I will not command any of you to join me. But if you would accompany me, our chances multiply."

"I see no choice in the matter," Synod said. "Death there or death here, what difference might it make."

"Depends on the nature of that death," Leftworth said.

"You said we are *ronin*," Áine said to the cook. "Ronin seek treasure. You said it yourself. *There* is treasure." She pointed out the viewport to the majestic fortress-ship.

"I am not ashamed to admit my fear," Leftworth said.

"I admire your honesty, cook," Áine said. "But I would admire your bravery more."

Leftworth's face flashed anger, not shame. Something stirred within him.

"I have shown my bravery many times over. I will do what needs to be done to survive, ser, but know that I will not allow you to put me in a fool's position, especially in such a dangerous place as a deathship."

"You have my solemn vow that I will not waste your life—your lives—on some vainglorious crusade," Áine said. "Tell me, scholar Grimlar, what could we find aboard that wonder that might aid in our journey?"

Grimlar's third arm rose up from within his robe to scratch at his goatish beard.

"Aetheric crystals, yes," he said. "Enough for a journey across systems. But first, we need astrological survey data. That would be a matter of locating a spirit we could persuade to give us the information."

Áine nodded, invigorated with a purpose, a quest, beyond simple survival. They were coming around.

"Is it really that simple, then?" Leftworth asked.

"No," Grimlar said. "That is a deathship. There is no guarantee any of us would survive if we stepped aboard."

"How did it get here, scholar? *Why* is it here, now?" Synod asked.

"I do not know."

"Is a demon piloting it? Will we find ghosts and goblins aboard, eager to eat our flesh and pluck out our eyes and teeth?"

"Those are just stories…"

"Are they, though?" Leftworth asked, his eyes wide and face set hard. "We have to know what we might be up against. Does it not seem suspicious to you that your college summoned evil upon Gorgon's Head, and now evil has answered the call?"

"Enough!" Áine snapped. "What choice do we have? If we do not seize this opportunity, what then?"

Grimlar shrugged.

"We take our chances in this system and hope the spirits guide our vessel to some safe harbor. I am not a navigator, and I know little of this place, save what was told to us during our campaign preparations, which was very little. Mostly declarations of our great lord's impending victory. I cannot even tell you why we are here beyond the ministry's crusade propaganda. Perhaps they told you more."

Áine shook her head.

"I am a column leader in our lord's infantry, not a senior officer. I knew only the main points of our battalion's battle plans, but what happened on Gorgon's Head did not reflect the projections of our briefings."

"Forgive me, ser," Leftworth said, turning to leave the command bay. "I must attend to the kitchen. If we must step foot into nightmare, let us at least do so with full stomachs. This may be our last opportunity for a hot meal for some time." He slipped into the corridor, quiet and quick.

Grimlar raised an eyebrow at Áine. She turned to look back out at the deathship, which loomed larger than before, the distance between the two vessels shrinking as they drifted inexorably closer. For each blast of thrust to keep the landing boat at distance, the deathship drifted twice as close. It seemed the decision to rendezvous was made for them.

14.

The shipboard spirits needed some coaxing, but ultimately agreed to guide the boat to one of the portside docking bays. Grimlar had told them they would be landing on a larger vessel—*a frigate of some size and uncertain origin*—but had declined to mention that it was an ancient deathship spat out of the darkvoid itself. The spirits suspected Grimlar withheld some part of the truth, but they were disinclined to ask questions for which they might receive troubling answers.

The landing craft floated closer and closer, matching the speed and rotation of the behemoth fortress on its approach. The survivors watched the deathship drawing nearer via a viewscreen set in the main cargo bay, where the soldiery had conducted drills while in transit. It was the widest and most open space on the vessel, though that was not saying much. Áine recalled her time spent in a similar vessel while it was interred in the belly of the carrier. The monotony of close combat drills, formation command practice, physical training, and the cleaning of the boat's passageways and chambers had gnawed away at all of them. Even in these extreme circumstances, she did not look back fondly on that time.

On screen, the camera zoomed in on a great subplate built into the massive hull of the deathship. The visual feed clicked through various magnifications until the camera focused on a circular aperture cut into triangular sections that, with a signal from the boat, pulled apart. The boat fired corrective bursts of aetheric blue light to maintain its course.

Grimlar grumbled something as he ran his three hands over the wooden console near the far side of the chamber.

"Problem?" Áine asked.

"No, not really," he replied. "The spirits sense something is amiss. Radiological noise they do not recognize. I am trying to convince them we are in unfamiliar space and they are tired, but that landing here will help us reach our terminal destination."

"Unless *this* is our terminal destination," Synod said, eyes on the viewscreen. Shadows overtook the display as they passed through the aperture and into the deathship.

The boat shuddered to a landing. Metal-on-metal impact reverberated up through the hull and into their bones. Lights cycled colors on nodes throughout the bay, signaling breathable atmosphere and readied hydraulics. Grimlar pressed a series of runes, and the ramp's mechanisms hummed to life. Pressurization made their ears pop. Áine put on her helmet. Her visor improved her vision in the low light, and her lenses displayed a reticule that searched for possible hostiles. They held their weapons at the ready.

The deathship was countless shades of dark metal and alien stone drawn from worlds that had long ago seen their suns go dark. Jagged shapes and irregular patterns cut walls, chambers, platforms, and doors roughly double the size of an average human. Tubes of opaque glasslike substance held wires that rushed with aetheric blue light. The air tasted different, as if it were not recycled but blown up out of a great subterranean expanse. Cool, tinged with a tang of metal and the dust of millennia. But breathable.

Áine went first. The others followed close behind, with Leftworth bringing up the rear, his aetheric crossbow splashing green light against his chest and face. He paused to lay a hand on the runes that faced out from a panel on the hull. Bursts of air shot out from seams in the hull as the hydraulics engaged, raising the ramp back up to seal the boat.

"What if someone comes knocking, here?" Leftworth said. "I don't want to be wandering this labyrinth without a way to escape."

"The spirits have a pact with me," Grimlar said. "They will not lower the ramp for anyone but us."

"Unless they're offered a better deal," Synod said.

"Let's not spook ourselves any more than we have to," Áine said.

They followed her to the edge of the docking bay. A rectangular hall with rounded corners led away from it. A line of faintly pulsing blue light ran along the ceiling, leading straight on, beckoning. Áine paused at the threshold.

"Should we try this way?"

Grimlar shrugged. Synod stared into the gloom. The running lights faded into darkness in the vast distance.

"The light seems strange," the levyman said. "As if there is a fog ahead, or..."

"I should tell you something about the deathship," Grimlar said suddenly. "The darkvoid is not just a place. It is like—like weather, or a presence. It can affect us."

Synod turned his attention to the sorcerer.

"You can feel it more than us. Because of your..."

"My prevous exposure and practice," Grimlar said, his eyes bisected and dark, his sharp chin and beard more goatlike in the dim chamber. "But it will affect all of us, sooner rather than later."

"Are you trying to scare us?" Synod asked.

"Have you not seen enough to be scared already?"

"How long do we have until we go mad in this place?" Áine asked.

"I am working on such a conjecture," Grimlar said. "We may never go 'mad,' as you say. Or we may turn on one another at the first sign of conflict. It all depends on how much we are willing to trust one another, because what lies ahead is unknown to me."

"Then trust this, if not your own eyes and ears," she said, raising her sword. "Trust mine armor and determination to see us through."

The knight stepped into the corridor, her heavy footsteps on metal floor plates echoing ahead of her. The men followed in bravery and fear.

15.

Metal corridors and bulkheads gave way to labyrinthine hallways of weird stone. The aetheric blue light, running along the ceiling, bent at right angles down along the walls to the floor.

Elaborate wrought-iron sconces in leaf and spiderweb design held ice-blue cylinders. Áine cautiously approached one. Grimlar handed her a match; it sputtered and caught as she struck it. She put the flame to the cylinder. It released anise-smelling smoke and cast flickering illumination into the dark hall of stone. Leftworth, his crossbow bolt glowing, joined her at the sconce to run a hand along the wall.

"How is this possible?" he asked, his voice a reverent whisper. "Is this some illusion or synthetic material? Plastic made to appear as stone, stretched over metal?"

"It is stone," Synod said, running his bare fingers over the surface nearby. "This is no trick." Pulling a crystalline clyinder from its holder just below the low ceiling, he joined its tip to Áine's, sending up more light. The tip burned, but the rest was safe to hold. He lowered the crystal torch to survey the floor ahead of them. Ash and dust were undisturbed.

"The darkvoid infuses the deathship," Grimlar said. "It penetrates our minds and draws up from it our memories, our ideas, our conceptions of reality. It may be conforming to expectations. Or it just might be a stone chamber, as it appears."

"What people would build a ship like this?" Leftworth asked, the worry on his face made heavier by the flickering light of the torches. "Odd angled halls of stone cutting through alien metal..."

"Perhaps this ship is an amalgam, collected piece by piece over the millennia, by the darkvoid itself," Grimlar said.

"You know an awful lot about the darkvoid," Leftworth said grimly.

"I am a scholar."

"I did not know scholars were permitted license to explore heresy."

"You should report me to the local priest or ratcatcher."

"Enough," Áine said. "We—" She was cut off by bursts of light that appeared in the darkness ahead. Two at a time, at evenly spaced intervals. The crystal torches, springing to life, one set at a time, alighting to advance toward them.

Flickering light and shadow moved across faces, helm, armor. The air tasted of burning wick and smelled of melting wax. Áine thought of her vision on the beach and the appearance of the deathship. A steadiness of spirit overcame her. Not of determination, but of acceptance of the path she was meant to walk.

"The ship itself lights our way," she said, in reverence.

The stone hallway led deep belowdecks at a steady decline. Eventually, Áine called for a halt. Through the amplified vision of her helm, she saw the end of the hallway awaiting them: a great wooden door clasped in decorative metal. Stone demons or gargoyles flanked the portal, wings wrapped protectively around their shoulders, their mouths and eyes open in wicked laughter, as if finding humor in the interlopers' hesitancy.

The door creaked open in welcome.

"Wait, ser."

Leftworth joined her at her side. He knelt and set his crossbow down, then shuffled off his pack. From his belt he drew a rod, which telescoped out with a flick of his wrist, extending its reach many feet ahead of them.

"Hold up that torch, if you would." Áine raised the burning cylinder in her left gauntlet.

Leftworth guided the extended rod over the stone floor ahead of them, letting it dip and press down from time to time. As he swept it back and forth, he shuffled forward, bent low, probing the path ahead. Before Áine could ask what he was doing, the cylinder's tip depressed one stone several yards ahead, which recessed and clicked.

"Down, ser!" Leftworth dropped the probe and put a hand on Áine's armor. He could not push her down, but the gesture convinced her to crouch. The door at the end of the hallway suddenly clicked shut. The gargoyles on either side were drenched in shimmering shadow, and their eyes and open mouths glowed red-hot. Jets of orange fire erupted from between their sharpened teeth, floating slowly toward the space around the depressed stone. Leftworth buried his head in his arms and felt the heat wash over him. Áine crouched as fluttering embers of the fire sprayed harmlessly over her armor.

When the trapped stone clicked back up and the gargoyles' mouths went cool and dark, Áine helped Leftworth back to his feet.

"Well done, Lam," she said. The man gave her a half smile. He removed his cook's turban and found brown singes along its white fabric. "What a strange device for a cook to carry."

"Very strange indeed," Synod said. "How did you know it was trapped?"

"I did not, not for certain," Leftworth said. "If our lady here had not paused so, I would not have thought much of it. But I have learned to trust instinct, and hers was trying to tell her something."

"Perhaps we should all listen to that voice while we are aboard the deathship," Áine said.

"Indeed." Synod's face flickered between light and shadow, his eyes on Leftworth, who stepped carefully ahead, feet and toes moving lightly along the stones that might spell their doom. He reached the door, then paused to crane his neck forward, his eyes running along the frame. Satisfied that nothing was amiss, he poked a single finger to the door and pushed it open. The great portal creaked on metal hinges in want of oil, but otherwise revealed the way forward. He stepped through.

Áine and the others—their eyes on the gargoyles—

followed cautiously behind.

16.

The door led into another stone chamber, wide but shallow. Cobwebs stretched from low ceiling to four stately sarcophagi. The air tasted of dust. Water accumulated on the stone ceiling above, which was pockmarked with green moss and stringy growth. The room felt different, as if they had passed deeper into the recesses of the earth, not merely stepped through a door.

"Does this feel like the deck of a starship to you?" Synod asked. Áine shook her head, then turned to look behind them. Grimlar stood at the back of the room, the last one through the door.

"Grimlar," Áine said. "Would you step to the side, please?"

The scholar stepped to his right, his head tilted in query. His eyes followed hers, settling on the wall behind him. The door was gone.

Áine rushed back to the wall, raising the torch as if its light could cast away an illusion that bewitched them. She ran her armored fingers over the surface, searching the old stones, crumbling mortar, and green moss for the door through which they had all just passed.

"A refraction portal," Grimlar said. "I would need

some time to calculate its origin point. I am sorry I missed it. Does anyone have any chalk?"

"You may have been distracted by the thought of imminent immolation," Áine said. "I was."

"What's going on?" Synod asked. Leftworth was focused on the sarcophagus nearby, kneeling down to sweep his eyes over the cap.

"The door is gone," he said. "But the scholar does not seem too concerned."

"There may be a way to restore the door," Grimlar said. "A simple trick, really. But we need data on the ship's layout."

"What about hidden levers?" Leftworth said. He stood on the far side of the sarcophagus, bent over. He struggled with something. A grinding, stone-on-stone sound. Ancient metal gears clicking and clacking into place. A shaking of the floor.

The four sarcophagi slid to the side, grinding away to reveal shallow blue stone staircases leading down into darkness. Áine kept her hand on the wall. Still no door, but at least they had options. She approached the stair revealed by the sarcophagus over which Leftworth now stood. The cook struggled with the stone lid.

"Help me with this, would you?"

"Perhaps we should let the dead rest," Áine said.

"I would say we have already disturbed them. One push from you, ser, and this will be open in no time."

Curiosity got the better of her. She helped remove the stone lid, setting it carefully onto the floor. Leftworth peered inside the sarcophagus. The others gathered round.

Within the stone resting place was a human

skeleton, its flesh long gone. It wore a helmet with a full faceplate, its flat eye slits glimmering with ruby material not unlike Áine's lenses. Devil's horns protruded from the top of the helmet. Spiked pads protected the skeleton's shoulders, and a thin chainmail shirt stretched down its chest. Its arms held a longsword that pointed down toward its feet. The rotted-out remains of leather and clothing were piles of dust and errant scraps along its body.

"How long has it been here, do you think?" Synod asked.

Grimlar reached inside to pull at something along the skeleton's neck. With his other hand he reached in with a sharp knife. A quick *snap* later and he removed a charm on cut string. It glimmered in the light of their torches. Grimlar held it up high for them to see.

It was a small thing, no bigger than two inches in diameter. Silver, untarnished, with black gems inlaid in a familiar shape. A dark bird. Perhaps a raven taking flight.

"This has some similarity to our lord's noble crest, yes?" Grimlar held it close to Áine for her to inspect.

"One bird is like any other."

"Perhaps," the sorcerer said. "Or, perhaps, this warrior is from our world." He returned the charm.

"How did some distant cousin of ours come to be entombed in a deathship?" Synod asked. "Hey, what are you doing?"

Behind him, Leftworth was already working open the next sarcophagus lid. It slid across the stone with a painful groan, then thudded to the floor.

"Perhaps they found the ship as we did," Grimlar

said. "When they were meant to, as we were."

"Do not get spooky on us, wizard," Synod said.

"This one died peacefully," Grimlar said. "No scarring of the bones, no weapon or shrapnel marks. Skull looks intact."

"We should be so lucky," Áine said. She looked to Leftworth. "What are you doing?"

"My lady, the dead have no use for these," Leftworth said, holding up a pair of rings and a gold chain necklace, all of which glimmered in the low-frequency light of the party's torches.

A flick of his wrists and a snap of his fingers, and the jewelry disappeared. He reached back in for more.

"Thieving from the dead is hardly honorable," Áine said, even as she was tempted by the sight of the jewelry. A young knight's pay was not considerable. One expected to be rewarded with seized lands and treasure won on campaign in the Outremer, but Áine was beginning to suspect that such promises of wealth and grandeur had little weight behind them. How could a knight seize and hold land if their column was wasted in a pointless attack? How could her men form a garrison if they were all dead—or undead?

"Are all cooks so good at thieving? Your hands move with great deftness." Synod joined Leftworth at the sarcophagus. The air got thicker. Something was up.

Leftworth smirked.

"Perhaps all those hours cutting potatoes have paid off."

"Indeed."

"I believe we can find something for a peasant-soldier to retire on, here. Perhaps something for his pretty wife? We have not searched that one. Would you help me remove the cover?"

Synod raised his pike to his chest crosswise and shoved Leftworth, sending him stumbling back.

"What's this about?" Áine shouted.

"Who are you, thief? Speak the truth now, or I will beat it out of you!"

Leftworth pressed back against the stone wall. The light flickered in the crypt, making his features shift and uncertain.

"Lam Leftworth, cook." There was icy steel in his voice. A hint of warning.

"That is the name you have worn since I found you rummaging in the camp," Synod said. He lowered the pike to point the tip at Leftworth's belly. "Perhaps there is more you should tell us besides a simple name."

"Careful with that, old man."

"You are no cook."

"Did you not enjoy the roast, Corporal Synod?"

Áine stepped forward to separate them, but Grimlar placed a twisted, malformed hand on her shoulder plate. He shook his head.

"Were you one of ours, or theirs?" Synod asked.

"I am sure I do not know what you are talking about."

"Say the word. Or should I?"

"What word, old man? Has the deathship made you mad so soon?"

"Do you have Leftworth's blood on your hands?" Synod asked. "I wonder how many died for your deception."

"What is this about?" Áine asked.

"He is shinobi," Synod said. "Spy. Thief. Assassin."

Áine furrowed her brow.

"One of ours, or one of theirs?" Áine asked.

"Do you have blood on your hands?" Synod said, pressing the pike's blade forward a perilous inch. "Perhaps Lam's blood? Hmm? Murdered and replaced early on in muster, when no one would know his face?"

Leftworth—or the man they had called Leftworth—grimaced in pain and held his hands aloft, pressing himself back against the stone wall as flat as he could. Áine stalked forward to join Synod, her powered armor frame imposing over the diminishing Leftworth.

"Talk," she said through her helmet, her voice modulated with synthetic menace. *"Talk or die. Both would suit me."*

Shadows passed across Leftworth's features. His face, twisted in fear, showed calm. Acceptance.

"I enlisted as a volunteer." His voice was flat and impassive. His eyes showed no fear. "There was no need to murder or lie. Your lord was eager for bodies. He was in a rush to reach Gorgon's Head. You were an officer, Áine. Tell me, did the campaign seem organized to you? Did it seem like you were expecting spies? Could you even name your enemy?"

"Heretic forces seeking to make territory in the Outremer their own," she said. "From there they would launch terror attacks into our system, or those of our allied neighbors. We were to capture and hold holy land."

Leftworth smirked.

"That is all? That is all they told you about us? That describes nothing. Less than useful."

Áine put her fist to the wall, right next to Leftworth's head.

"I anger you because I speak the truth. Tell me, Ser Kard, what were your objectives, aside from seizing glory in battle? Capture Gorgon's Head? Please. We landed on a thin strip of beach and were pinned between an entrenched enemy garrison and the ocean. The battle was lost when it was drawn up. I never had the opportunity to make a report. I did not *have* to. This crusade was doomed from the outset because your lord was a fool. We are lucky we are not dead."

"You *are* a spy," Synod hissed. "We should kill you."

"And what would that accomplish?" Leftworth said. "I am a spy for the other side—a side that is broken and dead, as is yours, thanks to the work of Grimlar's colleagues. You call us heretics? That necromancy—forbidden art—did its grisly work all too well. I am a cook that fed your men for half a year and managed to survive the horrors your lot unleashed. I am a man who has skills that can help you navigate and survive this deathship. Are these truths at odds? And speaking of odds, what are yours, down a man—especially one who might know scouting, trap finding, deception, and stealth?"

"We cannot trust you," Áine said flatly.

"Do you think I can trust *you*?" Leftworth asked, incredulous. "Are you all what you say you are? A knight with a sword stolen from the dead. A levyman who lives when his comrades all fell. A sorcerer who is more monster than man." He placed a hand on Synod's pike blade. "Look at us. Look at where we *are*. In this place of horrors and miracles. We will not survive this on our own. We might not even survive this together."

Synod and Áine had no answer for that. After a time, Grimlar spoke up.

"We should not linger in one place for too long. We should choose a staircase and descend."

"Can we go back the way we came?" Áine asked.

"Yes, but to do so, we need map data to reorient ourselves."

"It sounds to me like you need a scout," Leftworth said. "A sneaky shinobi would do nicely in a situation like this."

Synod looked to Áine for a decision. She turned from them both.

"Which way, then, scout?" She asked from the center of the room. "Four stairways down. Which path might extend our lives?"

Synod gently swung the pike's blade away from Leftworth's stomach. The shinobi exhaled in relief, his face pale in the strange light of the chamber.

17.

The wizard and their familiar found them standing in the shadow of hulking stone monoliths. The structures were arrayed before a wide viewport through which mists of darkvoid and aetheric energy swirled. Violet and crimson clusters of gas and light drifted across black heavens pockmarked with glimmering green starlight. Blue-green aetheric energy danced in jagged arcs from cloud to cloud. The monoliths—vaguely humanoid in oversized form—reflected and refracted the cosmic light to delirious effect as the wizard's fell incantations reverberated throughout the wide chamber. Luminous words seeped into their minds, spreading corruption along neural pathways, poisoning connections, rerouting synapses to insidious effect.

The psychic slash struck Grimlar first, his thoughts blurring and malforming. The others swayed on their feet, eyes glazed as they viewed the swirling cosmic wonders beyond. Leftworth—or the man who called himself by that name—stumbled forward to catch himself on the base of one of the humanoid monoliths. Áine dropped her sword and fell to a knee. Synod slurred out words of confusion, then warning, holding himself upright with his pike.

The sorcerer, recognizing the danger, let himself fall forward, rolling into his shoulder with a *thud* against the stone floor, then kicking himself onto his back like a drunk. He searched the darkness behind them for the threat.

BEHIND US, he managed, a psychic burst of urgency transmitted via aetheric waves to his companions. The words came out strong and clear, the effect amplified by the darkvoid suffusing the ship and his own body. Leftworth stood up straight and Áine cleared her head to reach for her sword. Synod snapped to a fighting stance, pike blazing blue with aetheric power.

Grimlar pointed into the dark, using the levyman as a lodestar upon which he struggled to focus. There, to the left, was a faint glow within swirling shadows. Grimlar commanded his claw to point at the distortion while Synod's pike led him straight toward it. The sorcerer held his breath and focused his mind through the tumbling, disorienting words of the enemy wizard, marshaling the darkvoid that had mutated his body to resonate with the veins of power that cascaded throughout the ship.

Bright purple sparks sputtered from his fingertip, misfiring, burning the flesh before igniting like an ember caught by the wind. But then a sphere of red energy localized just beyond his fingertip and shot forward, into the dark, past Synod, toward the illumination that was the wizard's flashing eyes and white teeth, sharp and angular.

The darkness broke. The words of wonder and pain

ceased for a few precious moments, leaving headaches and confusion in their wake.

The wizard was tall, clad in a shimmering silver robe with an oversized hood that made them look like a viper preparing to strike. Seeing the orb of darkvoid energy moving toward them unerringly, they smiled wide, shifting hands to catch and redirect it—before splitting into a kaleidoscopic flurry of limbs, silver cloak fabric, and multiple transparent visions of bodily form. The orb passed harmlessly between those ghosts, a wicked, fanged smile of triumph on their many faces, outlined in rainbow colors, disorienting and vibrant. Grimlar summoned another sphere of destructive power, his poor finger mercifully spared the burning of another misfire.

The wizard's visages—five or more, depending on the angle—floated outwards and orbited the incoming ball of darkvoid energy, allowing it to also pass by harmlessly. Synod tried for a thrust of his pike at full power, spilling blue aether light in a form-perfect attack. But this, too, was dodged with precision and sparks of rainbow radiation. Áine charged recklessly as Leftworth struggled to aim his crossbow.

Grimlar did not recognize this magic. It was as alien as everything else on the deathship. He knew of no counterspell or technique that could overcome this glamour, nor could he risk his limited power by mindlessly casting away in vain. The wizard had not counterattacked, yet, but even with the additional pressures of Áine and Leftworth's attacks soon to follow, it was only a matter of time before more poison words flowed and their minds and bodies were caught in that deadly tide. He had to think.

The wizard's dexterous magic could have another source. One nearby. One close enough to refract and amplify its power, but just out of reach of threats. Grimlar's goat-eyes searched the darkness around the wizard's many glowing forms, probing the crevices and alcoves of the stone corridor from which this threat had emerged. He looked for any sign of movement, of light, of—*there*. At the edge of the corridor, where it met the opening of the grand monolith chamber. Hidden in rippling, synthetic shadow, a tiny, malformed blue-grey face with bulging black eyes and quivering lips, wrapped in black cloak. A familiar. A kobold or dwarf, from the look of the horrible little freak. A lesser servant of an adjacent plane—conjured easily and banished just the same.

Grimlar pushed himself back to his feet and stalked forward, grateful that the warriors distracted the wizard, who even now was beginning to speak again. Moving through miasma, Grimlar's muscles struggled to coordinate and his bones rattled to keep balance in such uncertain flesh. The others struggled valiantly against the degradation of reality that flowed forth from the wizard's lips.

The familiar had no such trouble. Its small, warped blue face reflected sputtering neon light as its thin lips worked to form words that refracted and amplified the original spell, spreading its area across the monolith chamber in a cascade that would doom them. Grimlar pointed with his left hand and extended his thumb leftward on his right. He gathered his remaining strength to speak a word—a simple word, one every sorcerer bound for a battlefield might learn. A word of force and power that, when amplified by the rumbling engine of destruction that was an aetheric energy field, could crush a warrior in armor. He need only crush this vile goblin.

Antilight was a malignant projectile, splintering across the vast distance of the chamber to the corridor's edge. It collided perfectly with the kobold, sending it flying back and upward at incredible speed, its little feet kicking and arms flailing within its black robe, its blue face and deep black eyes frozen in a mask of surprise. The amplifying sorcery broke. The creature splattered, head first, against a stone wall, spraying blue blood and discharging its brain matter like pus from a lanced boil.

Synod felt the surety of his strength return. The pikeman charged forward, spearing the wizard in their side as the glimmering rainbow light failed and phantom bodies coalesced into a single target. The chamber air sizzled with the aftereffects of the magic volleys and the ringing drone of darkvoid.

"Do not kill him! Do not kill him!"

The others pointed their weapons at their fallen foe, who sat against the chamber's stone wall, nursing their wound. Neon blue liquid had spattered against the wall, the floor, and the wizard's silver robes. The silver hood had fallen back, revealing a waterfall of shimmering blond hair. A woman. Her beautiful face was twisted in pain, snarling in fury, thin nose and blue lips under sharp azure eyes that glared daggers.

"Speak not again, wizard, unless spoken to, and carefully," Áine said, holding the sharp tip of the greatsword at her enemy's throat. Grimlar knelt at her side to examine the wound. Glowing blue blood flowed freely from where the pike's blade had cut through silver cloak and flesh alike.

"I have never seen magic like that before," Grimlar said, genuine respect in his voice. "What tradition do you follow? What school do you come from?"

The wizard glared at him, clearly in pain.

Áine set her sword upon the magnetized plate on her back and knelt down. In full armor and helm, she was as imposing as any foul spell or curse. Her voice came out synthesized and angry through the voice modulator.

"Why did you try and bewitch us, wizard? What would you have done with us?"

The woman curled her lips into a sneer before losing her composure to a wave of pain.

"You will die," Áine said. *"Answer me and we may yet attend to your wound."*

The woman's eyes flitted around them, defiant, searching for some advantage.

"Your familiar is dead," Grimlar said. "I splattered its vile brains against the corridor. It will not be coming to your rescue. That is how we broke your spell."

The woman's eyes flashed with anger before becoming moist with sadness.

"Bastards," she said.

"ANSWER ME," Áine said, leaning in close, her visor lenses flashing red. *"Answer our questions, or die."*

18.

The wizard had a ship. She would not give them her name—such a thing might give them power over her. She would rather die. But she bargained for her life with the promise of escape, with the temptation of a vessel that could translate through the darkvoid if they could procure the crystals necessary to entice and empower the spirits.

Synod applied a healing patch to the woman's side, finding her glowing blood beautiful and smelling faintly of blooming flowers. The patch took, and she was stabilized, if weakened. She did not thank him for repairing the damage he caused, but spoke to Áine and Grimlar with plain answers to their questions, offering little resistance. Leftworth eyed the woman with a smoldering anger that threatened to spill over into bloody violence. The woman would only glance at the shinobi, whose desire for revenge was plain.

"I have been exploring the deathship for over a year, maybe longer," the wizard said, her words tinged with pain. "I spend no more than a week aboard for each delve. Time does not work here the same as it might elsewhere. You will discover that soon enough."

"You assume we have not been here as long as or longer than you," Grimlar said.

"Your inexperience was plain. I was able to get the better of you because you were unwary. You gawk at dangerous things as if they are petty wonders set up for stupid pilgrims." She nodded toward the monoliths and the viewport.

"What brings you to the deathship?" asked Grimlar.

"Likely the same thing that brought you," she said. "Treasure. Opportunity."

"Banditry, you mean," Leftworth said. "You meant to kill us."

"Only if you were trouble," the woman said, risking a look in the eye. "I would have taken your lady's power armor and whatever useful trinkets your goat-man carried. But I would have left you alive otherwise."

"To die unarmed in this ship? That is murder all the same."

The woman shrugged.

"What are you really looking for?" Áine asked. She removed her helm to look upon the wizard with her own eyes. The woman was beautiful and clean—she was not covered in the filth of weeks of bloody and dusty campaign. She was vibrant and fresh in a way that they were not, and thus their eyes and other senses found her intriguing, among other things.

"Take me to my ship and let me leave, and I will tell you what I know of the deathship," the wizard said.

Áine pursed her lips and shook her head.

"You will guide us to your ship and we will decide what to do with you. Perhaps we will disarm and abandon you to these endless and vast corridors, as you meant to do to us."

The wizard glared at the knight, considering her next words.

"Careful," Grimlar advised. "I give you fair warning as respected practitioner of the arts. We have overcome much to survive. My companions will not hesitate to do worse than relieve you of your equipment and fight alone. Especially that one."

The woman's eyes flicked toward the shinobi and back to Grimlar in acknowledgment.

"Where is your starship?" Grimlar asked.

The wizard gave a slight tilt of her head.

"North of here. I can lead you to it."

"We may not need your ship, but we do need survey data and crystals. Can you offer us those things?"

"If you spare my life, I will provide them both from mine own stores."

"This is too simple," Áine said. "What are you really doing here, wizard?"

The woman took a moment to gather her strength. The loss of blood made her tired. Speaking was painful.

"There is a consciousness here," she said, voice flat, despite her pain. "A great spirit moves among the ship's various systems. I seek communion."

Grimlar rubbed at his chin.

"What goblinry is she on about?" Leftworth asked. "Nothing good can come of this."

"She does not seek contact with just any spirit," Grimlar said softly, his words tinged with awe. "She seeks communion with the deathship itself."

The wizard offered a pained but satisfied smirk.

"I will parlay," she said. "I will get something from it.

I will know the god of metal and space and stone, the god of the veil of death, and seek its favor."

The others fell silent. Water dripped in the distance, its sound echoing down innumerable corridors.

"What could you offer it?" Grimlar asked, genuinely curious. The wizard arched an eyebrow and gave the goat-man a naughty smile.

"That doesn't matter," Áine said. "Lead us to your ship and provide us with what we desire, and we will release you to your own mad schemes. But I warn you: the first hint of betrayal, or any act of aggression against us despite our mercy, and we will destroy you."

"I could walk better if I could draw power from the darkvoid," the wizard said.

"Then you will walk slowly," Áine said. "On your feet, wizard. Grimlar, ensure this one cannot betray us with a fell word. You will find us less merciful should you try to harm us a second time."

19.

Their prisoner led them in the direction she described as "north," cutting through various corridors and across great chasms of stone and metal. They passed more monoliths not unlike those they had found near the viewport, as well as ramshackle huts built from conduit panels and stacked stone held together with glistening wires the color of pink sunset. But they saw no sign of the dwellers who had built those structures. That brought equal parts relief and worry.

The wizard kept her silence for a time, careful to keep her thin lips together, the eyes of the party upon her with hostility and fear. An hour into their journey, she spoke up.

"I see now. You were soldiers. You are alone, now, and lost."

The words vibrated in the air as the group passed under a great conduit of lacquered metal that twisted and contorted across the wide but low ceiling like the belly of a great wyrm. White steam leaked out of cracks at the corners of each twist, cool and humid. As they walked on, the steam descended to become a mist that obscured the path ahead, glistening with moisture.

"What we are is not your concern," Áine said, her sword's crystal conduits pulsing with blue aether energy in the dim corridor. "So long as we are merciful."

"But it *is* my concern, as you are my captors," the wizard said.

"We will release you when we have what we need. When you pay penance for your unprovoked attack."

"Who was it that slew my familiar? Was it you, goat-man? How did you do it?"

"Careful, my lady," Grimlar said. "Our patience has its limits."

"Does it, though? I think you are not some band of hardened mercenaries. You are scared, confused. Lost. You are not showing mercy by sparing my life. You are showing bad judgment."

"Perhaps we should correct that," Leftworth said, his voice drifting out of the shadows.

"I could have killed you all, yet you keep me alive. You have to know that nothing I can offer offsets the danger I represent. If you do not, you lack the wisdom to survive this wondrous and terrible place. You will all die here."

Áine brought her gauntlet down across the back of the woman's head, lending the blow just a fraction of her considerable strength. The wizard grunted and fell to her knees.

"*There* it is," the wizard said, her words coming painfully. "The spirit necessary to survive the deathship."

Áine wanted to hit her again, but Leftworth hissed for silence from the shadows. He approached the knight to lay a hand on her raised right arm, then pointed into the mist ahead. Áine cycled through her helm's various light-modes, searching for heat signatures and figures in the dark but finding none. She shook her head but said nothing. Leftworth raised his aetherial crossbow and pointed it into the mist while holding up his free hand in signal to Grimlar and Synod, who moved to the walls of the corridor and crouched low in its shadows, eyes ahead.

"Another test of your mettle," the wizard said, returning to her feet slowly. "Another opportunity to—"

She was silenced not by Áine's gauntlet, but by a vision of an oil-like shadow that floated across the floor, carried on the mist.

"Let me cast a spell, let me—"

More ovals of shadow and mist flowed out of the gloom ahead. No one moved.

From the slicks of shadow popped up creatures of sinewy darkness, figures stretched and gaunt, with snapping mouths of jagged black; long, limber arms of glistening gloom; hands and sharp fingers probing outward. Hideous laughter filled the corridor, reverberating and echoing from each of the creatures that emerged from its own impossible shadow.

Leftworth fired his crossbow, the bolt of green light illuminating the corridor as it harmlessly passed between the phantasms into the beyond. Drifting shadow-fingers stretched toward them. The wizard captive, no longer waiting for permission, raised her arms up in a Y-shape, shouting out the opening words of a spell. The shadow-fingers lanced through her forehead and her body went slack. Her feet and robes left the ground to hover over the metal floor plates.

Leering phantoms slid past her, rolling forth on

clouds of mist and shadow, their glee evident in their twisted smiles of jagged night sky and the anti-light of broken stars in empty eye sockets. A long, spectral, outstretched finger probed toward Áine, but was reflected off her helmet with a sputter of aether spark and a hiss of ozone. The phantom withdrew with a pained grimace.

Another creature floated forward, both arms and many fingers outstretched to pierce Leftworth's exposed flesh. Áine stepped up between them. The fingers glanced off her armor, but there was a cost: her power level dropped noticeably, a readout of percentage points in her visor decreasing by a few precious spinning numerals. The display dimmed, and painful shocks marked the points of contact.

Grimlar pulled a vial from his belt. A bright pink liquid shimmered within. Liquid sunrise. He held it in his left hand while his right searched for and produced a short sword from the folds of his dark robe. His third arm emerged to pop the cap from the vial, releasing a bittersweet scent of flowers—of lovers entangled together on a beautiful summer day, with nothing to do but one another. He poured the contents over the short blade, and the liquid bubbled and sizzled when exposed to air and metal. The sword glowed faintly as with the first rays of sunlight peeking over distant mountains. The smell was spring. Life, perpetual.

Living darkness floated towards him, deadly fingers outstretched. He dropped the vial and grasped the hilt with his hands, his third arm withdrawing into the luminous folds of his robe. A phantom, bold and focused on slicing its outstretched fingers through the sorcerer's head, ignored the danger the blade represented.

That was its last mistake. Grimlar slashed his weapon in a wide arc, cutting into the creature's raised arms and separating shadow-limbs from its body. A howling of pain and anger filled the corridor—electronic distortion transmitted through fraying wires.

Synod closed ranks with Áine and Leftworth, seeing that the knight's armor offered some protection against these ghastly attacks. Along with the shinobi, he moved with Kard as she made to parry the drifting, almost casual reach of each phantom as they tried for their brains. He kept the knight between the horrors and himself, finding opportunities to thrust his pike safely around her wide form.

Leftworth risked a step out from behind Áine to fire, landing a shot center mass on one of the phantoms. The aether bolt exploded on contact, releasing a cloud of light and the smell of wet, rotten wood put to flame. The phantom disintegrated.

Emboldened by this minor victory, Synod charged his pike so that blue energy flowed along crystal wires, sputtered, and lanced from the edge of the blade.

Áine swung her sword to knock back grasping fingers. The phantom repositioned to her left, its focus on her, as Synod's charged weapon pierced its side with a squeal of tearing, rubbery shadow-flesh. The pike became stuck as the creature groaned in pain and reached for the offending weapon. Synod overcharged, spending precious aether to do so, until it dislodged itself from the phantom with a burst of heat and bubbling, liquid dark. The spirit collapsed into a puddle of goo at Áine's left foot.

With a heave of her greatsword, she parried another

attack. The doubled their efforts to chip away at her. Her sword slashed wide in a blur of blue aether that radiated from its crystal inlay. The phantoms fell easily to her counterattack, even as fingers found her helm, her shoulders, and her legs, *tick-tick-ticking* her power levels down. She had to end this fast.

A bolt of green exploded a phantom at close range. Leftworth stepped up to her right, another bolt already manifesting in the flight groove. Synod moved up on her left, slicing the charged blade of his pike back and forth in the dark like a dancing blue firefly.

A burning slash of pink light heralded Grimlar's arrival in the melee. Shadow-flesh snapped and leering, inhuman forms melted into pools of acrid dark that bubbled and stank of chemical decay.

The wizard stood suspended in the air where she had been touched by the phantoms, her head raised and eyes open, her arms to her sides as if readying a spell.

She neither moved nor breathed but merely *was*, solid and immune to the prodding of their hands and unresponsive to their words. Whatever dark power had done this to her, saving her—even if they had been inclined to do so—was beyond the group's knowledge and abilities.

Grimlar mused on theoretical methods as more of a thought experiment, but it was Ser Kard who suggested that they simply let her be. The wizard surely meant to betray and kill them at first opportunity, ship or no ship.

Leftworth was quick to agree with the knight, and Grimlar and Synod made no argument against it. Her fate would be her own.

And so they journeyed on, warily eyeing the strange mists and shadows that surrounded them.

20.

They passed through a deck lit by flowing tendrils of darkvoid energy flowing through a stories-high viewport. On the far side of the great chamber, a great blue skeleton welcomed them with a friendly grin. The eye sockets were tall as a man and crawled with shadows. Shoulders hunched forward, arms spread wide over the deck below, the titanic ribcage perched above a door cut into the bulkhead upon which the giant rested.

Synod had never seen anything like it in all of his years. As they approached, he sensed it moving—shifting and leering in patience, waiting to strike as soon as they were within reach. Good sense prevailed, and he reminded himself that ambush might be more effective in a place with such an obvious distraction. He scanned the deck for threats, finding only columns of metal, low rises of stacked stone, and the view of the darkvoid energies in the space beyond the great viewport.

Grimlar had told them to look for energy conduits— lines of flowing aether that might guide them in the direction of some critical system or reactor—but the many halls and chambers through which they had passed had offered little in the way of logic or utility to discern how its structure was laid out.

More than once, Áine had asked herself: *How can this ship* be?

Each time she kept her nervous query to herself, for the answers Grimlar could provide were cryptic and laced with madness. He would be the first to succumb to the darkvoid's dread influence, considering his advanced state of mutation. While his counsel was necessary to survive this place, she did not want to offer him any further opportunities to indulge in abstract thinking and display unhealthy, gleeful wonder at their predicament. It was unnerving.

"The only door is the one ahead, beneath Ser Bones, there," Áine said.

"An ominous doorman, if there ever was one," Synod said.

"He looks jolly enough," Leftworth said, levity in his voice. "Perhaps we could ask him for directions."

Grimlar sat down, his robes rippling like the waters of a stream flowing over flat rocks. He produced his pipe and glass jar of flower, packed the bowl, and sparked it with a snap of his fingers. The acrid smoke of the cannabis wafted over the chamber as he coughed through the first pulls.

"Is now the time for that?" Áine asked. "Are there spirits here to consult?"

Grimlar, his alien eyes red and watery through the smoke, nodded and pointed to the leering skeleton ahead of them. Had the great skull shifted ever so slightly to look down upon them? Did it smile in welcome, or leer at their impending doom?

Synod looked from the ossiferous titan to the sorcerer before joining the wizard on the deck.

"Let me try that."

Grimlar giggled through a mouthful of rolling smoke.

"You are not trained in the arts."

"You know little of the boredom of farmers and fathers."

As they shared the pipe, the skeleton's gaze was upon them, its smile sinister and silly, a beacon glowing in the refracted light of the swirling cosmic illumination.

Grimlar and Synod, thoroughly stoned, announced at once, speaking together, and then over one another, that they should accept the skeleton's invitation, posthaste. They laughed as they stood up, sharing some whispered joke. The others followed.

Beneath the great skeleton was a wooden door clasped in iron, set within the bulkhead. It swung outward on hinges that creaked for want of oil. Inside was a domed antechamber, its ceiling high but humble in scale considering the vastness of the space through which they had just passed. The air within, rather than carrying the metal-tinged taste of the air recyclers, was heavy with burning wick and melting candle wax.

Recesses held humanoid bones in repose, covered in disintegrating burial shrouds and attended by low, melting candles. Someone had laid flowers within several of the chambers for the dead many weeks or months ago, now dead themselves and mere shadows of their former vibrancy.

The domed ceiling was decorated with a menagerie of hand-painted horned demons and luminous angels making war and love among swirling cosmic phenomena and constellations overflowing with blood. The angels—winged humanoids in splendid silver armor and suffused with green light—fought against or alongside handsome or curvaceous demons. Some held one another as they bled out in their arms, while others were embraced in the act of sex. Áine found the painting compelling but deeply puzzling, unsure of its message. Perhaps it recorded a grand war or a single battle. Perhaps it communicated a moral or an idea lost to those who lacked the cultural reference to grasp it. Maybe it was simply what the artist liked.

They passed beneath the domed ceiling and followed a narrow plaster hallway to a door only large enough for them to pass through one at a time. Áine took the lead, careful to sweep her eyes over the door for trip wires or other signs of trap, but, finding none, pushed it open and stepped into the inner sanctum.

Here the floor and ceiling were wide circles, with the curved walls forming a great cylinder. Light filtered down through stained glass, illuminating the chamber in a splendor of shifting blues, reds, and greens. At the far end of the sanctum was a massive greatsword totem, point down and embedded in the tiled floor, carved from soft stone and plated with gold along the edges of the blade, hilt, and handle. It shimmered, dazzling in the light of a hundred candles.

Before the greatsword knelt a massive knight in powered armor of a radically different design than Áine's. The suit was blue, with folded metal and flared cups along the joints, shoulders, and waist. Ridges and curves in the design, purely ornamental, emphasized musculature within. To the left of the kneeling figure was a real sword that was no totem, one that dwarfed even the wide greatsword Áine carried on her back plate.

The knight stood up, armor shifting and sliding, and turned slowly to face those who had interrupted his meditations. He towered several feet over even Áine. His helm was a demonic gargoyle's face growling in threat.

"Greetings," Áine said, not an ounce of fear or trepidation in her voice. "We are travelers, seeking shelter and succor within the deathship. We mean you peace, if you would have it, and do not wish to disturb you at holy prayers."

Synod raised an eyebrow at the knight and kept his pike at his shoulder. Leftworth remained in the doorway, pressed against the frame, crossbow pointed at the floor. Grimlar stood behind them all, hood pulled over his head so as not to offend with his appearance. A goat-headed, darkvoid-touched sorcerer could never be too careful around holy types.

After an interminable pause, the tall knight flicked his gargoyle faceplate up, revealing a nominally human visage glowing a haunting, calm blue.

"Hail, travelers," his voice boomed, loud without shouting, in the small sanctum. "I was offering my prayers to the dead who have passed through in pilgrimage across the deathship." The blue face flickered and warped, a projection in snow and static. The massive knight reached down for his greatsword, then held it to his side, point downward. It was wide as a levyman in padded armor and taller than any of them. The interleaved ribbons along the blade marked the work of a master craftsman. Áine had no doubt it was a weapon of great power, especially if swung by such a behemoth of a man, if a man this spectral giant was. "I then asked God to hold within their hands the life of the one I was sworn to protect, but who now wanders alone."

His face was suddenly a wash of grey static. It reformed with a hiss of energy and a pop of ozone. His "head" was a display screen mounted atop his hulking form, and his face no more than a hologram in blues and greens. That face considered them. "Might you have seen a maiden in white, dressed in the habit and robes of a novitiate, wandering these dark halls and catacombs? Her name is Saleh, and we were separated during a battle many days ago and have yet to be reunited."

Áine stepped forward, boldly, head upright, showing no fear, meeting this knight as an equal—if not in size, then in manner and station.

"You carry an oath."

"Yes. I cannot leave the deathship until it is fulfilled or I die in its pursuit. Either outcome will suit me."

"I am sorry, ser knight, but we have encountered no such novitiate. We were waylaid by a wizard and her wicked familiar, but no one of priestly magic. Tell me, ser, what is your name?"

He raised his head high. "I am Tahir, Knight of Sorrows, sworn to guard the ladies who make pilgrimage to the darkvoid deathship."

"People make *pilgrimage* here?" Synod asked. "Why?"

The knight's large, blue hologram eyes fell on the pikeman. Pride showed through the crystals of the display screen.

"Few places in all of creation offer such holy wonders

or damnable terrors," he said, voice tinged with awe. "The Order of Sorrowful Sisters has seen fit to send its novitiates on pilgrimage for centuries. We Knights of Sorrow are pulled back to service from death to give them the protection they so richly deserve on a quest of spiritual discovery and atonement."

Synod, sensing the religious fervor that danced along the edge of Tahir's words, chose to remain silent. Tahir, seizing an opportunity to evangelize, continued.

"Know that the face of God is hidden in the darkvoid, but may be revealed to those of resounding faith and gentle humility. Some believe God lives within the fell lights of the deep energies that accompany the ship. Others—myself included—have seen and experienced them within the endless halls of the deathship. The shipboard spirit is an angel of their innermost court, guiding this vessel on its righteous path through the deep dark."

This stunned the group, who, unaccustomed to such heresies spoken of so plainly, remained politely silent in the giant knight's presence. Grimlar smiled at his companion's discomfort and spoke with an amused humility.

"We thank you for this catechism, Ser Tahir. Is there some way we might help you in thine quest, or perhaps you could help us in ours? We seek survey data to locate our vessel, crystals with which to fuel our departure, and astrological charts to guide our way."

Tahir considered this, then reached behind him to his campaign satchel. He withdrew a pair of red candles, wide and heavy and wrapped in gold foil. Grimlar's eyes grew wide in shock.

"If you were to find my charge, please tell her to meet me here, at the Sanctum of the Sacred Skeleton," he said. "Or, if you would be so brave, to escort her here yourselves. The deathship is dangerous, as you know, and so I offer you resurrection candles as advanced payment for your help, whether you find her or not." Grimlar, no longer so cautious, shuffled forward hastily to accept the candles.

"Thank you, Ser Tahir. You honor us with your trust and with your gracious gift."

Tahir's eyes flicked to Ser Kard.

"One may be burned in the event of death to come, at your discretion," he said. "The other must be burned for a death in the past, for the circle to continue, for the circle to close. Do you understand?"

"I believe so," Grimlar said. Tahir ignored him and repeated the question to the knight. Grimlar gave her a look that said *go along with this*. What was so special about the candles, she could not guess.

She nodded in her ignorance. That pleased both the knight and the sorcerer.

"You have been good company in mine hour of need, but I must resume my search, and I bid you do the same. I know not of start charts, survey data, nor crystals, but will search for them all the same as I look for Saleh." Tahir pulled his pack on, then slung his titanic sword to his hip, where it clicked into place with a magnetized hum.

"Before I go, one word of warning. Beware the Knight of Mist. He wanders these halls, looking to test his mettle."

"What knight is this?" Áine asked.

"A foe not unlike me in countenance, but beyond any of you, I would fear, although I mean no disrespect," Tahir said. "It was he who fought me near to second and true death, forcing Saleh to flee. It was only the intervention of the frogmen that distracted him and saved us both. He is a revenant-knight, like me, a spirit bound to his armor, but devoid of holy purpose and the promise of rest at the end of his hajj. He moves like a ghost but fights like a demon. If you were to see him, or one like him, I would suggest flight."

"We are learning to move quickly," Áine said.

"He does not relent. He will make many more victims upon this vessel before his time is ended."

"He is one of your order?" Grimlar asked.

"Yes. But driven mad by the energies of the deathship. I have been here many times but have not stayed longer than a few weeks. He has spent many long decades wandering its halls and been subject to its excesses."

"How can a place of holiness drive one mad?" Leftworth asked. "You said God's angel commanded this vessel."

"You must not know much about God, and the terrors they can inspire, even and especially in their holiness and power," Tahir said, softly. "Perhaps your companions might tutor you in matters of spirit. Farewell."

They parted to let the knight pass. He moved through the sanctum to the great door and beyond, leaving them in the quiet of the chamber to contemplate his words—and the lives and deaths of those who had made pilgrimage aboard the darkvoid deathship.

21.

Triangular panels of pink- and blue-tinged glass refracted starlight and the haunting illumination of cascading darkvoid energies. They formed a cathedral, glimmering atop a hill at the far end of a grand chamber, its luminescent spires rising high into hazy darkness framed by the great viewport beyond. The chamber itself was many times the size of those previous rooms through which the doomed fellowship had journeyed. It was also home to a village on the plain below the synthetic hill.

To Áine, the houses appeared not unlike those in the villages that surrounded her lord's keep, complete with a common square, a well, and room to trade. The pink and blue refractions of stars and swirling cosmic energies passed over the village like the glowing aura of an angel. There was no sign of inhabitants, recent or otherwise. As they approached the edge of the commons, resonant organ music flowed out of the glass cathedral.

Grimlar and Leftworth stole off to search one of the larger houses for supplies. Synod and Áine watched the cathedral sparkle in the cosmic twilight and listened to its sonorous music juxtaposed with the tinkling of glass.

"Are you a man of faith, Synod?" Áine asked, her voice flushed with wonder.

"My mother certainly hoped I would be, considering the family name," he said.

"I don't know it."

"Perhaps the education of the nobility is imperfect, then, ser."

Áine gave him a sidelong look, unsure just how much of that remark was meant as insult, and, if it was, how much of it was comradely, and, beyond that, what measure of such things she should tolerate lest she lose her grip on command. Such was her insecurity, even after all they had been through. Perhaps the moment— like so many others here—called for flexibility and tolerance. She gave him the benefit of the doubt.

"A deficit of learning among my rank would explain more than a few of our present struggles," Áine said, removing her helm and allowing the corporal a smile. The light from the cathedral passed over them again, warming her face.

"My heart longs for what lies within," Synod said, eyes on the wondrous structure before them. "To be able to walk in there, and sit through the rites and rituals. To worship."

"Why don't you?"

Synod stood silent for a moment, his mind drifting.

"We do not know who or what is inside, or how they might see the gods, God, the deathship, or us," he said.

"No. But say the music we hear now is played by some automaton, that there are no living beings or dangers inside. Would you venture within?"

Synod tilted his head, remembering something.

"I do not mean to bother you with my mean concerns," he said. "Forgive me, ser."

"Death awaits us around every corner but boredom stalks us just as savagely," Áine said. "Tell me what troubles you, that it might pass the time, and that I may learn something of you."

Synod closed one eye as if struggling to focus on the glimmering cathedral.

"I once told God that I hated him for what he allowed in this world." Synod let those words hang between them, punctuated by the soft, rolling hymnal played out on an organ within the glowing miracle beyond. "I told him he was sick, and that he hates us. That he cannot love us. That no god could and yet allow all this war, death, and misery."

Áine considered this. She always understood the gods as plural—fickle and jealous, yes, but ultimately communal in their spiritual relationship to humankind. Synod's singular use of the word "God" spoke of another way, much like Tahir's. Perhaps the pikeman was admitting to more than simply impious thoughts. Were there sects and cults within their country, within the ranks of their lord's army? She supposed there would have to be, given the number of soldiers and support labor involved in raising and deploying a legion from their homeworld to the Outremer. In her youth, she had been disinterested in the strictures of religion, going through the motions at worship or giving declarations of faith as embedded in oaths and ceremony as part of her duties as a knight and lesser noble. *Heresy* was a dirty word, but one she had not given much thought to. Was this heresy, now?

And if it was, did it matter?

"You feel you have committed a grievous sin in saying these things. Is that what you mean?"

Synod nodded.

"Do you have children?" he asked.

Áine shook her head.

"I have—*had*—three," Synod said. "Two sons and a daughter. All three of them—all of them—at one time or another, told me that they hate me. That they hate their father."

"Is that...typical?"

Synod laughed.

"Oh, of course. Of course it is. Do you know what my response was? I was raised in the old-fashioned ways, far from the cities and academies with their strange philosophies. I should have reacted with anger, with the belt or the rod. That is what *my* father would have done. That is what he did."

The music in the cathedral swelled.

"Each time it has happened, it was love, not anger, that I felt. It was the outstretched hand I offered, not the closed fist. I felt *love,* ser. I saw in them all the hurt and pain of the world, all *my* hurt and pain, and understood that their childish hate, their intensity of feeling, no matter how strong it may have been, could never challenge my love for them. Their anger was a puddle swallowed up by a sea of my love."

Áine considered this. She had never desired children. Her martial life had seemed to preclude the possibility, at least until she was relegated to some command staff or support position that might provide more stability. Her desire for men had been muted at best in her time as a knight and soldier; she had seen them more as brothers, considering the difficult and dirty conditions through which soldiers and knights served. She *understood* men, belonged among them. Now, the women. Those were strange creatures. Many were tough and athletic like her. Good fighters. But soft and strange, too, mysterious and alluring in a way that she felt she could never be.

"I wonder if God is like that," Synod continued. "In my moment of grievous sin, did God see me as someone who is hurt and broken, in need of his repair? Does he see all of us like that, all of the time? Or does he hate me for what I have said and done? For what we have all done in this cursed world?"

The organ music stopped. The soft glow of the cathedral walls dimmed, all the energy flowing out of the building, rendering it dark and silent.

Later, Grimlar and Leftworth returned, their packs laden with crystalline curios but no food, nor tangible evidence that anyone had lived in or even passed through this strange village for some time. While the cathedral drew their wonder, its silence and resplendent glow were a holy thing that they chose not to disturb, and thus continued their sojourn through the deathship.

22.

They made their way through a complex of corridors built at perfect right angles and paneled with wood or a synthetic material made to resemble it, and emerged into a massive, open deck filled with agritrenches from which great trees and plants overflowed across the metal floor, roots finding unlikely footholds in the cracks between deck plating and grates, given succor by the cosmic light and darkvoid radiation that filtered through titanic honeycomb viewports overhead. A humid mist suffused the area and a layer of fragrant, grey soil muted their footfalls on the metal deck.

A fortress-temple rose gradually from within this mystical forest as they approached, stately columns carved from ancient wood polished with dark lacquer, sloping roofs over its main building and attendant towers covered in interlocking monk tiles with chiwen dragon heads set at the corners. Beyond the initial rise of the main keep was a singular and stately pagoda, its many eaves spreading outward, the leaves of a blossoming, red flower absorbing the fruitful radiation and purple light that seeped through the viewports high above. Gold plating shimmered and glowed, reflecting the light in sensual twists and pleasing refractions. The splendor of the temple gave the party pause, much in the same way the glass cathedral had the day prior. There was still room in their hearts for wonder, even in this grand fortress of terror.

The temple compound abutted a great bulkhead in the vast distance beyond, cloaked in darkness and vertical overgrowth. Artificial canyon walls stretched on either side of the vast chamber, granting the temple a remarkable defensive position within both the natural beauty of the forest-field salient and the architectural wonder of the deathship's design.

"How could such a thing exist here?" Synod whispered.

"How could it not?" Grimlar replied.

"It dwarfs even the troop carriers in the fleet," Áine said. "It must be large enough to house thousands."

"Perhaps it houses only spirits, like the village," Leftworth said.

"We shall discover the truth of that, then," Áine said. "Be wary, but keep your weapons low or sheathed. We are likely watched, even now."

As they approached the fortress-temple, crops pouring out of the agritrenches and climbing across the deck, they found a well-worn path through the growth. They passed outbuildings created in the same architectural style, with those flared, sloping tile roofs and exterior walls painted red, purple, and gold. Smoke drifted up from some of them, as it did from the temple complex itself. Shadows moved within the huts and small houses they passed. They were not alone.

Great defensive walls of red stone and gold rose up to meet them, framing an imposing golden gate fit to repel a siege. Atop the walls were spikes, sharp and silver, glimmering in the light, well maintained and anything but decorative.

A low hum approached them. A crystal the size of a large dog and the shape of a dagger's blade, blue and luminous and flanked by two smaller shards, floated down from above. A voice spoke to them in a quick succession of languages, until it spoke words that their translation matrices could comprehend and refract.

Who dares approach the Shadowkhan Temple?

Leftworth's eyes went wide at the name.

"Ser Áine Kard, knight-errant, Grimlar the scholar and scryer, Arturo Synod and Lam Leftworth, men at arms. We are wanderers here, seeking food and shelter from the hospitable and kind. We seek to trade for aether crystals. But most of all, we hope to find in you peace and friendship."

Grimlar raised an eyebrow at her honesty. Áine shrugged.

"Let's try the truth and see how far it gets us," she whispered.

The crystal went dark, morphing from blue to grey, and floated up and away from the gates, just as they shuddered to life to open inwards in welcome.

"The truth opens many doors," Synod said, wonder in his voice.

Inside, the grandeur of the complex was now even more apparent. The keep was taller than it had appeared in the distance, as were its attendant towers and the great pagoda beyond. They entered a wide courtyard of well-trod stone surrounded on all sides by statues of fierce warriors with facial features exaggerated to the animalistic. They held weapons or bared their fists in odd poses, representing the fighting styles and techniques taught there. Beyond the stone guardians were steps that led up to the main keep, where imposing wooden doors remained closed.

"This is no temporary shelter built by survivors," Grimlar said. "This puts to shame even the cathedrals of our home country."

"This is familiar to me, somehow," Leftworth said, his arms tense. He kept his crossbow slung over his back and paused for a moment, as if carefully considering his next words. "I was trained in a place such as this. It was not nearly so grand. Those who taught me the shinobi arts spoke of hidden temples where grand masters studied and taught their craft. I assumed they were folk tales for initiates."

"Is this some glamour, meant to lure us in with an idea drawn from Leftworth's mind?" Áine asked.

"I do not believe so," Grimlar said. "But I have been smoking much of the wizard's weed, and my ability to differentiate between varying threads of reality and dream is fraying."

"Our lives depend on you, sorcerer," Leftworth said.

"As does mine, and the adaptabiliy of my mind, for which the smoke is both balm and boon. Perhaps I should smoke now to read the energy of this place and our immediate future. Care to join me, Arturo?"

Footsteps echoed to them across stone. A lone young woman approached, brown hair cropped short, wearing a vest over a thin yellow shirt and light pants. Her skin was lightly bronzed from hours spent outdoors—or what passed for outdoors aboard the mighty deathship—and her hair and eyes were a complimentary shade of brown. She stopped a few feet away, pressed her hands together, and bowed.

"Welcome, honorable wanderers, to Shadowkhan Temple. I am called Koh. I remain at your service as attendant and guide while you are guests of the temple." She completed the bow and stood upright, keeping her palms pressed together. She was thin but her muscles were well defined, and her slight smile and sparkling brown eyes spoke confidence. She moved with the grace of a trained dancer, but the single sai, its central blade threaded through the sash at her waist, spoke of another discipline entirely.

Áine removed her helm, laying eyes on the girl for the first time. The way she carried herself, her accent, the tinge of her skin—Koh was unlike anyone Áine had ever seen. She was beautiful, but not in any sort of courtly manner, as the young woman lacked all makeup or pretention to performative femininity. Áine had never given a hoot about such things.

"You, uh, honor us with your hospitality, miss, um, Lady Koh," Áine said, finding her voice not quite working the way she meant it to.

"Just 'Koh,'" she replied, flatly. "Come. Our master invites you to speak with him. *That* is a great honor, o knight." She led them across the courtyard and toward the steps of the central keep, where gold-trimmed red doors swung inward in welcome.

23.

Koh led the party through hallways of immaculately polished wood, the walls adorned with grand paintings depicting ancient battles, mythical warriors wielding aetheric weapons, and stylized cosmic landscapes. Stringed instruments played snatches of a haunting melody. Incense and firewood smoke drifted to them in subtle and calming waves. The scent of roasting meat and steaming rice made their stomachs growl and their mouths salivate.

They passed people of all shapes, features, colors—some like Koh, others like those of their homeworld, still more of exotic heritage whose skin tones, facial features, hairstyles, tattoos, and manners of language were as diverse as the cosmological and terrestrial wonders the party had witnessed of late. They wore uniforms almost identical to Koh's, or slightly diverging thereof, the differences presumably based on rank or station. Some—initiates, likely—wore short brown pants, sandals, and stark white shirts, their heads clean shaven and their eyes held low as the group passed.

"They have not taken our weapons," Synod whispered. "Very trusting of them."

"Something tells me they do not need to," Grimlar said. "Do not underestimate them."

"No," Leftworth said, eyes wide with wonder. "That would be a deadly mistake."

At a formidable set of double doors, Koh reached for a silk rope to the side. She pulled it once, twice, then bowed toward the doors. They opened, revealing an audience chamber of great depth, its ceiling held aloft by red columns adorned with swirling dragons in bronze and iron. The floor was of smooth-polished tile made of black-speckled red quartz. At the far end of the room was a dais, upon which a man sat between two women, all of them of advanced age. Their eyes sparkled in the dim light of torches and braziers.

Koh led them to the three and bowed deeply, whispering. Words were exchanged, low and quick, and Koh stood and turned sharply to face Áine and the others.

"Grand Master Liu grants you audience, honored guests. Respect has been given to you, and hospitality. We ask that peace is returned to us, in both word and deed, for the time you spend among the disciples of the Shadowkhan Way."

Áine gave a slight bow of her head, unsure of the protocol. This seemed sufficient signal for Koh, who left the group before the three elderly masters.

Grand Master Liu was stately and in perfect confidence as he sat cross-legged upon a dais. He wore only modest brown pants and a red sash over his shoulder. Muscles like iron wires moved under papery skin. His eyes surveyed them with an intensity that made it difficult to meet them for long. He stroked a wispy white beard in contemplation.

"As Grand Master, I welcome you to Shadowkhan Temple, and grant you asylum here from the wonders and terrors of the deathship, for as long as you wish to remain our guests," he said. One of the women at his side struck a small bell with a hammer, sending out a ringing vibration through the room that bounced off their bones.

Áine stepped forward, helm in her left arm, and took a knee. The others, seeing her gesture, joined her, heads bent low.

"Grand Master Liu, I am Ser Áine Kard, knight-errant," she said. "These are my cadre, survivors of the Battle of Gorgon's Head: Grimlar the scholar and soldiers Arturo Synod and Lam Leftworth. We find ourselves at the mercy of your hospitality." Grimlar raised an eyebrow at her continued reliance on the full truth, but considered the wisdom in honesty. "You have shown us great respect, care, and consideration, especially as we are strangers wandering the halls of this deadly fortress. Your generosity and strength must be great in equal measure to extend such gracious trust."

Grand Master Liu gave a slight smile and tilted his head down toward the knight.

"Do we have anything to fear from you, Ser Kard? From any of your companions?"

"Fortune laid a path for us to your temple. We merely seek shelter for a short time, and perhaps kind direction on our quest."

"Both I can provide you," Liu said. "But know that our generosity has its limits. Those who see our kindness as weakness discover only too late the extent of our strength, even of the least among us in the initiate ranks."

"Understood, Grand Master," Áine said. She looked to the other two masters, their faces wizened but kindly. Áine thought of her own grandmother, and almost laughed picturing her dressed in monks' robes and performing martial arts.

"May I ask of you some questions?" Liu asked.

"Of course, my lord. We are your servants."

Liu nodded. "You spoke of a battle."

"At Gorgon's Head, yes. The local moon."

"The deathship has transitioned again, then?"

"It appeared shortly after we left the upper atmosphere," Áine said.

Liu turned to his right, then his left. Wordless communication passed between the masters. "Have you been aboard a deathship before?" he asked.

"No, Grand Master. We knew of them only in legend."

"This is a place of great wonder, but also of danger. You should rest here for a time."

"If it would please you, Grand Master."

He offered a warm smile and held up a hand, palm flat.

"I appreciate your respect and formality, knight-errant, but you may relax. Do you have questions for me?"

"Yes," Áine said. "What is this place?"

"You are aboard a darkvoid deathship. One of the oldest and mightiest of that fleet. As for our local space position beyond, you would know more than I. Here, the Shadowkhan Temple is home to hundreds of students and followers of the Shadowkhan Way. We hold to the tradition that our way began here, in fact, developed by the ancient grand masters who, in isolation and infused with the energies of the darkvoid, created a martial art and path to enlightenment unlike any other in the known world. Now, a question for you: Why were you fighting on Gorgon's Head?"

"For our lord's honor," Áine said.

"As foolish a reason as any to lose one's life," Liu said. "Your lord's honor was not satisfied, I take it, since you are not with them now, either in victory or in death. You are lost and alone, begging for charity from monks. Your motley party appears to me as ronin—or, worse, bandits. Perhaps 'errant' is too kind a word for what you really are."

This turn caught Áine off guard. He had lulled her into comfort with promises of rest and shelter. She paused, gathering her thoughts.

He is expecting me to change my story, to admit to some deception or additional motive on our part.

Then, coming to the same conclusion as Áine, Grimlar spoke to her without speaking.

This is a test. Careful.

"We seek crystals and astrological data," Áine said. The truth had gotten them this far.

Liu considered her face, and her response.

"Few ever intend to walk the paths of dishonor, but sometimes our lives demand it of us, or we demand it of our lives. Remember, knight-errant, that there is always a choice, even when one is alone, desperate, and hungry."

"Yes, Grand Master."

"Know that this temple is open to all, save for

criminals, bandits, and mercenaries who seek to enrich themselves at the expense of others. Warriors from across the realm travel here for our tutelage, risking much in the journey and even more by walking our path. You, however, have stumbled upon our humble temple as a drunk might bump into a holy shrine after a night of overindulgence. I consider that fortunate for you. Whether it is fortunate for us remains to be seen."

"May we train here, Grand Master?" Leftworth asked. "I have heard of your chamber of ninjutsu, and wish to study your techniques."

Áine turned back to Leftworth with a raised eyebrow. Liu stroked his wispy beard with thumb and forefinger, a pleased smile on his face.

"So quick to reveal yourself, eh, shinobi?"

"For a chance to gain your tutelage? Yes, Grand Master." Leftworth bowed his head low, eyes to the ground.

"The deathship is our home, our ark, the dwelling place of our gods," Liu said. "We take in pilgrims and show them the light of our path. Those who stay join our body and give themselves in service to the temple. Those who leave, leave stronger, with more wisdom, and spread sparks of the light of our way across the vast night. It seems your master, or your master's master, may have been one such spark, young shinobi. I wonder, will your flame be a beacon to others lost in the dark, or will it be a funeral pyre?"

Liu clapped his hands. Koh reappeared at the back of the room.

"You will all be given food, shelter, and the service of apprentice Koh as our guests. We have chambers dedicated to many techniques and schools of discipline, including the shinobi arts, weapons, and unarmed combat." The grand master's gaze settled on Grimlar. "We have a small college of scholars who weave the darkvoid, too, but their tutelage and counsel are limited to those who enter their chamber knowing some semblance of the art already. You appear to have more than a passing familiarity with the aether and darkvoid, sorcerer. Tread carefully among our scholars, and give respect in all cases, even and especially when they answer your queries with silence, and they may accept you."

Grimlar bowed his head in acknowledgment.

"You are welcome to stay until you are ready to continue your quest. But respect our temple as guests. Any trouble you cause will return to you tenfold. The kindness you show will likewise be multiplied."

"We are honored," Áine said, putting a fist over her heart. "Thank you, Grand Master."

"You will be humbled, I should think," he said, smiling. "You have learned one way to fight, o knight. There are many martial paths, but few as demanding as ours. I hope you will take the time to learn some of the basic techniques of our initiates."

A bell chimed. Incense smoke flowed up and over the three elderly masters. Rainbow light illuminated them from behind, washing out their features and forms. They faded from view into candle smoke as a swirl of myriad colors.

24.

Áine slept a dreamless sleep of exhaustion, lost in the comfort of a bed with clean sheets. Rest—real rest, deep and true, for the first time since departing for the Outremer.

Upon awakening in the little room enclosed by sliding bamboo doors and paper walls, she found her armor and sword untouched in a pile next to her bed, along with a fresh set of clothes. White shirt, pants, undergarments of various sizes to choose from. Her own underclothes and mesh suit had been washed, folded neatly, and set in a pile nearby. Whirling cosmic gases, reflecting starlight and moonlight, illuminated the hallway that adjoined her quarters, signaling what passed for morning aboard the deathship.

Once dressed in the white garments, she followed the smell of eggs and coffee to the mess hall, a large, open chamber with a cool stone floor, open rafter design, and long tables where the monks congregated in small groups to eat and drink quietly. Lam waved her over to a table with the others on the far side of the room. She acknowledged him but went first to stand in line for a plate of scrambled eggs, steaming green vegetables, and rice balls, along with a porcelain cup that she filled with brown coffee poured from a metal decanter. Lam's meal on the landing craft had been a blessing; hot, fresh food here in the depths of the deathship was a miracle.

The men were in good spirits, chatting about the luxuries of a private room and fresh clothes. Grimlar wore a new robe, one in the same brown and white style as the monk's standard uniform, but threaded throughout with dark purple foil. He kept his hood up but drew no curious or hostile looks. Despite living on a deathship, none of the others showed signs of mutation. Still, the scholars of whom the grand master spoke had yet to make their appearance.

After a time, the mess began to clear out, the monks rising from their tables and working to clear plates and cups, then sweeping and wiping the tables down. Koh approached Áine and the others.

"You have the opportunity to rest or to join us in our exercises," she said. "Lam Leftworth, the grand master has given you permission to enter the ninth chamber, where you might learn from Master Hayabusa's teachings. Grimlar the scholar, you may enter the seventh chamber and find our college hard at work. They are busy, often single-minded in their pursuits, but your knowledge of darkvoid magic practiced in the wild will certainly inspire them to conversation."

"Such is a start to greater things," Grimlar said.

"I would invite Arturo Synod and Ser Áine Kard to join me in the training yard."

Synod put his coffee down.

"Do you know the pike, miss?"

Koh smiled with confidence.

"As apprentice, I possess familiarity and skill with pike, pole, scythe, hammer, spear, tonfa, sai, dagger, short sword, and more," she said. "You will find our initiates have great competency with many weapons, and work toward expertise with at least two."

"Perhaps I can teach your whelps a thing or three."

"We would be honored," Koh said, her soft smile now an amused smirk.

The group stood. Koh raised an eyebrow, then nodded toward the dirty tableware. Sheepishly, they started cleaning up their own mess. She joined them. Áine couldn't remember the last time she had to clear a table. Not having her nobility weigh upon her among these men felt good.

The training ground was a great octagonal stone courtyard behind the central keep and in the shadow of the pagoda. The air was cool and ideal for morning drill.

While Grimlar and Lam sought knowledge among their own kind elsewhere, Koh led Áine and Arturo through kata for each of the beginner's weapons: the pole, the scythe, the hammer, and the tonfa. Peasants' weapons, easily concealed or procured. Both of them struggled with the unfamiliar weight and movement of the tools after drilling and fighting so long with sword and pike, but their minds soon picked up on the patterns, on the subtleties of weight and hand position.

Koh was neither pleased nor displeased with their progress or lack thereof; she merely guided them through each drill until they could repeat them satisfactorily.

"Our way teaches personal and community defense," Koh said, eyes on Áine's muscular form as she completed a three-step routine with the tonfa sticks held close against her forearms. "Nobility and the wealthy do come to us, but not in the same numbers as those who are poor or lack the privilege of squires and powered armor." Those words had a bit of an edge to them. "These are simple weapons for simple people. We train those who would stand against the oppression and terror of the powerful and the unjust, using what tools might be at hand."

"I don't understand," Áine said, catching her breath. "What good does it do the poor to become monks, here?"

"You would not expect the poor to know how to fight, except perhaps as disposable infantry for some lord's vain crusade?"

Áine bristled at Koh's question. She had been trained to see the souls under her command as tools, weapons shuffled around a battlefield. Numbers on a data slate. Men and women to do the hard labor of setting up and breaking down camp, of carrying out the orders of their betters, of fighting and dying when told.

There were times when Áine felt at odds with the way her peers or betters spoke of the soldiers they led, but being of a lower rank, and not wanting to seem as a sympathizer with the lazy and ungrateful of the common rabble, she had kept her mouth shut. She had only engaged in the petty ritualistic humiliation that passed for discipline a handful of times, and only when her exhaustion and frustration were at their peak. This was no point of pride, now, faced with Koh's barbed question.

"The powerful often do not expect the unexpected," Koh said. "Why would illiterate peasants know how to fight, to organize, to sustain a campaign where they are outnumbered and outmanned? Those of our way who return to the world, to the field—we give them the tools they need not only to fight, but to teach, to grow our way."

She gestured to the far end of the courtyard, where a small group of monks were donning blue and grey robes, wrapped up in white cloth belts and adorned with backpacks and pouches by attendant initiates. "These warrior-monks prepare to depart our temple, and the deathship itself, to respond to calls for aid, to return to avenge a wrong, or simply to wander and avail themselves to those in need as the gods reveal such opportunities."

"You are anarchists," Áine said.

"We spread sparks, and some of those sparks become flames, and we burn away the dead and atrophied wood of the world."

"You have ships here?" Arturo asked, leaning against his pole.

"We count many ship captains among our friends," she said carefully. "But these ones will take stoneway gates to their destinations."

"You have gates, here?" Áine asked. "There was rumor about one on Gorgon's Head, but..."

"*We* do not have gates, no," Koh said. "The deathship does. Whether it will reveal them to you or not is an open question."

"How do the—the disciples—find their way back to the temple? The deathship moves, does it not?"

"There gates' destinations are fixed, even if the gates

themselves are not. As for starflight, there are signs in the heavens by which the deathship's movements may be understood. Techniques that perhaps your goat-man can learn, even.

"Some who leave us return. Many do not. Those that do bring with them books, technology, wealth, recruits for initiation. Some bring back husbands, wives, or even children. Some return to recruit more to join them in matters of war and honor. Our temple ebbs and flows upon the cosmic tides. As the energies of the darkvoid flow, so too does our order. But we have discussed enough. Return the weapons to the rack." Koh pointed at the far side of the courtyard. "We train with the body, now."

When Áine and Arturo made no movement, Koh stomped her foot and clapped her hands. Her lovely voice became a low growl.

"*Move!*"

They did as they were told.

25.

Would you consider remaining here?" Áine asked the men over a hearty dinner of rice balls, steaming wooden bowls of seasoned vegetable stock and strips of beef, and generous cups of hot, sweet wine.

No one spoke at first, sensing a test from their lieutenant.

"You are not bound to me. Our lord is dead. Speak freely." Saying those words was like removing chains from her own mind. "There is opportunity here. Work, food, knowledge." Áine's eyes fell on Grimlar. He had changed robes yet again, wearing now the light blue and purple-trimmed robes of the Shadowkhan college of sorcery. Did not something appear different about him? His features were hidden in the shadow of his robes, but she was certain his face had changed.

"I would counsel against any of us making decisions about our future until the true nature of this place has revealed itself," Grimlar said. "But I do admit to its initial charms."

"You speak as if there is deception here," Áine said.

"They house both a sorcerer's college and a chamber

of the shinobi arts," Leftworth said between slurps of soup. "Deception is key to both disciplines."

"Are we in danger?" Synod asked.

"We are always in danger aboard a deathship," Grimlar said. "It remains to be seen what kind of danger."

"Would these mean us harm?" Áine asked.

"They seem hospitable," Synod said.

"Perhaps the danger—or the deception—has not presented itself, yet," Grimlar said. "We should be cautious. We should learn what we can, and rest, while we figure out what to do. But do not join this order without understanding what you are signing up for."

Áine refilled her cup with sake from the bottle. The hot drink went down pleasantly in her throat. She couldn't remember the last time she drank alcohol so freely.

"Our handler, Koh, mentioned something to that effect," Áine said, letting the buzz loosen her tongue. "These monks are ideological. Revolutionaries, even. Their outlook is sure to have made some enemies over the centuries."

"They welcome us because we have martial power, and some use to them," Grimlar said. "It is clear their spiritual beliefs are genuine, or genuine enough to provide succor to strangers such as us, but already they train us, give us weapons, or instruction in the shinobi and darkvoid arts. They treat us as guests, but they hope we are recruits."

"They are fighting a war," Synod said softly, in sudden realization. "They need soldiers."

The others shuffled uncomfortably in their seats as

the weight of the truth settled on them.

"Why not just be forthright with us?" Áine asked. "We would have accepted their charity either way."

"The shinobi is taught that deception is the first and last rule of warfare," Leftworth said, reaching for the bottle of sake. Dried blood was smeared across the fingers and knuckles of his hand.

26.

The days that passed were not long enough for Áine to master the fundamentals of movement and weaponry of Shadowkhan, but they were enough to start her down the path. On the third day, she lost all of her progress, forgetting where to place her feet and hands, the movements and coordination becoming clumsy and disjointed. Koh whacked the back of her head and her butt with a bamboo reed, shouting out curses in a language Áine's translation matrices gave up on. She was grateful for her ignorance.

On the fourth day, she felt as if she were starting all over again, her muscles sore and her movements slower than ever.

On the fifth, her body adjusted to the movements and, while she was still not confident in the dozens of kata routines that were more akin to dance than the sword-fighting maneuvers she was used to, she earned her first bit of genuine praise from the apprentice.

"Slow is smooth, and smooth is fast," Koh said, nodding, watching Áine turn her hips and shoulders to flow from one form into another.

Synod, to his credit, received more blows from the

bamboo reed than Áine did, but never once cried out or faltered, and did not complain about their tutelage— although he did complain about his middle-aged body.

"At what point can an aging man set aside the drill yard and the field?" he moaned. "When honor is satisfied, when our enemies are dead, or when I meet my end, I suppose. Which end to toil might arrive soonest, I wonder."

Deep into their second week, they met Koh in the courtyard. She waited for them with two brown vests slung over her muscular forearms, extended outwards.

"You grasp the simplest of our concepts to avoid injury in practice," she said, producing a grim smile from Áine. "These are the vestments of initiates. They are yours to wear as long as you would bear their honor and burden." Áine and Synod accepted them with a bow.

"Initiates cycle through the chambers and receive instruction from the masters and their cadre," Koh said. "They commit to the rigor and discipline of the temple. They stay for as long as they wish and for as long as they wish to try. Advancement is based on the good, sound judgment of the apprentices and masters of each chamber. Achieving rank means more responsibility. It means leadership. Sometimes it means deployment to the field, beyond the safety of our walls and perhaps beyond the deathship itself. It is a hard life, but one worth living, as you will serve the innocent and protect those who cannot protect themselves. Such is the offer we extend to you, without obligation or expectation."

Áine and Synod bowed their heads low.

"Must we make a decision now?" Áine asked.

"No," Koh said. "You are guests of the grand master.

You have been given the honor of joining us as initiates, or to remain as guests until such a time as you may depart."

"We hoped to find astrological data and crystals for a journey," Áine said.

"We have not forgotten. A second audience may be arranged shortly, after the work of the tournament is complete."

That caught Áine's attention.

27.

The chamber reverberated with the murmuring excitement of a hundred monks. Initiates, apprentices, full monks, scholars, and masters alike gathered across the flat, wooden bleachers around the stone-carved arena with a padded canvas square at its center. A red floral design marked the springy canvas, bright and vibrant, its configuration calling to mind the swirling cosmic energies visible from the temple's courtyard.

The grand masters sat on a dais overlooking the squared circle on the far end of the arena, adorned in brown robes with sashes of crimson that marked their rank, their bald heads reflecting the soft light of torches set at each corner of the square. Great banners hung along the walls, emblazoned with hand-painted characters of a script Áine did not recognize.

"'Victory over self,'" Leftworth said, pointing to each in turn. "'Honor over glory.' 'Spirit of desire,' maybe, 'strength of arm and wisdom.'"

"I would think being a thief and assassin would leave little time to learn letters and calligraphy," Áine said.

"You would think wrongly, ser," Leftworth said. "My

hand well remembers the proper grip of the quill."

"If you write half as well as you cook, I might order you to take dictation of my annals of war," Synod said, taking on the airs of a disinterested noble. "My successors should know the extent of my bravery in campaign." Áine let slip a snort. That drew smiles from the men.

Two initiates entered the arena, carrying great cymbals. They crashed them together. A second pair followed, carrying marching drums and pattering out a cadence familiar to any soldier. A third pair entered on the far side of Áine and Leftworth, wielding torches that blazed blue fire and warbled out a strange but pleasant melody that stimulated the ear and mind.

Upon reaching the canvas square at the center of the arena, the initiates let their instruments fall silent, save for the blue fire, which hummed a subdued, melodious tune, underpinning the ambient noise of the chamber. Master Liu stood up on the platform at the short edge of the arena. He raised his hands, his lips moving, but his words were lost in the reverberations of the music of the blue flame. Some signal passed from him to the initiates, monks, and masters as the entire arena erupted in a great shout—a pair of phrases that Áine found both exhilarating and chilling.

HONOR FOR THE GODS.

BLOOD FOR THE DEATHSHIP.

The arena fell silent. The blue flames reached high. The torches around the square and the chamber were subsumed by blue fire. A high-tempo rhythm of drum, cymbals, gong, and synthesized instruments brought the crowd to their feet. The monks' excitement was a raging storm, a fury of pre-combat lust, ribald and charged with adrenaline, easily the match for any tournament or jousting crowd for which Áine had fought. The hair pricked up on the back of her neck. Synod stood and pumped his fist. Leftworth, usually more reserved by his training and general nature, stood tall as he nodded his head and clapped to the overpowering music. The first two combatants approached the canvas square and ropes.

The music and shouting did not stop as the referee, a monk in orange vest adorned with a white sash, stepped under the ropes that divided the stretched-canvas square from the baying crowd. Blue light reflected off of his shaved head as he pressed fist against open palm. He bowed to Liu and the other grand masters. Receiving a curt nod as acknowledgment, he turned toward the two fighters and gestured with outstretched hands for them to enter. The crowd cheered as the fighters took up their positions. Bowing to one another, they listened to the terse instructions.

The words of the referee reverberated throughout the arena, amplified by device or magic.

"Fighters, ready."

The combatants bent their heads forward, raised their fists, and stepped out into fighting stance. The referee held a hand between them.

"Engage!"

A roar from the crowd. The referee retreated to the ropes as the fighters circled one another, each looking for an opening. Eyes low, arms raised in parallel to protect their faces, shoulders bent forward, they wore wrappings on their arms and hands, flashing white. Bare feet on taut canvas stained with sweat, ash, and blood. Their movements left trails through time in the light of the blue fire. The rose of crimson on the mat awaited their blood.

A fist probed out, followed by another. One-two. *One-two.* Connection to the defender's arms. Shouts from the monks in the stands. A leg swept forward, striking shin, causing a stumble. Roaring approval. Fists raised high. People shouting and bodies colliding, pretense of form and precise strikes giving way to the scrum of close combat. Separation by the referee. Orbiting, striking, deflecting, breathing. Dodging. *One-two, one-two-THREE.* Pained grunts. The slap of fist on arm flesh. The inevitable pull, fighters drawn to one another like celestial bodies, two halves of a beautiful, electric whole. Áine was of the crowd, and the crowd wanted pain, wanted impact, wanted resolution.

There was blood before it was over. There was more blood when it finished, a fighter with fist held high by the referee, their opponent on a knee with palm pressed against a trickle of blood from a split above their right eye. The crowd—Kard, Synod, and Leftworth among them—cheered for vanquished and victor alike.

Áine had seen and participated in armored tournament fighting, but the rules were stricter, the proceedings slower, and bodies could still get mangled. This, without armor or weapons, felt more personal, more impactful, even if it was called before serious injury could occur.

She was excited. The trepidation of the invitation was gone. Seeing it, experiencing it, she wanted to be a part of it now. She was ready.

28.

The crashing of cymbals and the pattering of militant drums broke through the noise of the celebrating crowd. Two initiates gestured to Áine from the aisle at the far end of the benches.

"Wish me swift victory," she said.

"We shall wish the blood be kept from your eyes," Leftworth said, nodding at the fighter who had just lost.

"Remember that you are not wearing your armor," Synod shouted as the crowd cheered for the winner. Áine couldn't decide whether that was genuine advice or if he was teasing her.

She stepped out of the bleachers and followed the two initiates down the aisle to the roped-off square. They parted the ropes above and below so she could climb up and step through. The crowd reacted with a cautious cheer. She looked down at her hands and arms as the initiates wrapped them in fresh white. Their movement trailed that pleasant blue afterimage effect from the strange torches. When the initiates were finished, she moved through a simple kata to warm up: striking out, returning to defense, and shifting the position of her feet and shoulders, not wholly unlike the techniques of pugilism with which she had some limited experience. But this was faster, if more considered, and the technique had to account for strikes from the legs as well as the hands. She understood the mental stack of having to carefully consider so many variables, and knew that whatever the outcome of her own battle, she would have to spend many years training to be the match of any monk beyond the rank of initiate. She hoped her opponent was, if not a guest of the temple like her, then at least inexperienced.

The ropes on the far end of the square parted, and through them emerged a familiar face. Koh was even more beautiful in the shimmering blue light of the torches. Her wide brown eyes caught Áine's and held them hostage. Her lithe body was wrapped in form-fitting white, with a vest and leggings of light blue befitting her rank. Wisps of trailing light followed her as she moved, marking her as a lovely specter in an erotic dream, not some foe to be punched and bloodied on canvas.

Koh must have read surprise—or something else—on Áine's face, as her impartial mask slipped from a determined frown to a knowing smile. Áine blushed.

"Expect the unexpected, knight-errant," Koh said softly, her words clear to Áine through the noise of the crowd. Áine shook her head and raised her arms in fighting stance.

"*Fighters, ready,*" the ref said, his words reverberating throughout the stone chamber. Áine nodded. Koh swapped stances as if she were performing dance moves in a ballet. Áine recognized the first two, but not the third or fourth. Koh settled with her left foot forward, her forearms bars defending her pretty face.

Her smile disappeared. Áine saw only violence in those lovely eyes.

"Engage."

They circled one another for a few moments, the crowd shouting encouragement for Koh and insults for Áine's form. As the adrenaline hit Áine in its initial waves, she felt slow and weak in her movements. But she was experienced enough to know that this was merely the prelude to her body's adjustment to imminent violence, and that it would perform when called upon. She soothed her mind and shushed the voice that urged her to *strike, strike now!* and allowed time to tick by. The attacks you do not make are just as important as the ones you do.

Koh floated forward and back out of Áine's orbit again, teasing her with subtle advances and withdrawals, hoping to coax an ill-considered strike. Áine's training had only provided the basics of familiarization and beginner's forms, but she had other training to rely on, too. She wondered how well a form-perfect advance of her own discipline would fare without the protection and weight of knight's armor.

She did not have to wait long to find out. Koh slipped toward her and, sensing her reluctance to take the initiative, offered a kick to her left thigh and a grazing punch to her right temple. Áine shook off the first blow and managed to dodge the second. Koh's offense was little more than a probe, however, and confirmed what she suspected: Áine was not sure of herself. Koh stepped forward, spun to avoid a strike that Áine wisely withheld, and twirled into a punch straight for Áine's face, giving her good opportunity to test her defense. The knight raised her forearms and absorbed the blow, but the shock of being hit left her slow to respond to the follow-on move.

Koh's kick reached her stomach with no dispute. Áine lost her wind and stumbled back, catching her balance on the edge of a fall, her body alerting her to pain at multiple points. The referee stepped between Áine and Koh, his face dour as he evaluated Áine for injury or inability to go on. Áine shook her head and resumed her form, her body tensing and releasing. Muted praise came from the crowd. Synod and Leftworth cheered her on, their words lost but their voices distinct. She set her eyes on her opponent, having survived her first attacks and remaining tall. Koh snapped her lips in a quick kiss toward the knight, unseen by others. Áine's pride, now wounded, flashed into anger—and anger was a potent weapon in her hands.

The referee withdrew. Áine stepped toward Koh slowly, determined not to charge in but moving into inevitable contact all the same. Áine knew they were playing Koh's game: fast strikes and tactical withdrawals, forcing confrontations on the monk's terms in a fighting style in which Áine was only a neophyte. She would have to find a way to take the initiative without exposing herself.

Áine moved in. Koh did not back up. The knight feinted with a right jab toward Koh's chin, locked behind her impenetrable forearms, and stuttered forward with half-steps to land her right foot against Koh's left knee in a downward thrust. The monk grunted and almost tripped and tangled them both up, but a quick shove from Áine sent them apart again. The crowd roared disapproval, but the referee did nothing to indicate foul.

In the half-second Koh took to regain her balance, Áine imagined herself in full plate—her shoulders wide and metal, her helm protecting her head, her runes aglow—and charged forward as if she were barreling into a column of infantry. Reaching Koh, she lifted her shoulder from the charge and snapped her feet out into the fighting stance they had drilled together. Standing straight up, she left her face and head undefended and twisted her torso to carry through each punch, *one, two, THREE*—landing fist against Koh's raised arms and through to her face, thumb or knuckle grazing forehead, ear, and chin. Áine gathered her strength and completed the combination with another downward strike from her right foot, this time clipping Koh's right ankle and sending her stumbling back, caught only by the ropes.

The crowd erupted—this time in approval. The referee was between them. Koh was already back on her feet, but Áine knew she had hurt her opponent—not just physically, but her gods-damned *pride*. The referee and Koh spoke in the language of the temple, confirming her willingness to continue the fight. Anger flashed hot in her wide brown eyes and blue light trailed from her body as she settled back into position. The referee reverse-chopped his hand between them to signal a continuation of the bout. Áine broke fighting stance to stand up straight, extend her left arm, and fan her fingers toward herself in invitation. The crowd roared. Koh growled. Áine adopted the basic fighting stance of the initiate to emphasize her point: she knew no fear.

Koh stepped forward, sure-footed and deliberate. Áine, emboldened by her successful strikes, would not allow Koh to re-establish tactical control of the fight, but also did not want to step into a trap. Koh's bare feet edged forward along the canvas toward Áine's own until they circled one another.

Instead of teasing, probing strikes, Koh threw herself into a roundhouse kick, strong and sure, at close range. Áine threw her arms up in clumsy defense and tried to duck to avoid it. The kick connected with her left shoulder and the side of her head. It hurt like hell, but did not knock her down or back. Koh was spinning back into place, preparing to send another kick out straight, her eyes wide and mouth open in a shout, as Áine abandoned her defense to charge toward her—arms extended, palms open and fingers pressed close, a last-ditch effort to interrupt what would surely be a devastating follow-up. Her palms struck Koh's chest and slid upward into her neck and chin.

Instead of falling back, Koh fought for balance and brought her right elbow down onto Áine's left shoulder in a painful shock, then struck her ribs with her right fist at close range. The knight suffered both blows with gasps and bursts of white-hot pain. The fighters broke contact as Áine rolled down and away, her hands hitting the canvas mat and pushing herself back up to her feet just as fast. She had clearly suffered the worse from that exchange, but Koh showed signs of pain, too, her face set hard. Gone was the amused condescension of the beginning of the match. There was a determination in Koh's eyes to put Áine in her place.

"Expect the unexpected," Áine said, just loud enough for Koh to hear.

29.

Something was wrong. Koh's eyes shifted away from Áine. The knight stepped toward her opponent, not registering the problem until the screams and shouting pulled her attention to the upper reaches of the arena.

Monks tumbled and scrambled over bleachers and down into the aisle. Strange men and women hopped through the doors into the grand fighting chamber, draped in blue and orange robes and wearing small caps, faces pale as the moon and eyes aglow with the purple of the darkvoid. Fangs, glowing neon green, extended from their blue-grey lips.

Cymbals and drums clanged. Shouts from the dais where warrior monks gathered around the grand masters in defense. The smell of burning wood and incense, of grave dirt and blood.

Neon fangs sank into the arm of an initiate who stood her ground in the aisle. Another of the pale-faced monsters grabbed her braided hair and yanked it upwards, exposing her neck as she cried out in pain. Purple eyes flared as verdant teeth glowed hotly in extension, then pierced through flesh like needles heated in fire.

The referee held onto the ropes, shouting for the doors to be sealed, when pale blue hands reached up from below and seized his ankles. His face contorted into a mask of terror. His voice collapsed into a screech of pain as the undead hands pulled him down with supernatural strength, squeezing through flesh and breaking bone with grisly ease. He tumbled beneath the ropes, mewling, where glowing fangs awaited him.

Áine was trapped in a recurring nightmare. No matter where they went or how long they fled, the dead followed—even into the depths of space. Her despair was spoiled by Koh, who shook her shoulder.

"Fight together, and we might survive," Koh said.

"Get me to my armor," Áine said, "and I guarantee we will survive."

Koh let her hand linger, her fingers lightly brushing Áine's shoulder.

"Don't let them grab you," Koh said. "They are stronger than they look."

"I have faced revenants before." Áine felt guilt rise up alongside her fear. *Have we brought the curse with us from Gorgon's Head, and laid it upon the very brow of our hosts?*

"Not like these," Koh said. "These are jiangshi." Áine was a little disappointed that Koh was not impressed.

Smeared in blood and eyes alight with the purple, smoking glow of darkvoid energy, one of the jiangshi climbed up onto the canvas. It angled its neck in an awkward, twisting motion to leer up at them like a beast, the referee's blood still dripping from its neon green fangs and pale blue lips.

Koh and Áine stepped forward as one, bringing their heels down upon its head, smashing its chin and face into the mat. The creature roared and spit broken teeth and blood. The women took turns heeling it in the back and top of its skull, adrenaline and years of training giving them the strength to crack and shatter bone. Mist rose from the cracks, its purpled brains writhing in blue-green blood that splattered and dribbled out against the mat. The creature moaned and went still.

Two more appeared at the edge of the canvas, hands on the mat. Koh assumed a fighting stance as she had in the contest. Áine did likewise, now comfortable with positioning her body for unarmored combat.

"Be merciless," Koh said. "Jiangshi retain nothing of their former lives. Evil spirits bound to empty bodies by rank sorcery. Do not focus your attention on the cards slipped into their clothes, belts, or pockets, or you may fall under their spell."

"Blood drinkers?"

"Yes. Life force. These are our temple's dead, in our burial clothes. This is personal insult as much as attack. Here they come."

The jiangshi clambered awkwardly onto the canvas mat, then stood up straight. A short male and shorter female, young when taken in death, not so imposing, except drenched as they were in vile liquids of recent death. Their eyes shimmered purple and their pale blue skin was spotted with green moss and grey decay. They raised their arms straight out in unison. They hopped toward Koh and Áine, lusting after their vibrancy. Hungering for their blood.

Koh lifted her right leg in a probing, light kick. When

the female jiangshi merely took the blow and continued to hop forward, Koh extended the kick up to strike her foot against the ghoul's chin and face, sending its head back and up with a *crack*.

It lowered its head down, slowly, eyes wide and face impassive, then pressed green fangs over blue lips with a hiss. Koh brought her leg back down, turned her hips, and made to strike with her left leg and foot, but the jiangshi caught the kick aimed at her stomach. Koh grunted but could not free her foot from the creature's grasp. It tilted its head, eyebrows raised and eyes wild, before turning its catch and forcing Koh to spin her body or risk having her ankle broken. She landed on the mat awkwardly, the wind knocked out of her, her foot still in the monster's cold grasp.

The male jiangshi advanced on Áine, one hop at a time. The knight raised her fists to her cheeks, unconsciously mixing the forms she had been taught here with the training-yard pugilism of her teenage years of squiredom. She advanced, fired off a jab to crunch the creature's nose, then danced to her right, putting herself at its flank as it shook its head from the disorienting blow. Áine struck again, one-two, landing punches on its left ear and knocking its burial cap from its head, revealing a tangle of decomposing hair that writhed with hideous, crawling things. Áine ducked to avoid its arms as it swung itself toward her in a lurching attack. She punched again in combination, then abandoned her form for a charge of brute strength.

The creature's hands grasped her torso with preternatural power. Fingers dug into Áine's skin, pinching her and eliciting moans of pain, but these noises were subsumed by her war cry. Wrapped up with the jiangshi, Áine pressed into a tackle, displacing its uncertain legs with surprise and strength. The jiangshi tumbled into its partner, knocking them both over and freeing Koh's trapped foot from the ghoul-girl's grasp.

Áine twisted her body and rolled away violently, dislodging from the creature's grip and landing on her ass on the canvas. Koh was already on her feet, running away from them to the corner. She wrapped her hands around the great blue-flame torch burning there, then kicked it loose from below.

The girl burned first. Her pockets were lined with paper missives from the living. The notes were meant to free her spirit from the worries and regrets of life, assuring her of love and kindness, liberating her into the spirit world without the burdensome worries of life.

They served their purpose, after all. The blue flame caught on the papers. The fire spread rapidly, smelling of mint. The jiangshi grew suddenly still. No shrieks of pain escaped those dead lips. There was only peace in sudden immolation.

As if lifted by strings, the male jiangshi now stood, legs ramrod straight, arms extended in threat toward Áine, who was scrambling back to her feet. It turned its stiff neck, eyes going wide as Koh approached, torch leveled at its flowing burial robes. It spun suddenly, straight arms nearly knocking the torch from Koh's grasp, long fingernails raking her arms and leaving three streaks of parted skin and blood in their wake. She cried out in pain.

Áine extended a straight punch to the back of the creature's head. It tilted forward, almost losing its balance, then slowly turned back to her with a dead smile, as if nothing had happened at all.

Koh recovered and shoved the torch forward, spreading the flames along his robes, working it to catch the burial papers as she moved in a semicircle around him. The jiangshi suddenly stood stock still, the fire doing its work, its flesh snapping and crackling like small branches in a campfire. The flames worked over a strange, hand-sized card woven into its belt, covered in bizarre characters written in green innk. That, too, served as quickening fuel.

A roar of some terrible, slouching spirit escaped its lips and it collapsed like a sack of twigs and branches. Bubbling slime the colors of the swirling darkvoid oozed out of its burial clothes.

30.

Synod and Leftworth scrambled down the bleachers, making their way down to the fighting square to reach Áine and Koh. Pale grey hands grasped for them, mouths alive with snapping green fangs. Jiangshi loomed over fallen monks, indulging in blood by piercing fangs through necks or draining wisps of life force—blue light that flowed from the eyes, noses, and screaming mouths of their victims into their gaping maws.

Synod wound up and punched one of the feeding creatures square on the nose. It went tumbling down the bleachers to a level below, but his fist reeled back with pain.

"Gods!" he cursed. "They are hardened by the touch of death."

"We need weapons," Leftworth said. From his training uniform's sleeves he produced a pair of short, flat knives, no hilt or handle aside from the dull plane of metal beneath the blades. He handed one to the pikeman. "Try not to prick yourself."

Synod accepted the gift and lunged for the creature that was hopping down the aisle toward them, slashing wildly at its face. It accepted the attacks passively, green blood leaking from fresh wounds, a smile at the edge of its blue lips and widening mouth. Synod shifted his attacks to its hands, which extended forward from ramrod-straight arms. Fingertips went first, followed by chunks of hand as Synod furiously chopped and hacked. The knife was fine and did its work.

The creature, oblivious to the pain but curious about the damage, brought its bloody stumps to its face, tilting its head in confusion. Synod and Leftworth slipped past it on the bleachers in the row below and reached the main aisle. Áine and Koh met them there.

"What do we do, ser?" Synod asked, acknowledging her with a nod but already facing his body and blade outward.

"We make for our rooms," Áine said. "I need to reach my armor, and you need your weapons."

"Use this," Koh said, handing Leftworth the torch of blue fire. "They are vulnerable to the flames."

The shinobi nodded to the monk with a stern, accepting look. They moved at a quick pace up the aisle, the two men glancing back occasionally to make sure the knight and monk kept pace with them. Leftworth swung the torch, keeping the hopping undead at distance, while Synod flashed the knife to slash or saw through any jiangshi who tried for them.

Soon they were through the doors and into the main hall. Shouting and the smell of smoke greeted them as they left the chaos of the arena behind.

"This is a planned attack," Koh said. "The main force likely came from our own cemetery, outside."

"What is the best way back to our quarters?" Leftworth asked.

Koh stepped up to lead them, guiding them through junctures and splits in the hallway, taking them down red-painted, wood-panel hallways freshly accented with sprays of arterial blood. They encountered a few bodies of monks, limbs torn off and faces frozen in screams. From darkened rooms, blue faces leered. Shouts for help and the names of strange gods. The hint of ozone on the air—perhaps the work of the sorcerers. Áine spared a thought for Grimlar and the Shadowkhan college, hoping they had put their skills to good use. She also hoped they would not make things worse, as had been the case on Gorgon's Head.

There was a mad dash across a stretch of open space between buildings. Outside, jiangshi patrolled in groups of two or three, hopping aimlessly over the bodies of the victims they had already claimed. Whatever resistance the temple might mount, it was not to be seen here.

Koh led them to the living quarters. They slipped in through the kitchen, where the initiates on duty hid beneath the working tables. Koh barked something at them in Shadowkhan shorthand, and they remained still and hidden.

After a time, they reached their quarters, the sliding bamboo and papered doors mercifully free of blood or evidence of damage, and they entered with relief. Leftworth stood watch at the closed door as shadows passed by. Synod joined Áine in her corner, immediately kneeling to help her into her armor, one piece at a time.

"Anytime now, mum," Leftworth whispered. "Monk. Take your fire back. I will get my crossbow." Koh accepted the torch and felt braver holding it, but the snapping flames and spiraling smoke would surely draw the monsters' attention.

Synod helped Áine snap her metal leggings into place, latching each section together as they magnetically sealed up and joined with the boots. Áine slipped a chain mesh undershirt over her combatant's simple uniform. Then they worked together to don the plate, lifting it over her shoulders and settling it down to join with the waist, where magnetized metal hummed as its systems came online. Áine extended her hands and Synod gently set the power gauntlets into place, feeling reverence at the ancient, instinctual honor of preparing an armored warrior for battle.

The armor's teal coloring became brighter as its component parts came together and runes ran hot with aether. Áine flexed her muscles within the plates, the interior padding suctioning to her robes and skin with the pleasant embrace of a lover's hug. As a pope might crown a queen, Synod lowered the helmet over her head. Inside, all was dark, until the red lenses on her visor lit up with a *zap* and system information cascaded down in crimson runes. Systems online, power at nominal levels.

"My sword," she bellowed, her voice amplified and distorted through the helm's speaker. Synod laid a hand on the wide, flat blade and handle, careful to lift with his legs as he picked it up and offered it to Ser Kard.

Áine accepted it with her right gauntlet. Power flowed from her armor into the sword, setting the aetheric crystals buzzing with blue-green light. She ran her left gauntlet over the freshly sharpened blade, then pressed it against her shoulder and turned back to the doors to their quarters. Koh looked at her with wide, awed eyes. Áine could impress her, after all.

Shadows gathered. Hands clawed at the paper and reedy wood of the door. Moans flowed into the room, inquisitive and hungry.

"Clear the door."

Koh stepped back. Leftworth, now holding his crossbow, retreated to the corner, his face illuminated green from the aether bolt ready to fire. Synod found his pike and his fingers moved surely over the pole, releasing a wash of crackling blue energy along the blade.

On the other side of the door, the hopping vampires clawed and pounded, the movement and voices within driving them mad with lustful hunger. Their eyes trailed purple darkvoid energy as they readied to feast on the living. Their dead mouths produced acidic saliva, dripping neon-green, in anticipation of blood.

The door exploded outwards. Heavy armor, driven by strange magic and the rage of the woman inside, sent the jiangshi flying.

31.

Áine Kard, resplendent in her teal armor, loomed in the broken doorframe, the runes and concentric circles carved into her plate aglow.

She reached down for the nearest creature, sent prone by her dramatic entrance. She wrapped her gauntlet around his head and raised it to meet her, dead eyes to the red lenses of her visor. It stared back at her stupidly, lancing out with sharp fingernails that dulled against her impervious power armor.

She squeezed. The armor lent its strength. The living corpse's skull collapsed, its eyes popping in unnatural directions, its pale, dead face disintegrating and its gelatinous brains liquefying to spatter against the polished wood floor. The jiangshi's arms went slack and its struggles ceased. Áine tossed it aside and searched for another recipient of her fury.

One such target stuttered back up to its feet, then advanced toward her with flat, emotionless face and eyes that sparkled purple with darkvoid energy. Claws and arms in burial dress wrapped around her hulking right arm, applying strength that defied the corpse's emaciated frame. Servos and gears whined as a yellow warning rune flashed in Áine's heads-up display, but the synthetic strength of her armor compensated for the embrace of the undead. She lifted her arm and the living corpse with it, carefully placing the ghoul against a wooden beam that ran the length of the hall's ceiling. She pushed. The beam cracked and shed splinter tears, but held.

The corpse was not so resilient. Its spine and skull cracked, then something within *popped* with escaping gases, and noxious green sludge poured out of its collapsing throat and chest to *slop* against armor and floor. Áine tossed the ruined body aside as hostile proximity warnings flashed on her heads up display. She caught a hopping jiangshi with her left gauntlet, squeezing at the neck to twist off its vile head.

Two others slipped past her into the quarters, leaping quickly into the hole where the door had been just moments before. Koh shouted a warning. Two blasts of green light cascaded out—the first going wide, the second finding its mark, burning a searing hole in the face of the first jiangshi to breach the room. The air crackled and a whirling power pike blade cleaved the others in two, vile heads to dead-blue toes.

Áine tossed aside the jiangshi's head and looked down both directions of the darkened hall. Koh joined her, blue torch blazing, with Synod and Leftworth at her heels, their energy weapons illuminating their faces from below in austere light. Screams and the sounds of battle carried to them.

"*Follow me.*" Áine trudged down the hall, obeying instinct. Her choice proved true. The first major juncture offered doors that led to a side yard of the exterior training ground. Áine stepped through and the others followed, weapons ready.

The ever-present night of space greeted them through the transparent segments of glasslike viewports that dominated this section of the deathship like an enormous dome. Darkvoid energy had gathered in persistent, clustered storm clouds that pressed against the ship itself and cast the temple in a wicked, purple light. Fog clung heavy and low to the courtyard, obscuring the other buildings and making distance beyond a few meters a hazy impression. Human voices shouted to one another in pain or desperation. Inhuman growls and wet, splitting sounds revealed what had become of those unlucky enough to fall prey to the jiangshi.

A burst of light from the far end of the courtyard caught Áine's eye. The snapping lights returned, heralding an uneasy electric presence in the fog. Human voices—chanting—bookended each discharge.

Synod and Leftworth stood at her flanks, weapons aglow with energy. Leftworth hopped in place as he psyched himself up for the coming fight. Koh stood just behind him, calm and still as a reflecting pool.

They moved forward with Áine leading the way by a few steps, her armor a bulwark against the uncertainty of what lay ahead. The fog parted. At her feet sprawled jiangshi in burial dress, pale blue skin scorched and blackened. Fallen monks joined them, throats torn out and wet with red, limbs clawed or carelessly scattered.

They walked slowly, navigating the grue and gore by suppressing their urge to run in favor of their desire for revenge against the creatures that had so violated this holy sanctuary.

Electrical discharge, blue and caustic, cut through the retreating fog. Áine lowered her sword to point directly ahead, preparing to rush forward at whatever fresh menace presented itself. Her imagination conjured twisted jiangshi, the undead golem of the beach on Gorgon's Head, and the phantasms that froze their wizard foe in the underhalls of the deathship.

The air cleared. A sorcerer in a purple robe turned to face them, face twisted in concentration and channeled anger. Around him was a broken circle of pale, motionless jiangshi in various states of dismemberment and ash, victims of the power that even now flowed between the sorcerer's fingertips. In his left hand he held a hexagonal mirror, the light of the darkvoid above and the temple torches below glimmering and refracting along its surface. The sorcerer's face was unknown to her. The brown eyes caught hers from within the folds of lustrous robe, going wide in recognition and inviting a smile to spread across his handsome face.

"Áine," Grimlar said, his voice the same even as his face was handsome and new, lacking both the goatish features of his maladaptation to the forces of the darkvoid's magic and the uncanny glamour he first used to conceal it upon their first meeting. Yet she knew him by his voice. Her heart swelled in relief.

32.

In the hours after the jiangshi poured out of the cemetery to swarm Shadowkhan Temple, the survivors counted the dead, slew the remaining straggler ghouls, and readied hasty hexes and wards to frustrate additional incursions of the undead.

These defenses included the hexagonal, hand-sized mirrors that Grimlar now carried and had used to amplify his own powerful magics. The light caught them from every angle, no matter how dim or faint, and strengthened tenfold in the reflection. While harmless to the living, the evidence of their power was in the number of incinerated jiangshi corpses that littered the temple grounds and halls. Grimlar kept his grasped in his left hand—his left *human* hand, not a hooved, mutated form, but whole and restored.

Áine wanted to speak to her companion about the change, but they were quickly enlisted for the long and difficult job of moving bodies to the cemetery. Áine's power armor made her an ideal candidate for this tiresome labor, as it allowed her to carry many corpses stacked upon her considerable shoulders. In this labor, she found no indignity or insult to her station. She was simply glad to be of service to the men and women who had given them shelter and invited them to learn their ways, however briefly, before tragedy and vile necromancy struck.

But as they worked throughout that long day, guilt gnawed at Áine. When Koh released them from their duties and told them to take a meal—warmed-over broth and rice, a feast considering the ordeal they had all just survived—and to rest, Áine's mind was free to torment her with questions and whispered implications of her role in bringing this terror to their generous hosts.

"Forgive me, Master Liu, but it is I who brought this evil upon you and your temple."

Áine knelt low before the grand masters in their chamber. She and Synod had polished her armor to a fine sheen in preparation for this audience. The blood had not come off easily.

Grimlar groaned and covered his now-human face. Synod tried to look anywhere but at anyone. Leftworth just shook his head.

Koh stood on the dais with the grand masters seated behind her, brows furrowed and gazes sweeping over these guests who had curiously but forcefully requested an audience so soon after the jiangshi attack.

"Speak, knight-errant," Koh said. At least she was not calling her *ronin*. Their help in the battle had earned them that much respect.

"We came to you from Gorgon's Head, survivors—

from both sides—of a battle," Áine said. "We found our way here, through great effort and trial."

As Áine lowered her eyes, her thoughts drifted to the faces of the men and women she once led, however briefly. She swept their accusing gazes away with a slash of her focus.

Grand Master Liu remained still, almost a wax statue in the dim light of the chamber.

"It is our belief that a cadre of sorcerers unleashed forbidden necromancy, a miasma of radiation that reanimated the battle-worn dead. There were...other horrors. Things worse than walking corpses. Things I cannot explain."

Wax hissed and wicks crackled.

"We may have brought this radiation with us, onboard the deathship. I fear we brought it to this temple. For that, I have dishonored myself, and you. I lead these men, and am responsible for them and their lives. I would ask, however humbly, that your judgment fall on me and me alone."

Moments passed. The others said nothing. Grimlar wiggled his fingers to generate idle sparks, not quite working up an aetheric charge. Leftworth mentally ran through a checklist of all the weapons hidden on his body. Synod found an interesting spot on the floor.

Liu stood up.

"You are a knight, and young, and not trained in magic. I will hear from your scholar, of whom our own college speaks highly." He turned to face Grimlar, who froze. "Tell me your assessment of the matter."

"Grand Master will know if you lie," Koh hissed in warning. Grimlar gulped and bowed low.

"It is…possible…we carry residual radiation with us," Grimlar said. "Likely, even, considering our proximity to both the deployment of the magic and our encounters with the undead on Gorgon's Head and the boat by which we fled the moon."

"Possible," Liu said. "Likely."

"Does that mean—does that mean we will become undead?" Synod asked.

"When we die, yes, it might," Grimlar said.

"Remain silent, soldier," Liu said. "Sorcerer. Does this *possibility* also account for the resurrection of our own dead? Was your colleagues' necromancy of a similar type?"

Grimlar thought that through.

"No," he said. "The necromancy on Gorgon's Head was sloppy, haphazard. Powerful, but ill-directed, much to the doom of my college and lord. These jiangshi are different. They move and fight differently." Grimlar raised his head to look at Koh. "Your servant mentioned the burial clothes of these nosferatu—they are your own dead."

"That is so," Liu said.

"Your cemetery is some small distance opposite the quarters, mess hall, and courtyard we frequent."

"Yes. So?"

Grimlar ran a hand devoid of hair and mutation along his clean-shaven chin.

"That we are responsible for their resurrection is increasingly *un*likely, then, given the distance and relatively low amount of radiation that we could presumably harbor."

"But not out of the question?" Liu asked.

"Nothing is ever out of the question when it comes to necromancy, Grand Master."

"Does your knight have it wrong, then?"

Grimlar looked to Áine, her eyes closed.

"I believe so. Hence my outburst when she first spoke. I do not doubt that the radiation is with us, but even with the four of us together, it is not enough to raise a corpse, let alone an army of them. These jiangshi are completely unlike the types we previously encountered. No. We did *not* cause this outbreak."

Liu offered a soft smile.

"I would ask that you counsel your young knight on the distinction between humility and foolishness," Liu said to Grimlar. "Her gesture, while meant to restore honor, may have had dire consequences for her and for those entrusted to her command. She is lucky to have one so scholarly and wise among her warband." Liu looked at Áine as a father scolding a child. "Your men, Ser Kard, are good fighters, and loyal. Their lives should not be so quickly risked on the whims of strangers, even ones who seem honorable and hospitable upon first impression."

Áine opened her eyes and flushed red in shame.

"Let me make my point further. If we would be damned and doomed for our hospitality and kindness to the alien, to the wanderer, to the stranger—then so be it. Shadowkhan Temple is but a breeze at the edges of the darkvoid's endless storm of time. Our doom will come as it does for all things. But that doom is not today. You are our guests, and returned our hospitality by serving as our defenders. Koh tells us that your armor, weapons, and aetheric sorcery were quite effective against the jiangshi. It is forgivable, then, that you kept certain details of your past to yourselves...and that you destroyed the door to your quarters in your enthusiasm for battle."

Áine blushed again, looking straight down.

"Be free of your shame, o knight," Liu said. "You did not summon these foes. Our great enemy did."

"Speak of this enemy, master, that we might help you find and destroy him," Leftworth said.

"You seek crystals to power your ship and the astrological data necessary to speed you from the deathship," Koh said. "We seek vengeance against the wizard who set our own dead against us."

"These jiangshi were disinterred from our holy cemetery, and brought back to life with spirit cards tied to their bodies." Grand Master Liu held up one such card, marked in blood with slashes of unfamiliar characters that, when focused on, gave Áine and the others a mild pain in their skulls. "This is the work of our ancient enemy, who has for centuries desired the site of our temple and the blood of our monks for his augurs and rituals."

"We have faced a wizard before, and prevailed," Áine said.

"Barely," Grimlar whispered.

"I'm just tired of evil wizards, is all," Synod said, to no one in particular.

The card Liu held in his hand burst into flame, the paper disintegrating into wisps of black ash and smoke. "We have waited long enough to resolve this conflict, and the price of that inaction is paid now by the blood that stains our floors and soil. This necromancer is older than we grand masters combined, a generational enemy, one not easily dislodged from his fortress within this quadrant's reactor complex. But you have a role to play in our vengeance, if you wish. We will pay for your participation, as is your due as mercenaries."

The thought of payment appealed to Áine. Of course it did. She had to look out for her men, now, and for herself. But the voice of honor remained. It spoke clearly to her.

"We could not accept such payment," she said. "You have been our gracious hosts, feeding us, sheltering us, clothing us." She stood tall, placing her gauntleted fist over her heart. "I, Ser Áine Kard, humbly offer my oath of service to the Shadowkhan Temple, until such time as their battle with this vile sorcerer is completed to the satisfaction of you and your council, Grand Master. I offer my sword. I accept it as burden in this quest."

Synod stood with an audible *crack* from his right knee, befitting his middle age. He stood at attention.

"Aye, my pike is yours, Grand Masters, for as long as Ser Kard quests, or until I fall in its pursuit."

Koh smiled warmly at them both. Leftworth stood, then walked forward to join his compatriots.

"Your shinobi have taught me much, and I will repay that investment by serving as scout, spy, and assassin in the coming battle," Leftworth said. He bowed low.

Grimlar, allowing the silence to linger, sighed.

"Ser Kard's sense of duty and honor is childish and foolhardy, and may yet get us all killed. But if she is committed to this foolhardy blood feud, then so am I, as fate and friendship have bound us together, even unto painful death. Oh, alright. I shall help you slay a necromancer." He stood, awkwardly, unsure of what to do with himself. "What is this enemy called?"

Liu gave a knowing smile to Koh, who nodded in acknowledgement.

"We can do better than tell you what he is called," she said. "We have discovered his true name."

Grimlar could not hide his surprise.

"You shall be the poisoned dagger that we set against his black heart," Liu said. "You shall strike directly at the hated and feared…Mumret-Kah!"

The grand masters stood in unison.

"There is much to prepare before the army departs. You must be purified in prayer within our sanctum."

Koh clapped twice, then pressed her palms together and bowed toward the grand masters. They faded away in smoke and a crown of glimmering rainbow-light, the tinkling of bells and the scent of incense marking their departure.

33.

Shadowkhan Temple was home to many shrines, chapels, recesses, and chambers of prayer. Áine found herself in one such sanctuary, the room small and cool, the stone gilded with a golden leaf overlay. Mirrors lined the walls and ceiling at intervals, creating a refractile, infinite sense of space, even if she knew that the chamber was no larger than their sleeping quarters.

The air was cool and flowed freely here with familiar, casual caresses, especially through the soft, thin gi she wore. Before her was the golden altar, rich with handcrafted detail: flat, platelike platforms of various tiers to receive offerings; fresh white candles burning red flame that smelled of cinnamon and young grass; a statue of an ascended master sitting at the highest level, cross-legged with hands held outwards in blessing.

Áine did not know the religion of the monks of Shadowkhan. Koh had told her they considered themselves as having none, at least in the way Áine understood it.

"Your goal is purification, respect, and life," the young woman had told her, just before reaching the chamber. "Enter the Mirror Shrine with that intent, and you will receive what you desire."

They were permitted to enter one at a time. They could bring a satchel with personal possessions, as the purification would be more effective with foci. Áine had gone first, pushing through the grand door adorned with bronze relief. Mythological figures tumbled over one another on its cool surface, animated by flickering candlelight in this subterranean stretch of temple deep beneath the central pagoda.

Battle. War. Constant. Unending throughout time. *Why?*

Now, inside, her reflection looked back at her from a dozen different angles. For a flickering moment she struggled to keep her balance, finding her footing by closing one eye and holding her focus on a single reflection. Her blue eyes were an anchor point on which she steadied herself. She put her hands to her head and ran her fingers through her hair. She had cut and washed it after the battle, allowing herself the luxury of hot water and soap. A part of her yearned for more such luxuries—rest, daily cleanliness, soft clothes, an opportunity to read, even—but she walked the warrior's path.

A giggle, soft and familiar. Wind chimes suspended from a porch overhang. Áine turned, and saw herself turning a thousandfold. There was the door, a rectangle tall and without mirrored surface, just behind her. There was nowhere else here for someone to hide. Yet, Áine felt eyes upon her all the same, in furtive, knowing glances.

She recalled Koh's advice.

Purification, respect, and life.

She looked to the altar. She let her eyes relax and

ran those words through her head.

I seek purification. I enter with respect. Life…

What did she want with life? Did she not possess it already?

Do I possess it at all? Or is does my life belong to others?

That was a voice she was familiar with. Doubt. Her own. Spoken to her in the dark watches of the night.

She shook her head and approached the altar. A small, handwoven rug offered soft comfort for those praying in the Mirror Shrine. She saw herself take a seat upon it a dozen times over. She slipped the satchel strap over her head and withdrew those objects she had chosen for purification. She had asked to bring her armor and greatsword. Koh had said that would not be appropriate, but that she could bring a piece of her armor or a smaller blade, and that it would carry the blessing back to her full kit. So it was that she removed her helm from the satchel, stern in its countenance, red lenses along the visor reflecting two more Áines who joined the chorus around her. This she placed on the first circular platform of the altar.

She removed the resurrection candle—the gift from Tahir, the revenant-knight—from the bag. Wide, heavy, the golden foil cool in her palm. The wax itself was bright red, a tone made all the sharper in the brightness of the Mirror Shrine. Áine was not sure if the gold foil was meant to be removed or not, so she placed the candle whole on the second platform. The third, and highest, she left empty. She looked at the configuration for a moment, then moved the resurrection candle to the topmost platform.

Her helm. *Purification.* Asking less than what might be fully offered. *Respect.* Tahir's red candle. *Life.*

She lifted a burning candle and brought the red flame to the resurrection candle. The wick caught easily and hissed to life. Áine settled in before the altar, crossing her legs as if to receive instruction from a master. She watched. She closed her eyes. The fire grew strong and wide, snapping in fresh life.

The smell of a wheatfield, of earth moistened by dew. The mud of the drill yard, horses and dogs in the field. The aroma of pots laden with stew cooked under the shadows of strange trees. Her master-knight's breath, tinged with ale and mirth in quiet moments huddled close to the fire. Her perfume was a lingering spirit, following them days or even weeks into sortie. The sacred oils of armor and sword maintenance. More, tumbling down through time back to her. The flame split and reformed, tumbled over the wick, spun in ever-widening circles, searching, searching for the moment its magic was needed...

Gorgon's Head.

The behemoth, towering over her, over them all. Soldiers scrambling, breaking in fear. The bodies crushed, the infantry wasted in wave after wave of charges, their own or the enemy's, exhaustion drawing them toward death. The hammer fall.

Her death.

Áine gasped.

She shook herself out of the vision. No. She did not want to see what lies beyond the veil of darkvoid. She could not.

But the candle offered that to her.

It offered to show her that moment of *potential* when she fell on those terrible sands. The terror. The glory.

The darkvoid is not the force of death, she thought, controlling her breathing, commanding her body not to panic. *It is merely the veil that separates planes...no, phases of being...*

The resurrection candle flared and burned down low, suddenly reduced to a puddle of wax in frozen cascade. Her teal helm gleamed bright, its angles alive with color and energy.

"One may be burned in the event of death to come. One must be burned for a death in the past."

It was finished.

Áine threw up.

34.

They moved with the vanguard through the fortress's outer underhalls, just behind the shinobi scouts. Leftworth served as messenger between the two elements, bringing word back when the scouts thought it wise for the assault team to slow or wait. He wore the traditional garb of the Shadowkhan shinobi: dark green cowl and jacket over armored pauldrons of low profile, with thin lacquered metal plates sewn into fabric pockets and connected by a fine chainmail mesh protecting his chest and stomach. He wore black climbing gloves and his arms and legs were padded to help him stay comfortable while crawling and to serve as light armor against hand-to-hand weapons.

So it was that they found the fortress of Mumret-Kah open to them, lightly defended by walking skeletons of synthetic metal, wielding aetherial crossbows not unlike Leftworth's. Their volleys were dangerous, but the cybernetic revenants moved slowly, and while their bones were metal and their eyes burned bright green with aether, they fell to the weapons of the shinobi and main column alike, leaving open the outer access points to the fortress. A match for a single soldier or a pair, perhaps, but not a worthy foe for the experienced shinobi and fighters of the vanguard.

Áine left her men at the front as she accompanied Leftworth and another scout back to the main force. There they met the warmaster in hurried counsel within a black alcove beneath great pipes that leaked neon-green steam. The Shadowkhan general, adorned in fine light armor and carrying a power spear twice his own height, heard the scouts' reports and description of the skeleton robots. He wrestled with two possibilities: one, they were moving into a trap, baited by light or nonexistent defenses; or two, Mumret-Kah had exhausted himself over the centuries, and more recently with his conjuring of the jiangshi to strike at the heart of Shadowkhan, and thus was open to attack.

With little to go on, he chose initiative. The attack would continue. The main force would present itself to the gates beyond this stretch of access tunnels. The vanguard and scouts would cut their way inside the fortress from below. With a nod, he ordered six sappers, all carrying great burdens of metal, wire, and fuel packs, to join Áine at the front. The knight, resplendent in her powered armor, led them back to her party at a run. Even burdened as they were, they had no problem keeping pace—a testament to the rigorous training of their tradition.

With a grunt, Synod turned the great metal wheel to redirect the flow of green-glowing aether from one transparent tube to another. Here was one of the reactor's many outflows, its energy providing cover for their activities but also distinct dangers. They did not want to be cutting through deck plating and energy conduits while they were full with enough aether to power an entire quadrant of the deathship. Such disruptions would undoubtedly draw the attention of Mumret-Kah—not to mention vaporize them all.

They debated which conduits should be active and which should be clear. Finally, with the clutch of pipes above them gone dark, the sappers began their work. They started by climbing along the curved walls, across active pipes and steaming vents, encumbered by their cutting packs and tools. Above, they found footholds on tubing and support beams, lowered their protective goggles, and lit their torches. Áine's visor and lenses protected her eyes from the white-hot light and heat. The others kept their eyes on the corridor in either direction, looking for roving skeleton automata.

They worked in shifts, two at a time, cutting through until dripping slag forced them to pause. They rested their torches while others moved into place, resuming the work and sending forth sparks and liquid metal to rain on the deck below. They were through the first layer in ten minutes, soon dropping panels and flaming debris as they made their advance. The second layer took the better part of an hour.

Time always moved fast on operations. Áine realized how natural it felt to be going to war again and was left burdened by her acceptance of danger, even as her eyes scanned for approaching mechanical death.

"Look out!"

A large panel, its edges white-hot, clanked down from above, slamming onto the deck and folding back on impact. Sparks streamed down from above. Torches went dark.

"The way is open!"

Áine walked beneath the center of the hole, seeing the space above them revealed in flickering light.

"Make way!"

The sappers climbed away from the hole, limber and their grip true. Áine crouched, then jumped with a great push of her legs. Her armor carried her up and through the hole to the deck above, landing on her feet, sword in hand. She found herself within a hallway, much smaller and more compact than the access corridors they had traversed below. The walls and ceiling were crystalline, but the floor recognizably metal, with vented panels revealing tubular contents aflame with the reactor's energies. No foes greeted her, just darkness lingering in the distance. She slung her sword back over her back, the magnetized plate holding it in place. She opened her satchel and produced metal spikes, already wrapped in thin, strong, black ropes. She knelt, then pounded all four spikes into points on the deck plating well away from the hole. Then she unfurled the ropes and tossed them down. They grew taut as her comrades caught them and began their ascent.

The sappers were the first over the top, wearing gloves and goggles, looking like bug-men with their cutting tools and fuel tanks, until they were in the crystal corridor and set their burdens down, only to replace them with small, handheld weapons drawn from the folds of their dark gis and robes. Some sparked portable torches, which cast blue light over the crystalline surface of the hall that refracted back to them tenfold. Grimlar, Leftworth, and Synod made their way up the ropes, grunting with effort and far slower than the monks. The Shadowkhan warriors waited patiently, pressing their bodies against the walls of the corridor and staring down into the gloom in either direction, alert for enemy patrols.

"These halls were grown, not built," Grimlar said when had pulled himself up into the corridor. "Magnificent." Six more monks of the Shadowkhan college followed him up with little effort. Even the monks' sorcerers were in incredible shape.

Leftworth held out a smooth, black stone in his left hand. It produced a holographic display of the fortress's lower levels, hovering above his palm, casting a pleasing blue glow.

"The reactor should be dead ahead," he said, his lower face obscured by dark green cloth.

"Should be?" Synod asked.

"Yes, or we're a level down, and have to cut through the ceiling again." He gestured up.

"We cannot cut through this material," one of the monks said, shaking her head. "Rather, we will not, because we do not know what this material *is*."

"Dead ahead it is," Áine said, resigning herself to the fate and fortunes of war. She turned to lead the spearhead deeper into the fortress. Low rumbles carried throughout the crystalline walls and ceiling. The metal panel flooring shook and tittered.

"The battle at the gate has begun," Áine said. "Leftworth, Synod, behind me. We are moving out."

35.

The reactor chamber's main doors awaited them, guarded only by twin robowarriors, passive and inanimate save for the nuclear-green fire that flickered within their skulls and the tubes that ran along the undersides of their rifles.

Leftworth pressed himself against the corner, angling his crossbow to point it at the nearest metal skeleton. To his right and against the far wall, a monk was on her belly, her single-shot aether rifle pointing at the far sentry. They fired in quick succession, dropping both skeletons with a pair of satisfying *thrums* and *cracks* as aether bolts sliced through the air and found the metal skulls of their targets.

"Watch that they do not rise again," the monk sharpshooter said, getting to her feet. "To the door!"

There was no question as to whether this was the right door or not. It was a tall, wide circle, just barely recessed from the wall and adorned with a cacophony of elaborate glyphs and runes. Grimlar approached, head cocked in contemplation.

"Can you open it?" Áine asked.

The scholar stepped forward and simply pushed. The

circle split, swinging open on groaning hinges.

"I can," Grimlar said, stepping back. He gestured for her to enter. "My lady."

Áine charged inside, followed closely by six of the monks, who fanned out on either side of the entry point, seizing the room, weapons in hand or their hands held as weapons. Inside, they found rows of computer consoles streaming data writ in descending lines of purple runes. A central walking ramp led down to the wide, angular glass window that wrapped around the far side of the room. Through the glass the great reactor could be seen, a titan's heart of green aetheric crystal, its inner light pulsing in time with the lifeforce of the deathship. Smaller formations sprouted from the larger crystals, flowering in radiant waves of dizzying green light.

Standing at the front of the room was Mumret-Kah. His body was wrapped in ancient funeral fabrics, more skeleton than preserved flesh. On his head he wore a crown of onyx stone, laser-cut to a perfect, smooth band, and at its center was a great blue and white crystal that stared out at his would-be assassins with the terrible countenance of an evil eye, made all the more unnerving in the wash of green light from the reactor behind him. His real eyes were long gone, leaving behind shimmering portals of deepest black. His face had disintegrated down to the bone, any remaining wrappings having long ago fused in place, becoming his new skin. He wore a chest plate of decorative gold and jewels in the rough shape of some vile stinging beast of the wasteland. Some trick of light or darkvoid animated the slouching creature into a roar.

DEATH, the mummy said, the word frightful and

powerful as it seared across minds. *DEATH FOR YOU AND ALL YOU LOVE.*

It raised its withered hands. Sparks of purple-red energy sputtered out in warning, followed shortly by bolts of liquid purple and red light. They spread like probing fingers across the control chamber, searching for flesh to fry.

Áine charged down the central aisle, sword held high, aglow with aether and the harmonic hum of her armor-body-weapon synthesis. The sorcerer's lancing beams caught the sword and shook it in her iron grip but failed to dislodge it. The sword served as a conductor, drawing in more lances until her sword was a tree of pure energy. This cleared the way. Synod and the first six monks through the door followed on her heels.

The others remained at the door. They produced small meditation rugs from cylinders hung at their waists. These they spread out in the corridor, then produced from their packs hollowed-out, orange squash. Within these they placed small candles that, when lit, burned sacred blue, visible through carved-out eyes and leering smiles, countenances fit to frighten goblins.

Grimlar joined them, eager to field-test this new technique. What good fortune he had, stumbling across this temple and its college, his teachers eager for him to join in campaign against a foe of immeasurable power. He had not been this excited since first lessons with his mistress of the darkvoid.

They sat cross-legged, hands pressed together in prayerful repose. Not only had they given him an opportunity to join in what was, to them, a holy battle against an implacable and ancient enemy, they had reserved him a seat of honor. Among the monks of the college on this decapitation strike, he was counted as number seven. *Seven*. A number of perfect completion. Grimlar lit the candle within his pumpkin and marshaled darkvoid energies for war.

36.

Áine and the monk warriors dodged dangerous spells and challenged their foe with sword, fist, spear, and bolt on the material plane. Grimlar and the Shadowkhan sorcerers prepared to face him on another.

To leave either his body or his spirit intact would be to invite Mumret-Kah's resurrection—and thus consign whatever desperate victory they might achieve today to the status of one skirmish among many, stretching far into a future of conflict and misery. No, the war would end today, one way or another.

Grimlar was in the corridor with the others, the door to the reactor control room open before him and allowing glimpses of a desperate physical battle.

When he closed his eyes, he sat among the glowing spirits of the scholar-monks upon the aetheric plane.

They sat in two rows of three, with Grimlar at the center rear of the formation. They faced forward, their carved pumpkins leering with faces of sacred blue fire. All around them was a mist-laden gloom: the uncertain, unfinished, gaseous materials of pure potential, not quite black, but absent light. The raw material of dream, anticipating the call to performance for the dreamer. They chanted the prayers of the Shadowkhan, harmonizing their spirits with the swirling energy of the darkvoid within and beyond the ship. Aether, darkvoid, the physical, the spirit—they all intersected here.

Grimlar finished the prayers they had taught him. He looked at his hands—shimmering with blue light and fully free of the mutations of the darkvoid that had marked him as heretic. He wanted time to get used to the feeling, if one could, of being pure mind and spirit, but it was not to be. Their foe was before them.

The desiccated creature emerged from a shadow that was smoke, stepping out from behind a curtain of absolute zero. His terrible gaze searched the void in disorientation, until he found the college arrayed against him. The necromancer attempted a smile, but his dried flesh could only leer, even if his black holes for eyes trailed energy and malicious anticipation of the horror to come.

"You are wise, o wizards of Shadowkhan, to strike at both spirit and body at once." He snapped fingers like dried branches, and a pair of fleshy candles set on tall bronze holders appeared before him. He passed his hands over each wick, lighting them with an idle thought. "Wise in *theory,* but weak and inexperienced in practice. Such is the fate of so many of our art. Eager and intellectual. Ill-practiced and ineffectual. You will die in this realm, *my* realm, and I will refashion your bones into cyber-servants. I will send your harrowed souls into the darkvoid screaming. They will cease to yearn for life anew, and will never again return to the realms of the living, for memory and terror of me."

Mumret-Kah clasped his hands together. The candle flames drew up in fury, casting fell light across the faces of the Shadowkhan college of sorcerers. The flames danced and formed many-limbed things in the air. Balls of blue meat sprouted limbs dripping in the amniotic fluid of dream. Eyes popped out of stalks. Teeth emerged from slavering mouths. Gleeful chittering as toes and fingers slid out of malformed feet and hands. Grotesque *slops* and *squelches* as flesh grew and distended itself into shapes fit for aetheric war.

A dozen, no, two, *no*, three dozen or more of the vile sub-goblins appeared, all malicious shapes, leering faces, bulging white eyes, and wide, blue mouths. They held scrap metal and shards of black glass in their stupid little hands, which they waved about clumsily as their rubbery faces babbled and bayed for blood. Their soft naked feet slapped the black ground as the malign forces of their summoning deposited them before Mumret-Kah, who held his arms out wide and laughed in triumph. The monks were nonplussed. Grimlar gagged.

"Kill them!"

The sub-goblins waddled forward in a ragged skirmish line, issuing war cries from twisted little mouths. The scholars were prepared. Moving their hands and chanting a simple hymn—much practiced with Grimlar before this assault—they finished the harmonic sequence by pressing their palms outward. Blue fire sputtered from the carved pumpkin totems, flames catching one another and spreading outwards, forming a transparent barrier of blue that bowed along the front of their formation.

The first sub-goblin died when it tumbled, face first,

into the shimmering aegis. Its ears, upper head, and skull plate microwaved into steaming goop. Its body, still pumped forward by dead signals sent to rubber legs, continued to march into the barrier, annihilating itself with nary a protest. The others carelessly marched forward to follow it unto death. The monks laughed as creature after creature pulverized and evaporated itself against the shield. The smell was of wet earth and fertilizer rotting in the sun. Grimlar held down his lunch.

More sub-goblins appeared, summoned out of the aether by Mumret-Kah. This secondary assault obeyed the shouted, frustrated orders of the necromancer to beware the danger of the energy field. They reached the wall of blue light and tested it with their knives of glass and metal. Azure sparks elicited fascinated yelps from the summoned horrors.

Mumret-Kah summoned one more batch and, seeing his efforts stymied, stopped and fell still as a corpse. Glass knife tips poked and prodded at the wall of light. Several came together, with little hands guided by babbled communication. They found a weak point.

The knives cut through. The shield was breached. A discharge of sparks and fire incinerated those smart enough to find the weakness in the defense but not so wise as to avoid the energy feedback. They melted into blue and green sludge, exploding and spattering the others in a shower of goop. Where their lower halves remained and melted, a break in the wall of blue fire was just large enough for the other sub-goblins to pass through, one at a time.

Grimlar shouted a warning, but the creatures were too fast. They sped through on tiny feet, knives up and razor teeth extended from floppy lips in grotesque smiles.

The monks nearest the breach scrambled back. Two were caught in a tide of the creatures, who moved with a swiftness belied by their silly countenances. Small bodies flew and spattered against the shield or plopped against the floor as the monks threw them off. Knives cut and tonfa slammed the little critters, but just as fast as they were struck back, more would emerge from the breach, laughing gleefully before latching onto the monks with murderous intent.

Grimlar pointed and whispered invocations to the spirits of the aether, satisfied to see winding bolts of green energy appear at his fingertips and strike true. He first reduced individual sub-goblins to charred meatballs of gristle and teeth, then spread his fingers and opened his palms wide, allowing the aether to fan out in a deadly tide while careful to avoid his comrades. The monks noted his defense and released fire from their eyes, deadly winds from their noses, or curses visible as multicolored, vibrating runes from their mouths.

When it was over, the sub-goblins lay dead or had retreated through the hole in the shield, but two of the monks had fallen—their bodies worked over by tiny blades and teeth, their eyes missing and limbs cut into bloody ribbons.

"Restore the shield!" Grimlar shouted. He kicked away sub-goblin meat and slop, then pulled the two dead monks to the rear of their sorcerer's formation. Their pumpkins went dark and decayed in accelerated fashion; their prayer rugs burned up.

Grimlar grabbed one of the monks.

"Do you do last rites? Prayer? Ritual for burial?"

The woman nodded.

"We cannot bury them here," she said. "But I know the ritual for sky burial."

"Close enough. It needs to be done, now."

She went and knelt by the bodies, producing small candles from the pouches along her belt.

"Shield is restored," a monk shouted. The breach had been healed. Relief—and sorrow—stretched across the faces of the remaining scholars.

37.

With two stations in the attackers' formation unmanned, Mumret-Kah saw his opening.

A black cauldron, steaming and overflowing with sludge, rose out of a swirling pool of shuddering blue energy at his side. The necromancer unhinged his desiccated jaw with a wet *clack*. Oblivious to the searing boil of the cauldron, he reached in, grabbed a handful of muck, and slopped it into his open mouth. His eyes went wide and white as he chewed, his head shaking back and forth to the rhythm conjured up from his dry throat.

He vomited the gruel back out, horking and shuddering with the effort. The vomitus formed a column before him, grey and glistening, human bones sticking out at odd angles. He spit one final mouthful and then produced a flame between his sickly fingers, and set it to the shape.

Fire spread across its surface, burning away the outer layer.

A woman, beautiful and voluptuous, appeared beneath the curtain of flame and steaming vileness. In her nakedness she glistened, large eyes alternating black and purple, and long, flowing dark-purple hair glimmering with strange light. She sauntered forward, feet padding wetly on the black floor, directly to the energy shield. Wings of taught, black flesh and tenebrous texture emerged from her back, heralding her approach.

Entranced by her beauty and the terror of her sudden appearance, Grimlar froze. Others shouted. She extended her hands to the shield. A shock greeted her and she pulled back. She turned around to stare daggers at Mumret-Kah, who merely guffawed in delight. After a pout, she turned back to the monks with a snarl. She pressed her hands against the shield and, with a grunt, pushed forward. Her lithe form belied a terrible strength, and the barrier cracked and then shattered like so much thin glass, shards raining down on the four remaining college sorcerers and Grimlar.

One of the men rose, still covered in blue sub-goblin gore, to face her. Another shouted and scrambled back, away from his own rug and pumpkin. The demonic woman, seeing these two break in fear so easily, reached for the one who would fight her, hands grasping his face and pulling him toward her in a mockery of a kiss. He kicked out, eliciting an annoyed groan as his knee connected with her naked stomach, but she was undeterred. She giggled and moaned in effort, pressing her hands together in a great *clap* that crushed the skull of the monk and splattered his brains and skull. She laughed in delight as gore rained down on her face and her hands were left glistening with brain matter.

The other monks stood up to fight. Grimlar shouted.

"No! Remain at your posts! Do not face her on her terms!"

The three remaining monks scrambled back to their

charred rugs and hurriedly assumed their cross-legged positions.

The winged creature turned toward them, arms wide, face and naked torso now spattered in blood. Mumret-Kah laughed and hurled insults in a language Grimlar's matrices could not comprehend, but their intention was clear all the same.

"Please, come closer, my loves," the demoness hissed. "Who else would like a kiss?" When the scholars held their ground, the succubus crouched to pull a leg off the torso of her victim. It came away with some effort and a tearing, cracking sound they would not soon forget. Standing tall and beautiful in her bloody gown, the creature took a few steps toward Grimlar and loomed over him, the leg of the fallen scholar held above her shoulder like a cudgel.

"What a snack you are." She bared her sharp teeth. But then something passed across her beautiful eyes. They narrowed in terrifying focus. "Something powerful is within you. Something manifesting slow and sure."

She snapped her mask of seductive confidence back into place, but Grimlar had seen the tell, and it intrigued him. "You have lived a lonely life. Would you like to join me?" She tossed her hair back in tempting, exaggerated movement. "The necromancer is only my master through his paltry summoning contract. Perhaps you and I could kill him, and then we could escape this place together, hmm?"

Grimlar felt his body respond to her words, the blood pumping within him in curious ways. To have a demoness of the darkvoid as ally, familiar, or lover would be quite the accomplishment for a sorcerer like himself.

They could navigate the darkvoid together, and escape the pull of this ship...

"*...and overcome the petty political struggles of men...find wealth and pleasure together among the stars, wonders of mind, body, and spirit. Not to mention, we'd fuck each other silly.*"

Her words slipped into his thoughts, and his thoughts were slipping into her words. Already they (*we*) had (*have*) such a connection! What power and pleasure might she (*I*) amplify and grow within him (*you*)? What secrets...

"*...of the darkvoid might we discover and alight together? I see now...You desire a tower, where wars and the vanity of lords are forgotten, and only study and the art matter.*"

Grimlar stood. The others shouted. The necromancer shouted, too. Why was she wasting time? There was killing to be done!

"*But that is not all, is there? You desire connection. Love. Fraternal love, but also romantic, and sexual, as all humans do, of course. As do I! And in the light of those loves, something powerful will grow. I see that tower, your tower—ours—built atop...built atop the thirteenth fortress of the thirteen world...and you are its master, and you accomplish things. Great things, borne of love and darkvoid sorcery, both.*

The winged woman smiled in delight—an explorer, a searcher, in her moment of great discovery. She set the leg down.

"I know not of what you speak," Grimlar said.

"*You know not yet.*"

Mumret-Kah shouted across the black plane.

"What are you doing, demoness? Kill them! I did not summon you to flirt with these vermin!"

"Do something for me, first," Grimlar said, ignoring his foe. "A pact requires sacrifice."

The demoness guffawed.

"You speak like a fool," she said out loud. "There is a price to be paid for the companionship and services of one such as I." She glanced at her fingernails as if in idleness and boredom, cocking her hips to the side. The gesture was overdone. Grimlar could read her, he realized. She wanted something. She wanted *him*.

"No. That one made a transaction to summon you," Grimlar said, motioning at Mumret-Kah. "You offer *me* something else. You offer me *pact*. I am interested. But I need to be wooed."

The demoness raised her eyebrows, then ran a hand down her side in invitation, as if he could have failed to notice her voluptuous beauty.

"Appealing. But I need more than that."

"No," she said, holding back her laughter. "Believe me. You don't."

"I have the gift," Grimlar countered. "I have the darkvoid within me, and thanks to the teaching of these, I have broken its hold over my body, and yet grown in it in power and knowledge."

"You are but a wolf pup at the edge of a deep and dark forest," she cooed. "Of it, but not its master. You are in great danger, and in fact may yet be consumed by the darkness that swallows souls whole."

"And yet you parley with me instead of obeying your master."

"Him?" She raised an eyebrow. "He got what he paid

for. I broke your barrier and made murder for him."

"Then do something for yourself," Grimlar said. "You see something in me you desire. Pay a dowry."

The succubus laughed, a melodic, frightening thing. Her eyes flashed purple darkvoid light.

"Usually, men and women pay handsomely for what *I* have to offer."

"And yet, here you are, negotiating."

"Your future is a tomb, here, now, without my help."

The female monk spoke up.

"What are you *doing*? Kill her!"

"*QUIET!*" Grimlar and the succubus snapped.

"What is your price?" the demoness asked, feigning fleeting interest. She put her hands on her hips.

"You did two things for your master," Grimlar said. "Do two things for me."

"And we have a pact? That is not enough."

"I will tell you the necromancer's true name," Grimlar said.

Her eyes flared.

"A good start."

"I am willing to negotiate finer details later, and would be so inclined to agree to terms favorable to you, o mistress of the darkvoid. I'm sure you can be quite persuasive."

She smiled. Her eyes flashed with desire. Grimlar's insides went all warm and mushy.

"Tell me your price."

"First, restore the one you dismembered, whole and healthy."

"I cannot do that here, as I owed *him*." She pointed back to the mummy-sorcerer.

"Then pluck his spirit from the void and return it to his body, unharmed, in the material plane."

She shrugged as if it were nothing.

"Okay. And the second payment to earn your pact, your mind, your power, and your flesh?"

"Help us kill the necromancer," Grimlar said. "Help us destroy the one whose name is *Mumret-Kah*."

The demoness smiled.

"I shall do as you ask, sorcerer." She stepped toward him, their pact already in bloom. She draped her arms over his shoulders. "And then you and I shall share *our* names."

"I...ahem, look forward to that."

She bared her fangs in vulpine smile. Beauty and danger, all in one. Grimlar audibly gulped.

"Yes. You *do*."

38.

On the material plane, in the liminal stretch of spacetime where the darkvoid deathship hovered over Gorgon's Head, within the reactor control room of its southeast quadrant, Áine Kard, Arturo Synod, Lam Leftworth, and the monks from Shadowkhan Temple fought Mumret-Kah to the death.

The necromancer was a slim figure, frightening in visage but not imposing, and yet he kept his attackers at a respectable distance, slashing out at them with jeweled claws and glaive, which whirled verdant and deadly in the flowing light of the reactor.

The monks probed with spear and sword, and the mummy advanced into their attacks, the jade blade of his long weapon striking in venomous arcs pleasing to the eye. Even in her armor, Áine was reluctant to commit to the attack, fearing the heat and whirring energy of that green-tipped weapon, not to mention the unknowable effects of the jeweled claw.

"Can you get behind him?" Áine asked Leftworth, who, in his dark shinobi garb, crouched low nearby in the shadow of a buzzing console.

"Give me the opportunity," he said, then slipped off

down the row, silently crawling on knee and elbow pads.

"Corporal Synod."

"Ser."

"Set your pike to maximum charge. We move in together. I don't know if my armor will protect me, but I'll stand just ahead and draw most of his attacks. I don't want you to commit to a strike. Just keep either claw or glaive off of me as best you can."

"Aye, mum."

"On me."

"Ready."

"Moving."

Áine advanced, willing aether into her sword. The necromancer turned his dried-out face to the knight.

"I have already killed those simple wizards on the aetheric plane," he said, his voice the rustling of dried corn husks. "They died painfully. As shall you."

Áine barely registered the taunt. The tip of her sword flashed out towards him in a probing strike. The glaive met it, making her arms vibrate with its shocking power. The jeweled claw whirled toward her. Rather than go for it directly, Synod wisely set his pike low and went for a strike against the mummy's forwardmost leg. The claw changed course at the last second, striking away the metal tip, almost grabbing it. It was enough to save Áine from receiving the counter.

She spun and swung, leading the blade from her left shoulder down to her right side, sending the heavy greatsword into the glaive's pole, forcing the necromancer to spend strength to keep it in hand and to fall back a few steps. She repeated the maneuver as the undead sorcerer regained his footing, forcing him to expend time and energy to deflect an attack powered by her armor's full strength. The claw flashed out again, trailing multicolored energy from its enflamed jewels. Synod was more aggressive this time, purposefully drawing out another fast parry. Despite Mumret-Kah's power and fighting skill, maintaining his focus across two planes against multiple opponents was taxing.

The monks moved in, challenging his right flank with elaborate kata of longsword and spear. Tonfa flashed sparks as they clacked together, a visual distraction. The mummy's back was to the reactor glass, but he was at an angle to keep both sets of attackers within slashing range of his weapons. It was just enough for Leftworth to slip in to position.

On the aetheric plane, the surviving scholars of Shadowkhan reformed their ranks, carefully placing the darkened pumpkins in a defensive line before them as they pulled their prayer rugs up in a neat row. The spectral bodies of the dead were covered in salt and prayer cards.

"Fools!" Mumret-Kah shouted. "I use the tricks of novices and pretenders to toy with you, and already you are on the verge of defeat! Hah-hah!" The necromancer held out his arms, and his body rose into the air. "There is still time to withdraw. For what I am about to call forth shall be your true doom. Hah-hah!"

"Now, my lady," Grimlar said. "We will cover your approach. Go!"

The darkvoid demoness smiled, her eyes flashing with the flames of lusty murder. She rose into the air, the toe of her left foot pointed toward the floor, her right leg bent as if she were a ballerina on stage. She coursed across the dark distance between the warring wizards, her path zigging and zagging, her body first in one place and then another.

Grimlar and the monks stood upon their rugs. They moved their arms and shifted their shoulders, turning their bodies away from and then toward their foe, pressing palms outward and pointing in choreographed fashion. They shouted the name of *Mumret-Kah*. Flames erupted from the pumpkins, forming a slow-moving ball of light and fury before them, passing beyond their line, gaining velocity and overtaking the demoness who skated her way toward their common enemy.

Mumret-Kah raised his arms, summoning pools of swirling green energy. From them arose glistening white skulls, jawless and attached to spinal columns that swayed like vipers. These he sent forward with a growl to meet the ball of fire.

The first floating skull-and-spine to meet the flames incinerated, screaming out in icy despair. But more rose up out of pools of strange energy, forming a shield of memento mori, of death in defense of undeath. These swarmed the demoness, who retreated into the gloom, appeared again elsewhere, and charged in toward her former master, only to withdraw as the clattering skulls-and-spines, dozens now, more, descended on her position. Others drifted toward the line of monks, sharp fangs visible in the rekindled light of the carved pumpkins, death's heads bearing down on them all.

This foe's power is beyond our estimation, Grimlar thought. *Áine, my friend—it's now or never!*

219

This foe's power is beyond our estimation, Grimlar thought. *Áine, my friend—it's now or never!*

39.

Green reactor light infused the control room with a pulsing, deathly glow. While the vanguard of Shadowkhan Temple was insulated from radiation in the room, they were not protected from the threat of sudden death that was every moment spent in the presence of Mumret-Kah.

On the aetheric plane, the fools were wilting under his sorcerous assaults. The demoness had turned traitor, yes—all the more disappointing considering her knowledge of the darkvoid arts—but in her betrayal she had merely married her doom to that of the wizard-monks who flailed against his spirit-self.

Here, in the reactor room, he had been less sure of himself. An accomplished warrior in centuries past, his skills had atrophied, and thus he had to rely on the magical strength of his jeweled claw and glaive. They had not let him down and, once the fools assaulting his spirit were dead, he could focus his full attention and powers to exterminating these vermin. Then it was merely a matter of attending to his cyberskeletons holding the line at the fortress gate and reinforcing their numbers with new recruits called out of deep sleep from the machine tunnels below...or from the corpses of the invaders themselves. The enemy army, such as it was, would break off its attack or die. If they fled back to their temple, he could pursue and lay siege at his leisure. Where the jiangshi had failed, his roboskeletons would not. He just had to survive long enough to see it all through.

Áine's aetheric power sword almost ended his plans prematurely. He parried it yet again with his glaive, sending waves of counterforce through the great blade. Only by the grace of her power armor did she manage to keep the reverberating steel in her hands—and at the cost of stunning pain. Synod and the monks jabbed and prodded with pike, sword, spear, and tonfa. They would make a mistake, a misstep, and Mumret-Kah's weapons would strike true. It would happen any moment. He was sure of it.

The evil necromancer's attention, divided between two planes, failed to notice the shadow creeping up behind him on his left flank, hugging close to the dark space beneath the window to the reactor.

Leftworth considered driving his knives into the creature's neck and back. They could cut anything, even dried and hardened wrappings and flesh. But instinct warned him off from a direct melee assault. What if the wizard had some secret defense? What if a backstab cost Leftworth his arm by way of malignant spell or curse?

Knowing this moment was more delicate than all

others, and sensing the success of the spearhead resting on his shoulders, he set his elbow on his knee and took aim.

When he was ready, he shouted.

"Hail, wizard!"

Mumret-Kah, his mind pulled in many directions at once, lacked the will to resist the distraction.

He looked back.

The bastard screamed in pain. Grimlar heard his cries over the shouts of his comrades and the clacking and snapping of the floating toems. Through the press of monstrous skulls and wriggling spinal columns, he could see the enemy necromancer doubled over in pain, holding himself up on one bent knee. Mumret-Kah put his hands to his face as black goo flooded out of his empty left eye socket. The green afterglow of an aetherial crossbow bolt illuminated his screaming face and the reflective black floor of this spiritual void.

Thank you, my friends.

Grimlar closed his eyes and searched within himself for the force that would destroy this powerful foe. The scholars of Shadowkhan had taught him much in very little time, as their elementary knowledge of the darkvoid was one of the first lessons mastered by their college initiates, and even shared among lay monks who sought to augment their physical strength with journeyman magic. They had taught him how to purge the corrupting touch of the darkvoid from his flesh, and in a few sessions of wrenching physical exertion and psychedelic meditation, they guided him to safely repair its warping influence on body, mind, and soul. Grimlar was the goat-headed no longer.

But some of it remained. It would *always* remain. He had seen to that. The demoness sensed it within him, and had thus bet on him over the ancient and powerful wizard who, by any other measure, should have been more than his equal.

But Grimlar knew lessons and secrets that the Shadowkhan scholars did not. His first mistress had been a heretic, a witch of the deep wood, both loved and hated by those to whom she ministered and plied her trade. He had loved her, of course, as most young men might love a mysterious woman of comely features and power, but she had kindly never used that against him. Instead, she mentored and shaped him as he grew into the powerful sorcerer she knew he would become, even if he could not see that future for himself. He was an augur for the forces of aether and darkvoid both, and she would not let such raw, potential talent go to waste because of the religious piety and strictures of a foolish noble lord who, in just a decade's time, would lead his army to ruin on Gorgon's Head.

They spent years together, training, studying, practicing the arts. One sorrowful day, when he found her missing from the remote house that was her home and his school, he knew she was gone for good, having fled the roving bands of witchfinders and the paladins who joined their mad pogrom.

He had wanted more from her, but she had given him what he needed to walk the dark path ahead. And so, her final and most important lesson was this: he would not have everything his heart might desire, no matter how powerful he might become. A boy—a man—would do well to learn such a lesson early in his life, and yet so many fail to do so.

In the absence of her protection and tutelage, and finding himself in a country increasingly in the grip of reactionary fervor, Grimlar hid his knowledge of the darkvoid. But he was dually trained, and so demonstrated his strength in aether to the college recruiters. Thus, he was spared the purifying pyres made for heretics and harlots and, instead, was made a junior scholar of his lord's college of sorcery, destined for crusade in the Outremer.

Grimlar called forth these memories and the vision of beauty and power of Lora the Cunning Woman. His hands worked the air and his lips whispered entreaties to the forces beyond the veil that separated life from death. His third eye opened, eager and spilling purple light and energy from his forehead, drawing in and transmitting out the refracted power of the darkvoid deathship itself.

His body called to the void. A musical laughter accompanied his disciplined thoughts. The succubus was in his mind—open as it was to hers now—and she helped him draw up those energies from the deep wells of painful memory. At first, he resisted her presence, putting up a wall, refusing to let another see his pain.

We are more powerful together, my love.

He relented. He let her in. She moaned—a sound and sensation intimate and pleasurable for them both—as she saw and understood the full scope of her new mate's potential and power.

Lora smiled at him with red lips, deep blue eyes, and flowing black hair framed by her drawn-up, purple robe, illuminated by candlelight.

She was beautiful, the succubus said. *You loved her very much.*

I think I still do.

She cannot love you back. Not in the same way.

No, I suppose not. But the heart wants what it wants.

Hmm. Well, we will have to work on what it wants, won't we?

Warmth and excitement swelled within him—feelings he had long thought dead. The demoness seized upon them, caressing those sensations into rivers of erotic energy flowing through him, past him, out of him.

Grimlar was not just a sorcerer. He was a door. And together, they opened him up.

Out flowed the darkvoid.

Explosive power shuddered forth, one with his spirit and thus sparing it of its destructive energies, streaking across the aetheric plane, unstoppable, from the living gateway to the foe who had haunted this quadrant of the deathship for centuries undreamed.

Mumret-Kah's screams of pain and frustration became cries of agony. Skull and bones and ancient jewelry melted into colorful, sparkling light and slag. Grimlar screamed, too, in victory and delight, and his demonic companion giggled in deeply satisfied amusement.

She had him now.

Smoke rose from his bandaged head. His bronze crown curled and melted, dribbling to the ground with a *hiss*. Bandages sloughed off as the preserved meat within boiled outwards, leaking through the funeral wrappings and spattering against the deck. Leftworth scrambled away, still on his back, as the mummy-king collapsed. Groaning, its jaw came loose and ejected a rush of blue vomit, a nauseating waterfall carrying frogs and scorpions that scrambled away to avoid drowning in vile ichor.

Synod leapt forward and stabbed his pike's blade through the sorcerer's throat, working the cutting edge until the neck melted and snapped, releasing the dark lord's head and sending it tumbling to the metal deck.

With a glowing aether bolt still embedded in its left eye socket, it stared at the shinobi in disbelief through the thin span of seconds in which its undeath remained. Then his face froze and his body seized up. Soon the flesh hissed and broke, becoming ash, the evil of Mumret-Kah gone from the universe forevermore.

40.

The monks buried their dead in the shadow of the pagoda tower. A pox of freshly dug graves riddled the earth. The initiates had reburied the jiangshi shortly before the assault against the reactor-fortress. Now, new graves were revealed for those who had fallen against Mumret-Kah and his deathly automata. Initiates, apprentices, monks, and masters were united here in death, interred in the imported soil of many worlds.

As the priests swung censers and intoned prayers, Áine stood with her men in a small formation at a place of honor near Master Liu and his council. Her teal plate gleamed, freshly cleansed, purified, and oiled, her helm in the crook of her left arm, her greatsword set in the soft earth, point down, at her side. Leftworth stared straight ahead, unfocused. Synod's soft eyes were moist, finding profundity in the burial rites of his fellow warriors.

Grimlar was a shadow in his dark purple robe, held in the grip of another darkness: that of the unnamed woman, attired in black funeral dress, veil drawn over her pale face. The woman had emerged stark-ass naked from a buzzing glass door of solemn light after they had killed Mumret-Kah's body and the magicians slew his spirit on the aetheric plane. Grimlar had covered her with his scholarly robes, treating her with even greater care and concern he might have shown another of their fellowship.

Áine, flush with adrenaline and the thrill of victory, had been focused on protecting the monks as they desecrated the necromancer's headless corpse to prevent his resurrection, and thus put her questions aside. But now, with the solemnity of a martial funeral to free her mind to reflection, she wondered at the sudden appearance of this creature who, despite her heavenly physical beauty, drew feelings of great unease.

The woman, sensing Áine's gaze, turned to reflect it with a sweet smile. There was no warmth there. Her eyes were light magenta and her black hair, perfect and long about her slender shoulders, held strands of fuchsia. Her appearance, her allure, her aura…they radiated with a sense of darkvoid.

She emphasized her embrace of Grimlar all the more, moving her arms over him in a fashion that verged on the improper, given the occasion. Áine would have private words with the sorcerer later, if she could pry him away. She frowned, self-conscious, and pulled her gaze back to the rituals.

These dead are honored, and will not be restless. I hope that one day, others will say the same of me.

Following the funeral, the survivors of Gorgon's Head

gathered in their quarters. Grimlar held up a frosted glass cylinder, in which a cluster of green crystals glowed faintly with a soft, calming light.

Synod leaned in close, his face cast in jade.

"All that trouble for something so small," he said. "The reactor crystals must be worth wealth beyond measure. These monks are rich."

"They care little for material goods, save to support their mission," Leftworth said. The shinobi knelt at a straw mat, his weapons and tools spread before him. He had been cleaning his knives, oiling his crossbow, and checking and double-checking his gear. They would be moving on soon.

"They will leave a garrison at the fortress," Grimlar said. "Mumret-Kah will not be the last to covet the reactor of a darkvoid deathship. They will have to guard it fiercely—as we must guard these crystals should we journey back to the boat." He covered the cylinder with a heavy cloth and pulled it into his robes, where his third hand—human now, and free of the goatish mutation—received it and disappeared into the folds. "We still need astrological data, of course. If we are lucky, the shipboard spirits will be able to divine a course to some familiar star."

"If we are lucky," Áine said. "Because there is no guarantee."

"No," Grimlar admitted. "And our craft's engines are not fit for transition at range. Our options will be limited."

Áine's eyes flicked over to the woman in black. Her gaze was fixed on Grimlar.

"And what of our new recruit?" Áine asked. "What

wise counsel does this nameless waif bring us?"

The woman turned to Áine and gave her a sharp smile. Áine did not like the feelings that stirred within her.

"Does she have a name?" Áine turned back to Grimlar, who was looking more uncomfortable than ever. "She is your baggage. Perhaps you would introduce us."

"Yes, about that, hmm." Grimlar cleared his throat. "This is...you may call her Esshi. We are, ahem, ah, working together."

Áine raised her eyebrows.

"'Working together?'" Áine asked incredulously. "She appeared out of a portal in the lair of a necromancer, and now you two are *working together*? She killed one of your fellow sorcerers."

Grimlar's face turned red. He feigned a cough.

Esshi moved to Grimlar's side and slid an arm around his waist.

"Working together," the woman in black said, emphasizing each word with her full lips. "And I restored them to life, as promised to my dear Grimlar."

"Good goddess," Synod said, amused. Leftworth just shook his head.

"Is there anything else to this story?" Áine asked. "Is she even human?"

"Yes, and, uh, no," Grimlar admitted. Esshi gave him a possessive hug.

"Should not we all decide who joins our outfit?" Áine asked. "I accepted some time ago that old ranks mean little now, so perhaps we should put it to a vote."

"Yes," Esshi said, her words those of a serpent. "Let us put it to a vote. Darling?"

"Aye," Grimlar said.

"Arturo?" Esshi said, eyes on the pikeman.

"'Arturo,' is it?" Áine asked, incredulous.

Synod smiled and nodded.

"Aye, ser. And *aye*. She makes for interesting company."

"Unbelievable. Leftworth? What say you?"

"We could use another woman about."

"This is mutiny," Áine said, exasperated.

Grimlar cleared his throat.

"Just know, Áine, that Esshi was instrumental in the defeat of Mumret-Kah. Her presence here will bolster my power, and therefore our chances at survival on this deathship and beyond. She is a good fighter, and has knowledge of esoteric subjects that will aid us in the challenges to come."

"And that's that?" Áine asked.

"That's *that*," Esshi said, enjoying watching Áine squirm. "You can still vote, if you want."

"*Abstain*," Áine snapped.

"The *ayes* have it," Esshi said, clapping her hands together. She reached for Synod and pulled him into an embrace with both herself and Grimlar, who looked more uncomfortable than ever. Synod seemed to enjoy the attention, a big, goofy smile on his face. "I am *so* excited to be among such handsome human men!"

Áine put her hands to her face.

"We, uh, should discuss more important matters," Grimlar said, pulling out of the awkward embrace. "We should decide, now, whether we remain at Shadowkhan, or if we make the sojourn back to our landing craft."

"Assuming it is still intact," Leftworth said.

"Or that we can find it at all," Synod chimed in.

"Yes, assuming that and more," Grimlar said.

"I have learned much here, but I desire to move on," Leftworth said. "My lord is dead, or may as well be, considering I was left to die on that moon, just the same as you. We have fought together and journeyed through hell, so I am content to remain in your company. We have something more valuable than the honor of service. We share trust."

"What would you do, given coin and the freedom to lay down your sword?" Synod asked. "Where do you end up, should the deadly Lam Leftworth survive the years ahead?"

Leftworth thought about this for a moment.

"I will herd deer," Leftworth said with a smirk. "I have always been fond of animals. And what of you, Arturo? What fate would you seek?"

Synod glanced sidelong at Grimlar's alluring companion. The woman winked at the pikeman.

"I desire to be home with my family," he said. "I wonder if my children survive, and if my wife has kept our homestead together. I fear that if the fleet returned without us, without me—she may be in mourning."

"Or she may have moved on," Esshi said. "You poor, lonely thing." She ran a conciliatory hand up and down the man's arm in comforting touch.

"Indeed, Lady Esshi. I do not know if we can ever make that journey, but I have to hold out hope that we will."

"Did you hear that, Grimlar? I'm a *lady* now. I like your companions. We will all be friends in the quick. Now, tell them what *you* see, my beloved. Tell them as you have told me."

"I have had…visions. Of a fortress, of a tower where I will discover and create great things. I seek now the wealth to construct that tower. We could secure that wealth, together, and build something worthy of legacy. Of song and story."

"And you, Lady Esshi? What is it you desire?" Synod asked. Charmed already, Áine noted. Would this new arrangement be three against two, or would Leftworth fall under her spell as well? These men were hers in fellowship, yes, but not *hers*, not in a way beyond her comradery and their voluntary deference to her command. This woman—even one so beautiful and desirable as Esshi, whatever her true nature—should be no threat to that fellowship. Right?

"Thank you for asking," Esshi purred. "The scholars of this temple have nothing more to teach my beloved. The moment I saw Grimlar, I saw potential. I saw a dark and terrible future. I want a piece of it. You are all lucky to be party to the coming storm. Grimlar—and others," her eyes flicked to Áine, "are beginning to see glimmers of that potential future. I intend to protect and tutor my precious scholar so that he might reach that full potential. I have not had such an opportunity in all my many centuries of existence. It seems quite novel, as do all of you. I am just so *taken* with this merry band of misfits."

"And what of you, ser?" Leftworth asked, sheathing his knives. "What is it you seek?"

Áine had been chewing that over for some time.

"Having been freed from the obligations of service by the death, defeat, or cowardice of our lord and commander, I yet remain a knight—albeit knight-errant. I am no monk to remain in quiet meditation and cleaning floors. I would continue to sojourn among trusted companions, to see what fortune or doom might be ours. As ronin, if we must, but as comrades all the same.

"What was it master Liu called us?" Synod asked. "A 'warband.' I like that. Sounds scary. We *are* scary. Fierce fighters, powerful wielders of magic, not to be trifled with. A proper *warband*."

The others nodded. Esshi smiled wickedly.

"Then we are *warband*," Áine said. "And we are moving on from Shadowkhan Temple, and from this cursed deathship, to see what fate awaits us in the stars beyond."

"If we find a spirit terminal, we can get the astrological data we need for navigation, and we can also petition for a manifest and map to find our vessel," Grimlar said.

"The monks must know of one nearby," Synod said. "They might even have one, here."

"I will see what I can find out," Áine said. "I will speak to our gracious host."

41.

No drills or prayers happened at this late hour. The blue-flame torches and synthetic lights of the fortress temple burned low, marking both night and solemn respect for the recently fallen.

Áine could not account for the warm, anticipatory excitement she felt, except perhaps as post-battle jitters, her body and mind processing the violence in which she had engaged and endured. There had been many close calls, too many desperate moments since they departed from their distant homeworld on this campaign of madness, and even more since fleeing the deadly tomb that was Gorgon's Head and boarding the deathship.

When would the fighting stop? Would it ever? When might the odds catch up with her, and with those whom she fought alongside, and now cared for deeply?

As she knocked on Koh's door, the excitement became nervousness. What did she have to fear? She merely wanted to discuss the logistics of moving on from the temple, of begging for supplies and directions to a spirit terminal with—

Koh opened the door. She stood, soft and radiant in her night robe, the top slightly parted to reveal the skin of her chest and the upper curves of her small breasts. Her hair was up and her face soft and moist. She had just finished bathing, no doubt, and here Áine was, bothering her.

"K-Koh," Áine said, stuttering such a lovely name. "I am sorry to disturb you, I..." Áine turned away.

"You mean to depart, soon," Koh said.

"Yes."

"Do not depart now," she said, reaching out with both hands to grasp Áine's left. "Come in." Áine allowed herself to be pulled inside. Koh slipped behind her and shut the door, turning a small lock into place. Áine looked around the room, finding it small and modest, but warm and inviting. Two chambers—a private bath in a small room, and a slightly larger room in L-shape, with a small stove near a table with two seats at one end, and a space for sleep, prayer, and books at the other. It smelled of lavender and candlewax. It smelled of Koh.

"We need to find a spirit terminal," Áine said. "Does your temple have one?"

"No, but there may be several nearby."

"*May be*, or are?"

"That depends on the tides of the darkvoid," Koh said. She tilted her head to the side, and candlelight danced across her face. Áine involuntarily wetted her lips with her tongue, and felt a desire to flee and to step forward, all at once.

"We have a vessel," Áine said, as if in apology. "We are not temple initiates. We do not walk the same path."

"Tomorrow our paths will diverge, yes," Koh said, her voice a hot whisper.

"Tomorrow?" Áine asked.

"Tomorrow," Koh answered. "Not tonight."

The monk stepped forward and, finding Áine tense but still, placed her soft hands on the knight's face.

"You are very pretty," Koh whispered.

"I have scars," Áine said, ashamed.

"I like your scars," Koh said. She leaned forward and placed her thin lips against Áine's, then pulled back to look up at her with half-lidden eyes. Áine, facing a strength she could not possibly resist, surrendered. She returned the kiss.

The young monk slid out of her robe, her firm, athletic body revealed in the soft light of night's desire. Áine had seen plenty of naked bodies in her time in the army, but what she had seen had stoked little of her desire, considering the filth and sweat of soldiering. This was different, and new, and exciting. In the soft curves of Koh's breasts, in the smooth contours of her hips and firm buttocks, in the darkness between her legs, Áine realized something about herself. She realized whom she might love, and who she might be because of that love.

Koh's body was pleasing to her, and, Áine realized, her own body might be pleasing to Koh. She removed her shirt, then lowered her pants and, with some reluctance, her undergarments, and stood naked before the monk who had been her trainer, opponent, and comrade.

Áine was several inches taller, and thicker with muscle in arms and shoulders from swordwork and her armor's weight, where Koh was leaner and tauter, but no less impressive for it. Koh slid her hands over the knight's body, finding her breasts, her hips, and the growing wetness between her legs. As the tips of Koh's fingers teased her, Áine released the tension that she had held onto for so long. As Koh kissed her neck, she relaxed further with exhalation, then pumped her own hips in rhythm with Koh's gentle, probing fingers.

Koh smiled up at her, then kissed Áine's chin. She pulled back to lead her to the modest sleeping mats, just big enough for the two of them. She guided Áine down, pulling her to herself, into soft embrace. Áine's hands, so used to wielding a sword, whose purposes had been set to fighting and death, found new purpose with Koh, as did so much more of her.

42.

As a visitor to the material plane, Esshi found the vainglorious constructions and inventions of humans both amusing and wondrous. Grimlar did not refuse her demand to wander the grounds, despite the late hour and his own exhaustion. It became clear she was leading him, following a ley line to a distant corner of the fortress monastery,

"We have not completed our pact's rituals," she said, holding Grimlar's human hand with her clawed fingers, possessively. "I am anxious to begin our partnership in earnest. As are you, I am sure."

"Yes, of course," he said, struggling to keep up with her. "I know there is much to discuss and learn, but...could it not wait until the morning? Preferably after a meal, and coffee?" Esshi did not acknowledge his questions. Grimlar, not for the first time, began to wonder just what he had gotten himself into. Fear crept into his thoughts and his voice. Part of him *enjoyed* the fear she inspired in him, too. What if she meant to devour him? And then: what if he *wanted* to be devoured by her?

They passed over the courtyard, which was empty this time of night save for the occasional patrol. Guards on the high walls looked down upon the artificial canyon and agriforest leading to the monastery. Flickering blue torchlights on the distant outcroppings high above marked scouts and sentries keeping watch at elevation. Even with Mumret-Kah dead, the deathship was a dangerous place, and the temple's defenses had been proven lax. Now they showed their strength with renewed vigor.

Esshi led him beyond the pagoda, which never failed to inspire awe in Grimlar in its height and design. That awe was shifting, becoming something else. Not quite jealousy, but…desire. A sharp longing for his own tower. One that he should build, and live within, and from within make his mark on some distant, haunted world.

Esshi led him past rows of old buildings from which flickering light spilled out through cracks in doors and around the edges of curtained windows. Here monks, initiates, servants, and even families lived and slept, and beyond these cramped streets, a hearty grove guarded its secrets.

Esshi released his hand and floated over a fallen log, then drifted deeper between bent trees and over scraggly bushes. Grimlar struggled to keep up, his robe catching on thorn and branch. He did not have to go far to reach her, but the alien forest made him work for it.

Before them was a two-story stone building, its circular roof sloped, its façade adorned with inward-facing triangular arrows at intervals. The twin doors were shut, secured by a cross of beams and fallen branches. The sky above was viewport glass and shimmering shield-energy, beyond which the night's stars burned bright and insistent. Grimlar could easily imagine they were in some primeval forest on a distant world, finding a religious site or holy temple on pilgrimage. Esshi opened her mouth in delight and salivation, running her pink tongue over her purple-glossed lips.

"This was a place of power and holiness for practitioners of the darkvoid arts, generations ago," she said. "So long for some, but not so long for others." She stepped forward and effortlessly lifted the first rotting beam, tossing it into the tree line as if it were nothing. Grimlar came forward to help, but found himself mostly getting in her way, and contented himself with removing branches and sticks as she removed the heavier obstacles.

When the door was clear, she put a clawed hand forward and pushed through. The door's hinges groaned, bidding them unpleasant entry. Inside, the air was thick with dust and an underpinning of incense and wax. Silence greeted them. Grimlar held his left hand aloft, and a vibrant pink light radiated out from a glowing orb in his palm. The chapel revealed itself: prayer rugs askew on the floor of the nave, shrines in alcoves hidden by cobwebs, the raised quire where the central altar stood draped in shadow. Golden figures sat upon the great altar itself, cross-legged and still, glimmering in the light from Grimlar's palm.

Esshi glided through the air, then ran her hands along the altar. She raised them to examine the dust that now covered her claws and palms.

"This will do nicely," she said.

"For what?"

The demoness whispered something, then pointed to

the idols on the altar. They began to shake and shimmer, then slid off and up, held aloft as if by invisible strings. With another whispered word from Esshi, they descended to the floor, then spun around, their fat faces and eyes turned away.

"Dust this off, will you? Use those robes."

Grimlar set his glowing orb to float in the air just above his head, then found old garments set on a railing at the edge of the quire. He ran them over the altar until it was clear of dust.

"You take instruction well," Esshi purred.

Grimlar folded his arms.

"Why are we here?"

"One more command," she purred. "Well, two, actually. But let's start with the first. Put your robe on the altar. Spread it out." Her teeth gleamed in the dim light from Grimlar's spell. Even in the gloom, she was more beautiful than any woman he had ever seen. He did as he was told. In his shirt and pants he felt cool, but not cold. The inner fabric of his cloak was a bright counterpoint to the darkness of this abandoned chapel.

"Final command," she said, smiling wickedly. She pointed to the altar, then raised her eyebrows in encouragement.

Grimlar felt a cold chill pass through him.

"W-what is this?"

"Our final ritual of bonding," she said. Sensing his hesitation, she walked forward, then laid her palm on his chest. Her hand was soft, but the long claws of her fingertips were pointed and tapped through his thin shirt in passive threat. "I *suggest* you remove the remainder of your clothes if you wish to wear them again. It might be a little embarrassing to beg a monk for clothes, with these in tatters."

She gave him a firm shove, and Grimlar backed into the altar. There was a predatory hunger in Esshi's eyes, and she stalked toward him one patient step at a time. Grimlar climbed up onto the altar, then began removing his shirt, the cold fear transmuting into something warmer. Something made all the more delicious by the fear he felt for the darkvoid demoness.

"Good pet," she cooed, as her hands worked to remove her own robes. They pooled at her feet and she stretched wide her tenebrous wings. Grimlar paused in removing his pants as his eyes fell on her breasts. She laughed, melodious and reverberating throughout the shadowed chapel, and helped him remove his boots. She then pulled off his socks and pants with impatience, straining the fabric when he proved too slow for her. She gave him the dignity of removing his underwear, then floated up above him. Grimlar lay on his back, facing the floating vision of beauty and terror above him.

"Is this your first time?" she asked.

"Doing this, *like* this? Yes, my lady."

She laughed.

"Close enough." She descended, her softness, curves, and weight upon him.

"Your name, now," she whispered hotly. "Your *true* name."

"Y-y-ours first," Grimlar stammered, his body shuddering in rhythm with her ministrations. Her hands worked him into a lustful frenzy. The weight of her naked breasts upon his chest was a pleasant restraint. Her legs pinned his own down. She angled herself toward his growing excitement.

Esshi smiled, then held his chin in place. She kissed him, softly, passionately. Her lips were smooth and moist, and the feeling and sounds she made sent waves of delight shuddering through his body, which was rapidly collapsing into total surrender. She broke the kiss with a smirk, and put her forehead to his.

"Your. True. Name."

Grimlar's self-given, secret name had been known only to one other in his life. Until this moment. Now he revealed that true name to Esshi, the woman of the deep dark. She hummed in response, her wordless voice a sing-song melody, her hands sliding across flesh and tuning him to her, unto her. She whispered his true name, over and over again, punctuating each syllable with a wet slide over his arousal. He writhed, but certainly did not complain.

Grimlar managed to pull himself back from the brink of ecstasy. There was still danger here. An imbalance. Much to his credit, he kept his head—so to speak—just long enough to make a demand of his own.

"Yours, now," he managed between hot gasps of pleasure. "Please, my lady."

Amused, Esshi granted him his request. She whispered her name in his ear. The sound of it was a waterfall in a forest glade, in which a sylvan, feminine spirit might bathe, and be spotted, and be loved on first sight. It was the rushing of the tide of lustful fascination, of a thrumming, persistent desire that drove one into desperate erotic fervor. It was sweet and satisfying beyond mere words, and it had belonged to her alone, until now. She gave it to him.

She reached down and slid him inside. Grimlar moaned at the initial warmth and wetness, immensely pleasurable. He was not prepared for what came next. She tightened herself around him, gave him an encouraging little giggle, and watched with bemusement as his eyes rolled back and his mouth dropped open in rapturous delight.

A wave of cosmic pleasure radiated from their coupling throughout his groin, cascading down his legs, washing up through his torso, his arms, and into his mind, which lit up with a kaleidoscopic array of irresistible explosions. Signals were overridden. Nerves were alight. His breathing almost stopped. His heart clenched still for a fleeting moment of pure delight. Then the wave receded, and his body was allowed its own commands, at least enough to keep things going, before further waves of pleasure rocked him and overrode everything else. Esshi enjoyed herself, too, holding his wrists down against his spread robe, angling herself to maximize her own pleasure.

Pact-mates, she spoke in pleasure, in his mind, in *their* mind, bodies and spirits as one, frightful and erotic and whole.

"Oh, oh gods!" the sorcerer gasped, before his breath fled him completely.

"Oh *goddess,*" she corrected him. "Your goddess, now."

"*My* goddess," he said, surprising her, pleasing her, just as she pleased him.

She nodded.

You will become powerful.

I will grow more powerful than you know.

We are together, now, and shall become greater for it. Greater than even you can imagine, demoness.

Esshi's eyes grew wide with amusement.

I am counting on it, my love.

Knowing she had little time, Esshi leaned down to kiss him softly as she gyrated her hips, bringing about her own hurried completion. His followed soon afterwards. They would have plenty of opportunity to build up his stamina later.

43.

Áine Kard, knight-errant, and Grimlar, scholar of the darkvoid, bound together in fate and fellowship, wrapped in the embrace of their respective lovers, dreamt the same dream.

A mountaintop fortress, illuminated by baleful bonfires along its imposing black walls. Lighting streaks across the black and red sky, revealing a singular tower at the fortress's heights, looming over the battlements. Rain falls in slashes. Clouds roil and churn as strange purple-red light emanates from within stained-glass windows.

Enter the great keep in the shadow of the tower. Hammers clang endlessly, keeping terrible rhythm. Halls of turquois stone glisten and shine in torchlight. Swirling blue-grey geists, draped in transparent shrouds, linger in pools of shadow or drift through the walls.

Continue into the armory, where swords, shields, pikes, spears, flails, and other instruments of war hang on hooks or stand in great racks. Enough armaments to outfit a small army. Enough for a *legion*. The cadence of familiar voices, shouting out in parade drill, echo throughout the halls and gloom.

Enter an adjacent chamber, full of wooden crosses bearing the chest plates and pauldrons of black-metal power armor. Helms with red monovisors peer out from shelves, gauntlets and boots and neck mantles—all similar in design to Áine's armor, but twisted somehow, more imposing, more demonic, spiked and inlaid with patterns not for standard aether energy but for another, darker form of power entirely.

Moving on: many chambers, rooms, home to servants and soldiery, faceless in shadow and moving in blur. A dining room and long table, fit for a warrior-queen and her knights, with walls adorned with great banners depicting the deeds of mighty warriors across bloody and doomed time.

Deeper now, to a council chamber overflowing with maps, scrolls, missives, and more; coinage stacked in towers to challenge the fortress itself.

Pass through double doors to another great hall, long and exorable, velvet and indigo carpet flanked by figures in dark plate drawn from the wicked armory. The royal carpet leads up to a dais on which an array of thrones faces rows of the black metal warriors. A legion, a dark legion of shining armor, alive with the purple, arcing energy of the darkvoid itself. The humming of latent power. The roar as they raise their weapons high, likewise crackling with darkvoid energy, unstoppable, dangerous beyond measure.

They call out names—no, titles. Honorifics.

Deathmage. Deathknight.
Deathmage. Deathknight!
DEATHMAGE! Deathknight!
DEATH-MAGE! DEATH-KNIGHT!

Áine woke up in sweat. She grasped for her sword, for her helm, for some token protection against fear, against the sense of helplessness she felt in the face of dark and mystifying visions. But in Koh's quarters, she was free of the obligation of knighthood, of the burden of her sword, if only for a night.

As Koh's hands found her naked back, caressing her, calming her, Áine wished she could be free of that burden—and of the black, phantasmal future—forever.

Grimlar opened his eyes and stared at the ceiling of the chapel, which was crawling with shadows and cobwebs. Esshi's eyes were aglow in the dark, her full lips a hungry smile.

"You saw it," she whispered, her voice honey and nightshade. "What awaits us."

"What was that?"

"You know."

He struggled to calm his breathing.

"I do not know or want that, whatever that was, whenever..." He closed his eyes, but the vision of the darkvoid legion remained.

Another detail, remembered suddenly like a whisper from an empty room: at the end of that great hall, upon the thrones of the dais, sat two figures, stately and regal. One in black armor like the legion, but more ornate, more fiercesome. And one in the black robes of a sorcerer, resplendent in swirling darkvoid energies.

"You may lie to yourself, but you may not lie to me." She shuffled closer, then, pulling the sheets off of herself, lifted a leg over his own. She sat up straight atop him, shuffling the softness of her buttocks along his manhood. It was no effort at all to arouse him yet again, even so soon. His fear subsided under the ocean of pleasure she offered him, but a spark of it remained. It always would, to say nothing of the fear he felt for her. But that fear was arousing, too, and, not for the first time, Grimlar wondered just how much his life would be changed by this woman from beyond.

As they coupled, Esshi spread her wings wide, her eyes never leaving his, her fangs bared, her mouth salivating—for him, and for their dark and terrible future.

44.

The map supplied by Koh, uploaded to Áine's armor and displayed from a holographic emitter on her wrist, offered three possible locations for a spirit terminal. Finding one would be a challenge. Successfully petitioning what they needed would be another.

One battle at a time.

Áine led them through a sublevel deep below the temple, accessing it via a network of secure doors that led from the cellars. Koh had been reasonably certain the underhalls were uninfested by monstrous foes, especially with Mumret-Kah dead again—presumably, for good.

But the deathship had taught Áine and her warband to never let their guard down. They moved through access tunnel after access tunnel, traversing the grated floors, the winding corridors lined with tubes and wires, and the steaming pipe and gearworks systems.

"Koh warned me that the ship changes," Áine said. The knight walked well behind Leftworth, her raven-crest hologram displayed at full parade-field strength in luminous blue, the red eye lenses on her helm's visor glowing in the dark, both meant to draw attention to herself and away from her companions in the dark. "But the map presents general landmarks. We need to be in the right place at the right time."

Leftworth, meanwhile, kept to the shadows ahead of them, dashing forward great distances, waiting at junctures, listening for movement. While he had appreciated the simple comforts of the temple, he admitted to himself that it was exhilarating to be back to his practice here, in the field, where he belonged. The humidity produced condensation on his dark green shinobi outfit and gathered on his crossbow and blades. He would have to thoroughly clean and dry his gear when they made camp for the night, assuming they slept at all over the next couple of days.

They walked for hours, pausing only to sip water or reorient themselves, until they reached the first possible location for a spirit terminal. The passage they followed ended at an alcove defined by winding bundles of large cable and ventilation structures that led down to a bulky, grey metal console.

The console was adorned with jewels for buttons and bulky, curved glass screens. No light or energy moved within. The world of spirits and their powers of computation was beyond Leftworth's experience and training. How was it that the dead could be so trusted with the essential, life-sustaining functions of a starship? Or perhaps he misunderstood, and these were not the souls of the departed but intelligences from elsewhere. *Or* were they merely energies feigning intelligence to put the users of such devices at ease? He shook his head free of such speculation. His job was to keep them safe, not wonder at the craft of ancient technicians and wizards.

Áine, her holographic crest casting the enclosed space in a hazy blue glow, joined him.

"Well done, Lam." The modulated voice was deep and rumbling, belying the often softspoken nature of the knight he had come to know. She turned and called back to Grimlar, who appeared shortly after with Synod and the strange woman, Esshi.

Synod, in his levyman's light armor and wielding his power pike, was ready for battle in these dark depths, but Grimlar and the woman in their elegant robes appeared almost as nobles being escorted through some technological slum.

She was pretty—easily the most attractive woman Leftworth had seen since leaving his homeworld to infiltrate theirs—and she smelled *great*, even here, but there was something about her he did not like, and that distrust went well beyond the fact that she had attached herself so effortlessly to the warband and their resident scholar. Áine clearly shared those suspicions, but Synod was quite taken with the lady, chatting her up and enjoying her smiles and laughter at his simple humor. Quite the flirt, that one, for being a loyal married man and all. Of course, that was nothing compared to Grimlar, who, while he *acted* disinterested and aloof, allowed her hands to roam freely over him, deferred to her every word, and disappeared with her at all hours of the day and night for things best left unimagined.

Movement caught his eye. Shadows shifted and a slight, almost unheard scraping emanated from the piping and cable bundles that stretched up and away from the computer console. Grimlar and Esshi were already typing away at the console's controls, the screens alight with datastreams, when Leftworth shouted to back away. To their credit, they did so without question or hesitation, trusting his command. As they backed up, he advanced, crossbow at his shoulder, and aimed at the source of movement and noise above them. The light from the green aether bolt set in the flight groove was enough to spill into and illuminate the recesses—and the small, green face and grey armored helm that poked up to spy him.

"Do not move, creature," Leftworth said, aiming his crossbow at the alien visage. It stared back at him with large, blinking eyes, its face wide and its mouth a flat line along its bulbous head. Soon, more eyes stared back him, set in faces all identical as far as he could tell, green and round and delicately armored, followed by webbed hands attached to thin, armored arms.

Áine joined him at the console and put a hand on his shoulder, encouraging him to lower the crossbow. She removed her helm, trading her frightening knightly visage for a softer human face.

"Greetings," she whispered. She held her other hand behind her, gesturing for Synod and the others to stay back. "I am Ser Áine Kard, knight-errant. This is my warband. Lam, Arturo, Grimlar, Esshi. We seek to use this spirit terminal in peace. We will leave it as we found it."

Many sets of round eyes blinked at her. Metal on metal sounds, the shuffling of moist limbs, the whispered babbling of inhuman language. The creatures revealed themselves in a tumble of armor and green flesh, clambering out from behind the pipes, tubing, and wires that, while providing some cover, could not have concealed adult humans. They wore thin metal armor like little knights, the helms with vertically slitted visors. They carried mundane spears, swords, shields, and simple metal bows and arrows, and stood on naked green feet with wide, webbed toes that matched their hands.

"*Grr-grr*-greetings," one of them spoke. This one stood closest to Áine and Leftworth, carrying a long spear—long being relative in this one's stature—and advanced toward them, the pointed end of its weapon kept up and away from them in neutral stance.

"We *arr-arr*-are the Knights of the Deep Keep. We do not wish to fight, but are capable *warr-warr*-warriors. It is only right that we warn you *al-al*-aliens, as you are strangers to this place, and may not know of our *prr-prr*-prowess."

Its croaking, groaning way of speech, as well as its honorable words, made Áine smile. She was content to leave her sword on her back. She offered a salute, her right hand straight and upwards, as if raising her visor in respect.

"Hail, ser knight," she said, the amusement in her voice clear to her companions. Leftworth thought that she had seemed lighter somehow, more jovial, since their final night at Shadowkhan. "We are strangers aboard this deathship. We seek this spirit terminal's astrological data to find our way. We will consult the spirits and continue on our journey as friends."

Strange words bubbled out of the frog-knight host.

There were a dozen of them or more, speaking in their own language that Leftworth's language matrices could not parse. It that sounded to Leftworth as the croaking and peeping of the frogs of the swamps. Their leader—or the one closest to Áine, anyway—spoke again.

"You may *cawl-cawl*-call me Sir Mire. This is my— your word—*warband*. We do not seek war, no, but will make it upon foes when honor calls for it."

"It is often called for, on board a deathship," Áine said.

"Yes."

"We have fought many foes here. We do not wish to fight you."

Sir Mire nodded slightly at this, then turned his frog-head to listen as his compatriots gurgled and croaked to him. He nodded again, then stepped forward another careful few feet. He held out his palm, revealing the soft, white skin beneath, spotted with black circles.

"*Trr-trr*-trade?"

Áine turned to Leftworth, eyebrows raised. He shrugged.

"What do you desire in trade? What has value to you?"

Sir Mire considered this by rubbing his webbed hand along the underside of his large mouth.

"It is not the thing that is important, but the *gess-gess*-gesture."

Áine nodded at this. She reached into the satchel at her waist, then produced a small pouch. She opened it and withdrew a pair of coins. The face of her lord—in his youth, more handsome, and very much not eaten alive on a beach on some moon deep in the Outremer—looked to the side in profile, stately and reposed. These she extended to Sir Mire.

"These coins are from our world, which is many systems distant. They are a reminder of our home, which we may never see again." She dropped them into his outstretched palm. He held them close to his face, examining them with a large, bulbous eye, before slipping them into a pouch on his belt. He then croaked, caustic and curt, and another, smaller frog—his squire, perhaps—shuffled forward, holding a small wooden box. He opened it, revealing to Áine a padded interior, home to several hand-length, ornate keys of a handcarved, smooth material. Bone.

"Of *grr-grr*-great use to travelers like yourselves, these ones," Sir Mire said. "Won or wrought at great cost to our *warr-warr*-warband.

Áine's face was solemn as she considered the keys.

"Many died for those coins, too," she said, which was true, but perhaps not in the same way. "You honor me with this trade." She went to select a key—the silver-lined one in the middle, but a rush of lavender perfume and a firm palm on her armored shoulder stayed her hand.

"No. We will need *that* one," Esshi said. She pointed her pointed claw to the red-stained skeleton key on the left. Áine took it and felt a rush of mountain cold. She heard the voice of a ghost, whispering solemnly—but then the moment passed and the key was secure in her satchel.

"Our trade is concluded," Sir Mire said. "A warning. Beware: a *wiz-wiz*-wizard."

"It's always goddamned wizards," Synod grumbled.

"We encountered a woman and her familiar, who attempted to bewitch us," Áine said. "They paid for their aggression with their lives. As did the sorcerer Mumret-Kah, whom we slew with the acolytes of the Shadowkhan Temple. We fear no wizard."

"What is death to a deathship?" Sir Mire croaked. "A second warning, then. An armored knight stalks these very halls, heralded by strange mist. Should the mist gather, you would do well to flee."

"We met a knight at a chapel, not far from here," Áine said. "He was kind and honorable, like you."

"He warned us of another," Synod said. "He was very insistent."

"Do not parlay with this other knight, do not seek to reason with him," Sir Mire said. Already his group was beginning to break position, moving past them to scurry down the dark halls beyond. "Run, if you value your lives. Stay and fight, if you *doo-doo*-do not."

"Thank you for the trade, your warning, and your kindness, honorable Sir Mire."

"Should we meet again, we will find one another in peace." The frogman put a webbed hand over his chest armor, then joined the others, who slipped silently into the shadows, graceful and sure.

45.

Grimlar and Esshi spent a moment looking over the ancient spirit terminal, searching for signs and symbols they might recognize.

"Here," the demoness said, pointing to a set of concave keys arrayed in a clustered spiral. Her claw tapped against the outer arm. "These mean *power* or *energy*, and *communion*."

Grimlar nodded at her to proceed. She pressed the buttons in sequence. The console began to hum. The screens flickered with columns of green text, flashing in brief salvos of light.

A lens projected a soft blue, semi-transparent skull that hovered above the keys. It rotated in place.

"Hello," Synod said. The others looked at him in surprise. The skull spun to face him.

"Greetings," the skull said, its voice light and reverberating. "You have awakened me."

"Oh, I am sorry," Synod said. "Were you sleeping well?"

"My sleep was troubled. What is your name?"

"Synod, my lady. What may I call you?"

"You may call me Miss Doss."

"It is a pleasure to meet you, Miss Doss. Would you be able to help us with something? We are looking for a docking bay."

"Working." The skull flickered. Bright blue light emanated from her eye sockets. "There are sixty-six docking bays aboard this deathship. Can you narrow your query?"

"Search for docking bays with operational systems," Leftworth said. "Those capable of receiving craft and remaining pressurized for human survival."

"Working." The skull rotated to face the shinobi. It opened its jaw, and a tumble of text and map data spilled out to collect in neat rows before it. "Twenty docking bays remain at full operational capacity, to include life support functions."

"Can you conduct internal scans?" Áine asked. "Look within that subset of docking bays in which vessels suitable for void flight are present."

"Now we are getting somewhere," the skull said. "Working." It vomited up a smaller array of data.

"Ten," Grimlar said. "And scattered across the four quadrants of the fortress. Can you give us descriptions of the craft within?"

The skull nodded. Streams of data flowed out of its nose sockets like ectoplasm, collecting against the ten locations. Grimlar leaned close. The data faded out.

"Bring that back, Miss Doss."

"I will, on one condition."

The group fell silent. Synod spoke up.

"Well?"

"Take me with you, Synod."

"I do not believe I can dislodge your console, let alone

carry it through a dangerous dungeon," he said.

"You will not have to," Miss Doss said. The console whirred and a panel flipped up, revealing a small set of gears that raised a bronze reception node. Between its tongs glowed a pulsing blue crystal, not unlike those Grimlar had taken from the reactor. "This binds my spirit to this plane, and to this console. I will reveal the location of your boat if you take me with you. I have spent many cold centuries bound to this node, to this console, and I desire novelty."

"Fine, great, all well and good," Grimlar said. "You can join the shipboard spirits in our transport's core. I have promised them release when we reach our destination. You can choose to remain or pass on with them."

The skull shimmered in a pleasant wash of blue light.

"These terms are acceptable. I will power down now. Place my crystal in your armor, lady knight, and I shall guide thee to thine transport." The skull hologram flickered and ceased; the console lens and screens drained of light and power. The crystal remained, a pulsing glow. The node *popped*, tongs releasing their grip. Áine reached for the crystal.

"Wait." Grimlar put out his hand to stay her grasp. He picked up the crystal, then held it up, passing it back and forth between his hands, examining it for damage and corruption. Finding none, he handed it to Áine. A compartment in her chest plate popped open, revealing three nodes. She placed the crystal in the center. Her suit whirred and, within her helmet, she heard the airy voice of the spirit emerge from the static.

Ahh. It feels good to inhabit the form of something else. I find this shape pleasing.

"Betray me not, spirit, or you will find mine armor less hospitable than your previous prison."

I could not do so even if I harbored you ill intent, o knight. Here, let me show you the way.

The holographic emitter on Áine's helm angled itself forward. The raven crest disappeared, replaced by a 3D holomap of this quadrant of the deathship. Áine's external vox modulator crackled and the voice of Miss Doss spoke to them from across the synthetic electronic wash of death itself.

"We are much closer than I would have supposed," the spirit said. *"I have taken the liberty of mapping the shortest, most direct route possible."* Dots of light appeared on the holographic map, representing their journey. *"Shall we proceed? I am anxious to leave this haunted tomb."*

46.

Shadows of soliders in familiar uniforms and armor beckoned to them from the dark. They called them by name. They asked: *Why did you leave us on that moon? Come back to us, comrades. The battle may yet be won...*

"*Do not listen to them,*" Miss Doss said through a wash of static in Áine's armor's speaker system. "*These phantasms mean us harm.*"

"How are they here?" Áine asked, expecting an answer from Grimlar. "How have they followed us into the heavens, into this place?"

"Perhaps it is we who followed them," the sorcerer said, hurrying ahead of Áine. The others moved at a fast pace, following the holographic map projected out before them from Áine's helm.

"You are speaking in riddles," Áine said.

"The shadows we encountered on Gorgon's Head are not consistent with my understanding of necromancy," he said between breaths. "I do not know how or why they were there, and I do not know why these shades harry us now. Perhaps it has something to do with time or gravity aboard and around the deathship."

Áine pumped her legs and drew on her armor's power reserves, sprinting ahead of the group to reach the next junction of metal corridors. Shadows grasped at them from alcoves, from the recesses between bundles of wire and pipes leaking white mist. Áine looked down both ways, seeing shadows gather along the walls and ceiling. She recognized some of the soldiers' faces, and her core went cold with despair.

Miss Doss projected a set of dots, leading them through a clutch of grasping darkness.

"This is not the path we took, initially," Leftworth said, catching up and watching the dots recede into the distance. "I recall a crypt."

"We may have been transported elsewhere or been subject to an illusion," Grimlar said. "Our memories may be affected by exposure to darkvoid radiation."

"So *much* darkvoid radiation!" Esshi said, wide eyes glowing purple in the dark. "I am excited to see what it does to you, my love."

"What it does to *us*," Áine said. "You will be changed, too, I would think."

The demoness revealed her fangs in a predatory smile. "A god is a process," she said.

"Come on," Leftworth said. "Let us hurry before these shadows block our way."

"The deathship is alive. Sentient, but not in the way a person is. Or parts of it are. That is what the voices in the static say."

"And what do you say?" Áine asked the spirit.

"We should keep moving. The mist gathers."

"What mist? What are you talking about?"

"Look to your feet."

Indeed, around Áine's metal boots, a low-hanging mist, blue and grey, swirled with the movement of the warband through the long, dark corridors of the deathship.

"What does it mean?"

"Ill omen."

"What does *that* mean?"

"Sir Mire's warning."

"Do not be coy with me, spirit. I will cast your crystal into the dark, and you will never leave this place."

"Neither would you. Do not threaten me, child. It is just that...perhaps the deathship can feel me. Feel us. Seeking escape."

"Why would that be a problem? Why would it care? It is vast and mighty, we are small and insignificant to it."

"Have you done insignificant things since boarding the deathship? You survived. You are covered in darkvoid radiation. Infused with it. It will be a wonder if you remain human for long."

"What are you saying?"

"Ser Kard." Synod stood before her, waving his hand in front of her helm to gain her attention. "We need the spirit to open the docking bay portal."

"I am going to disconnect you, spirit, and set you in a local node. I will take you with us, aboard our vessel."

"I have no choice but to trust you. But know that if I am left behind, when I find a way out of this crystal, I will

find you, and haunt and vex you."

"You haunt and vex me already. Now to your labor." Áine popped the crystal out of the node in her armor, then set it down in a cobweb-covered recess next to the sealed docking bay door.

"Did we leave this way?" Synod asked. "So much of this does not look familiar."

"The deathship changes," Grimlar said.

"As will you," Esshi said.

"For someone so charming, my lady, you sure know how to make a man shiver," Synod said.

"Oh I certainly *do*," she hissed, softly. Synod laughed nervously. Grimlar looked anywhere but at his companions.

The door groaned and opened in fits, the top and bottom portions pulling away from one another in pained separation. The warband slipped inside, weapons at the ready. Áine followed them, stopping to look back down the corridor. The mist grew heavier, rising several feet into the air. She remembered the spirit crystal, then plucked it from the node. The doors hissed and ground in pain, but shut again.

The docking bay was much as they had left it. The great doors were open to space, and the low hum of the energy field that protected the bay was a pleasing tone. The darkvoid energies beyond swirled in agitation, red and purple, like flowing gases in a pool illuminated by ghostly lights.

Before them was the landing craft, untouched and impassive, shimmering with the light of the mysteries beyond. Condensation gathered along the hull, even in the air that carried with it the icy chill of deep space.

"Something is coming," Esshi said. "Do not let my pact-mate die, knight."

"We are agreed that the sorcerer should live." Áine turned back to the sealed doors and drew her greatsword.

"Good," Esshi said. She looked to Grimlar, then pointed at a spot on the deck behind her several paces away. The sorcerer stood back and behind the demoness, not questioning her order or combat prowess.

"Perhaps you could be motivated to see to the survival of the rest of us," Áine said. "As friends and allies to your beloved."

"Well." Esshi raised her claws before her. Purple energy arced between her sharp talons.

"The mist gathers."

Áine pressed a release on her helm, and her mouth was revealed to the cool air of the docking bay. She watched her breath exhale as steam, a different consistency and color than the blue-tinged mist that clung to their ankles, that even now swirled and churned around them as a waterborne predator circling its prey.

Something scraped against the metal docking bay doors. The scraping became a probing, metal-on-metal sound. Then it *boomed*, an impact leaving no doubt as to its intent.

"Corporal Synod, on my left, several feet back."

"Yes, mum."

"Let my armor be your shield. Strike at range."

"Yes, ser."

More strikes against the door. Metal bulged and groaned.

"Leftworth, see if you can get a good vantage point on that door. Open fire the moment a target presents itself.

"As you wish." The shinobi slipped into long shadows.

"Grimlar, since you are infused with darkvoid, perhaps you can expend some of it in our defense?"

"I have something special in mind."

The doors bent inward, warping and preparing to give way.

"And our esteemed lady, Esshi—I would hope your talents extend beyond being a pain in my ass?"

"Just stay out of my way, knight," Esshi said, a crazed excitement coming over her. She leaned forward, biting her supple bottom lip, eyes wide and alight with boiling purple illumination. Her claws were arrayed above her head as a crown of death. Black wings stirred beneath the folds of her robes, pushing their way out through slits in the fabric to spread wide.

The doors collapsed inward. Follow-on blows knocked them completely out of alignment, curling them up and down, revealing a misshapen hole large enough for a warband to pass through. Mist drifted out to them from the darkness. Patient moments passed as they awaited the appearance of their new foe.

"Are you the strongest of your house?" A hearty, reverberating voice echoed to them from the dark.

The lower part of Áine's helmet resealed over her mouth. She held her sword at her right shoulder, then stepped forward, lowering the massive blade to point out, horizontal to the deck. She could strike, parry, or receive a charge in this familiar stance.

"What calls to us?" Áine asked.

"A servant of the deathship, o knight."

"Sent to stop us?"

"Or to strengthen you in fire."

"What?"

"Who can know the mind of a deathship?"

"It does not have a mind."

"Your ignorance is excusable. You have been aboard only a short while. Let my illuminate you with martial wisdom."

Darkness and shadow moved within the mist gathered at the blown-out docking bay doors. Armor glimmered in the light of the darkvoid. Áine was at first reminded of Tahir, the great revenant-knight in the shrine beneath the great skeleton. But this knight's armor was different, though no less fearsome. His helm and shoulders were adorned with demonic visage; bulging eyes upon his pauldrons. Twice as tall as even the tallest among them, with powered plate armor that was darkest blue and black, fists the size of great rocks.

The revenant-knight ducked beneath the wreckage of the doors to set foot within the docking bay. He held an oversized poleaxe, its blade alive with crackling purple darkvoid energy. The visor of his helm was a single, long eye, glowing red and trailing energy as he moved inexorably toward them.

47.

I call to thee, once more, warriors: are you the strongest of your house?" His voice was reverberation and echo, booming and ominous. He paused to lift the visor of his helm, revealing a curved glass screen for a face, upon which a malignant skull seethed, its eyes burning with darkvoid fire.

Esshi looked to Áine, giving her a nod to go on. *Say something.*

"The strongest of our house are all dead," Áine said, her voice echoing back to her weakly from the shadowy reaches of the docking bay. "We are what remains."

The armored titan considered this in silence. Then he brought his poleaxe across his chest and held it with both gauntlets.

"If you live, and the others are dead, then you are the strongest." He took a step forward, his footfalls heavy and thundering across the metal floor. *"I admire your knightly humility, ser. You shall make an honorable foe."*

"Please, ser, we—"

"I wish to test my might against yours."

"We do not wish to fight you."

"Death looks much the same with honor as without. I

have long forgotten my name, but know, in bringing about your death, that I serve the deathship, and soon, so shall you."

The titan-knight set his visor back down, lowered his shoulder, and charged, poleaxe held out with its tip pointed toward Áine, then brought back to his left in anticipation of a sweeping attack. Áine's sword was still pointed forward. She could hold or break.

She chose to hold. *Fuck it.*

The poleaxe's blade made for Áine's armor in a wide, sweeping arc as the revenant-knight bore down on her. Esshi leapt to the side. Áine stepped *into* the charge in the split-second before the blade found her. Her arms quivered with adrenaline and the flow of aether. Her blade split the titan's chest plate at its center, revealing hissing blue steam. The desiccated hands of spirits reached out from within, grasping at the torn edges to pull themselves free.

Even with the assistance of her mighty armor, the shock of the revenant-knight's charge into her sword was enough to knock it loose. Her hands unclenched in pain, the gauntlets losing their grip on the hilt. Her foe roared as Áine dropped to the ground, her sword clattering against the deck. His poleaxe swung over her helm, narrowly missing, but his right arm barreled into hers, stunning it into numbness. Damage warnings flared on her heads-up display, not that she needed the reminder.

The revenant-knight slid to a kneeling halt. Esshi floated above him, flapping her wings at a safe distance before diving down to work her talons against the flared armor along his neck. She fluttered away before his clumsy gauntlet could seize her.

This distraction bought time for her lover to complete his preparations. Grimlar pointed both hands at the enemy knight. Pools of spinning vapor appeared like numbers on a clock face. Lines of grey-blue matter erupted from each, then spread out in expansion, forming vaguely humanoid forms in the gloom and mist. The size of children, these muck-creatures waddled toward the revenant-knight, squelching and sure in their blind advance.

Another ghost—long-faced, all gangly arms and long fingers, no legs to speak of—slipped out of the wound that Áine's sword had wrought in the enemy knight's armor. He roared, then pressed his armor closed again with a groan of metal.

The first slime creature summoned by Grimlar reached him at that moment, grabbing his legs and holding him in place, a pillar of jelly challenging a giant. He grabbed at it, coming away with handfuls of grey-blue muck. His strength was such that he easily pulled free, but others piled in, determined in their mission not to destroy him, but to slow him down.

Green aether bolts cut through the dark, finding purchase in his neck and helm, *one, two, three.* These bolts shimmered as the revenant shuddered. Then he stomped his considerable legs and feet, the slime ceatures splattered, one after another. Leftworth prepared another volley, but the knight was already marching toward Áine, who was just now scrambling back to her feet. Synod stepped up, pike flaring with power, leveraging it in challenge and defense of Ser Kard. The titan grabbed the pike at its blade. Energy hummed and whined as it upcycled aether. The knight's gauntlet split and shook as it crushed the blade, suffocating its power at great cost to his own hand. Synod could barely hold on. The giant waved the weapon away, over his shoulder, and Synod went tumbling with it. He landed on the deck with a *crunch*.

The levyman had done well in buying Áine time. She was on her feet.

"Find my sword!" she shouted, to no one in particular. Then she ran. She thought to lead their foe away from the rest of the group, to buy them time to—to do *something*. The revenant-knight had already suffered several wounds from their short skirmish. He could not keep fighting on at this rate forever.

Could he?

Áine shoved those thoughts aside and focused on the only plan remaining to her: survive the fight. You cannot defeat an opponent if you are dead. That felt like good wisdom. Maybe she would live to pass it on.

She risked a glance back. The enemy knight mercifully ignored Synod, who lay on the deck, unmoving. Esshi floated down to the fallen levyman, eyes glowing purple with power.

The knight's charge brought much needed clarity to Áine's thoughts. She summoned her armor's strength and sprinted for the landing craft. The belly of the boat was a welcome sight—until she remembered that she did not know how to open the gods-damned thing.

"Grimlar!" she shouted. "Get this thing open!"

Her words were absorbed by a blast of purple lightning that streaked across the bay, spiking toward the charging revenant-knight and narrowly missing him.

Áine dove away from the landing craft as the knight

reached her far faster than she had anticipated. Metal groaned and snapped; powered armor pumped and fired off aether exhaust. On her back, Áine lifted her head to see her foe struggling to disentangle himself from the outer hull of the boat, now a ruin of impacted metal, venting out air from rent piping, sputtering electrical and aether charge from ruined bundles of wires.

"No," Áine gasped.

The revenant-knight dislodged his poleaxe from the ship. Flushed with the blue-green glow of aether discharge, he stood out in the dark, an irradiated monster ready to destroy them all.

"*No more trickery, knight-errant,*" the titan intoned, his voice like the hollow ringing of a funeral bell. "*Only combat. Find some honor in death.*"

"You speak like a pampered lord," Áine said, getting to her feet. She held out her gauntlets in fighting stance. "You waylay lost pilgrims and travelers. You stalk frogmen in tin armor. You know *nothing* of honor."

The revenant paused. Her words had wounded him in a way that none of their other attacks had. With a cry of fury, he charged this diminutive foe who dared lay insult upon his brow. He held his poleaxe out to his side to catch her in another sweeping attack.

Memories of Koh flowed to Áine, unbidden. Their night of love, yes, but also of their training, of their battle in the arena. The Shadowkhan Way taught them to move slower than their instinct demanded, but they traded that speed for deliberateness and strength. One could let the natural flow of the body's movements and kinetic energy empower them in close-quarters combat.

Áine stepped into the charge, focusing her aether-augmented strength by launching her left fist into the wound in his chest plate, then spun back and away at the last moment. He grabbed for her but only succeeded in knocking her off balance. Her armor adjusted for the fall and helped her brace her back foot, keeping her upright. More ghostly fingers pressed at the gaping, newly reopened slash in the revenant's chest. He dropped his poleaxe and used his hand to hold his armor shut. Instead of charging again, the knight stalked forward, patiently bearing down on Áine even as he struggled to contain the spirits trapped within.

Áine readied for another charge.

"Your wizard has your ship open," Miss Doss said.

"What?"

"Is there something you can use in the ship?"

It was as good an idea as any.

"He does not like being called a wizard."

"I will apologize to him if he survives this."

Áine turned suddenly and made for the lowered ramp. Grimlar was already retreating, light dancing between his hands. Áine stepped through a shower of green aether sparks and was aboard.

The revenant-knight walked up to the ramp and searched the dark for his foe. She was gone. Furious at being denied his prey, he stalked around to the aft side of the boat, finding an array of aether-fueled boosters. He grunted and swung his free fist, delivering powerful blow after powerful blow to the cupped shields and the grated vents, punching off metal and releasing sparks of green energy and blue-green liquid fuel. His fury was magnificent as he roared and smashed apart layers of shielding to reach and destroy the vital internal systems that allowed the vessel flight.

The boat was wounded well beyond the possibility of repair.

48.

Leftworth approached the enraged monster. He raised his crossbow, took careful aim, and fired. The green bolt struck true, into the right back shoulder of the knight. The blue-green fuel spilling out of the landing craft like blood sparked and alighted, consuming the knight's armor. He whirled around, enraged, enflamed, death and fire, fire and death. Ghosts pulled themselves free of his chest wound. He pulled his broken demonic-eye visor off, revealing his holographic skull-face flickering in pained static.

A bolt of purple light erupted from Grimlar's open left palm, followed quickly by one from his right. The darkvoid energy, concentrated and attuned to harmonization with the wild bursts of light beyond the energy field of the docking bay, melted off hot handfuls of slag from the revenant knight's armor. He turned to stare death at the scholar, but his legs took him on an inexorable course toward the shinobi, who hurried to reset the crossbow for another volley of aether bolts.

Inside the gun pod, Áine forced her bulky, armored form into the gunner's seat. Pieces of the armrests snapped off and clattered to the floor.

"Spirit, I am going to place your crystal in the console. Have you any experience with void guns?"

"My lady, I have never even heard the term."

"I am sure you are a quick study." Áine pulled the crystal from the terminal in her armor, then slammed it down into the waiting receptacle built into the wall of the pod. Light spread from the crystal throughout the transparent wires of the system. Those lines of light receded, then grew out again, as the spirit struggled to extend its influence across an unfamiliar network.

"Spirit!" Áine shouted. She flipped several large, long switches, summoning the aft spotlights. She turned cranks to train them on the revenant-knight. From this high up on the boat, he looked small—but Grimlar and Leftworth, nearby, were even smaller. "Spirit! Gods damn you, wake up!"

Áine banged her gauntlet against the wall. That did it. Blue energy rushed through wires encased in transparent glass, humming, all systems coming online. Áine swiveled the pod down, pointing out over the edge of the curve of the boat's hull, the damage to the thrusters visible even from her vantage point.

The revenant-knight stalked toward her allies. Áine found the titan in the display screen, placing him between the twin targeting squares. She flipped a switch on the lefthand grip, her right preparing to press the trigger. The screen flickered.

"Restore power to the gun, Miss Doss! I only need a moment!"

The spirit's voice crackled through the pod's comm speakers, quiet and distant.

"I do not...the strength...prepared for..."

"Then have the strength to die well, as we all must!"

"This...too great...burden."

Áine's wrath subsided. Her voice went low and soft.

"I know, spirit. I know."

The pod hummed and whined as energy surged. The targeting screen lit up, brighter than before, the wires shedding blue light, the turret controls alive in the knight's hands. Something above Áine burst, sending down a rain of green aether sparks.

The first shot went just wide. The knight stopped, then turned to look up at her, his holographic face a demon's masque of surprise and fury. One of Leftworth's bolts struck him from behind. A blast of purple, brilliant light sliced through his left arm, releasing it from his shoulder.

Áine put that miserable, inhuman screen-face between the targeting squares, and fired.

49.

The nameless revenant-knight, terror of pilgrims and travelers, blind vengeance of the deathship, was reduced to liquified biomechanical sludge. His weapon lay forgotten. His armor was reduced to puddles of steaming-hot liquid, deadly to the touch. Shards of his face-screen remained, pixelated out in terminal error.

Esshi helped Synod maintain his balance as he winced in pain. She helped him pick up his broken weapon. The blade was mangled beyond repair. The systems that infused it with aetheric power were dark, its channels shattered open. He shook his head and let it fall to the deck. Esshi pointed to the revenant-knight's poleaxe and helped him limp over to it.

Synod went down to a knee with a grunt, then examined the dreadful weapon. The blade was sure and sharp, and the telltale glow of aetheric crystals led up along the pole to the metal of the axeblade itself. His hands found the control module at the base of the pole. He depressed an azure jewel, and the poleaxe hummed to life, glowing brightly with power and the promise of imminent violence. Carefully, slowly, Synod took the weapon into his gloved hands, then lifted with his legs.

Esshi held out a hand to help him keep his balance. He stood and the poleaxe hummed with pleasure in his grip. He braced his legs for greater balance, then, with a grunt, swung the weapon outwards, back and forth, his arms burning pleasantly with the effort.

"Heavier and taller than I'm used to, by far," he said. "But with a little practice..." He brought the weapon to his side and set it straight up, as if he were falling into formation.

They looked to the boat. Grimlar disappeared into the hold. Leftworth followed him up the ramp.

"Are you well enough to walk?" Esshi asked Synod. He nodded, and they followed their comrades into the wounded landing craft.

The great sphere of hexagonal tiles was alive with light and color, the ghosts within aware that their home was in danger. A screen flickered to life, revealing swirling, humanoid mists floating in a plane of black and blue underlight.

"What is the meaning of all this? Who could fire *our* gunpod? We are detecting damage to the cargo hold and the engines. We *cannot* achieve voidflight under such conditions."

Áine pressed a gemmed button, which popped up a flap along the chamber's outer curve. A row of ten empty nodes awaited. She pressed the crystal into the leftmost one, then closed the flap.

The spirits on the screen stirred. Whispered voices of

the dead, quiet and incoherent, signaled their assembly and reception of the newcomer. The familiar skull appeared on the screen, confirming successful upload.

"You will have to explain to them that we are, indeed, stranded," Áine said.

"They know what I know, now," Miss Doss said. "They know you fought to save the boat."

"As did you."

"It almost killed me. Again."

"I know. Thank you for your strength."

The skull bobbed in the flows of the aether.

"Please know we meant to free you," Grimlar said. "I meant to free you all. But we are stuck here, aboard this deathship, as are you."

"We know," the skull said, acceptance in its voice. "We...appreciate it. We do not regret helping you."

"Should we power down your systems?" Áine asked. "What would you have us do?"

The skull flickered and bobbed, subsumed by spectral fog for a few moments, before returning in clarity.

"Leave the ship's power on. In fact, draw full power from this docking bay. I—we—think we know what the deathship will do next."

"What do you mean?"

"We have been prisoners in systems cleaved from broader networks for too long. We have conferred and reached a consensus. We seek a new experience. A new way of being."

"Do you wish to be released unto death, no longer bound here?"

"No, not yet. Entropy will destroy any mechanical

system in time. We desire instead…communion.”

“I do not understand,” Áine said. Esshi clapped her hands together, her face lit up in understanding.

“How exciting,” she said. “Come, let us do as they ask. I want to see this.”

The warband split between the spirit chamber and the bridge, activating systems in sequence, careful to channel and modulate power levels not to strain the spirits but to maximize the flow of aether across the boat.

They need not have been so careful. With the addition of the new ghost, their strength was more robust and durable than before, harmonizing with the fresh intelligence in a way it had not in decades. Motivated by the promise of new experience, the ghosts worked harder and faster than they thought themselves capable. Wires and display units lit up across the vessel. Screens and displays dumped out sensory input. The doors opened and shut, as if the spirits walked the decks.

With the boat humming and alive, the warband made their way back down through its corridors and hatches to the cargo hold. Áine tapped a still-functional screen near the breach as the others passed back out into the docking bay. She removed her helm.

“We are departing, spirits.”

“You have our thanks,” Miss Doss said. “We will see new regions of space. We will lend our wills to the great song. We will see and experience. It will be glorious.”

“Won’t it bear you ill will? For helping us?”

"It is beyond such petty concerns. Would a storm be angered by a breeze flowing in the other direction? Or does such a thing merely become part of the greater whole?"

Áine considered this.

"I am still me. I fight to determine mine own destiny."

"An interesting perspective. One limited by the illusory bars of your understanding. No, your destiny lies within the darkvoid, as does ours."

Something clanged against the hull. The power fluctuated; lights dimmed and then grew brighter, the skull on the screen shimmered and shook in destabilized digitized ecstasy.

"Good luck to you and your companions," Miss Doss said. "We shall be as one in…darkvoid…"

The screen became a field of deep, flowing blue, liquid clouds in spectral heavens, rolling and crashing against one another. The spirit was gone. Áine left the screen, making for the ramp. She joined the others outside of the vessel that had once been their salvation from Gorgon's Head. Now it would serve as something else for the spirits within. A tomb, torn asunder, now birthing canal for something new and wondrous.

Armored frogmen scurried around the docking bay, lifting panels from the floor using long metal tools. They revealed ports, bundles of wires, and connecting lines from the deck to form a network between the landing craft and the deathship. Visible through the docking bay's energy field, the darkvoid swirled, concentrated and luminous, in a state of excitement.

"It is good to see you again, my friends." Sir Mire of

the Deep appeared before Áine, webbed right hand to the side of his helmet in awkward salute. Áine returned the gesture.

"And you, Sir Mire. But, why are you here? Not that your presence is unwelcome."

Sir Mire pointed to the pool of slag that was the revenant-knight.

"We have fought that foe many times, and at great cost to ourselves. We owe you much for destroying him."

"Sir Tahir spoke of your bravery, and of the debt he owed you for intervening in a previous battle."

"Ah. A knight of great honor. We are blessed to know him."

"Sir Mire, what are you doing to our vessel?"

"It is wounded. It cries out to the deathship. We responded. There shall be a union. A joining. Not unlike—a mating." Leftworth chuckled and Áine raised an eyebrow.

"It is a holy event. You are blessed to see it yourselves. See, even now." Sir Mire gestured behind him. The armored frogs stood in a wide circle around the landing craft. The wires, tubes, and bundles connecting the darkship's deck to the boat glowed purple and blue, with energies flowing to and from the broken vessel. The frogs raised their webbed hands high, and the humming of inhuman throats and mysterious energies harmonized into a cascade of sound not unlike that of the swamp at night, rhythmic and soothing.

The wires and tubes went dark, and whatever power had once been within the landing craft was gone. Áine knew the spirits were no longer aboard but were elsewhere, within the great ship, now *of* the ship.

Sir Mire gave a subtle wave of his hand. The armored frogmen followed him past the landing craft to the outer edge of the docking bay, where they gathered to watch the swirling energies of the darkvoid at play in the cosmos.

Another rush of sound and vibration filled the bay, subsuming all else. The deck shook and the air warbled. Leftworth grabbed onto Áine's arm as Esshi, Grimlar, and the wounded Synod held each other upright amid the shaking. The frogs crouched, reverting to their animal-like forms, sitting still and balanced on all fours, even in their armor, which proved more flexible than it appeared. Áine recognized the skill and craftsmanship of their armorers and smiths to fashion such lightweight and flexile material, and she understood at once, much to her shame, that she had underestimated these creatures, even after all she had seen and experienced. There was still so much to learn.

The darkvoid deathship began to move, the entire superstructure pushed forward by a litany of unseen boosters powered by four mighty aetheric reactors.

The darkvoid energy beyond the docking bay swirled into a kaleidoscope of color and light, whirling gaseous clouds aglow, shimmering after-images of time, refracted space. Coming undone. Reforming anew. Light and sound and the fury of ancient suns, forgotten in the long forward march of time. X-ray effect; radiation infusing human bones with glimmering energy, starlight, particles that should be deadly instead unleashing something within and of the bodies built to temporarily house consciousness. The light. Slivers and glimmers of *universal* consciousness in partition. Elemental energies flowing from beyond space and time, through it, across it, transversal forward and back, the distinction meaningless from the correct perspective. *Darkvoid* being too reductive a term for such grand potential and beauty.

The face of her father, in radiance and love. The smiles of her comrades at rest. The embrace of Koh in pleasure. The smile of another—a dark, powerful woman whom she will one day love. Her own face, staring back at her, in warmth and understanding, at the end of all shame and suffering.

Visions of darkvoid-swept future:

A great tower looming over a mountain fortress, purple lightning striking across the sky. Within its highest window, Grimlar the Great, eyes alight with darkvoid energy, and at his side, his succubus consort, in power and radiance and beauty.

Another flash of unnatural lightning. The great doors of the mountaintop fortress opening, and rows of knights in deepest black powered armor, twisted and infused by darkvoid energies, marching forth. And at the head of their formation, a warrior of impossible strength, a knight-errant no longer.

Ser Áine Kard, warmaster of a legion of terror.

The darkvoid deathship transitioned into the malleable flow of space and time, and all souls aboard were bound to it dand with it, toward what destiny may await them.

50.

It was many hours later when the humans, the succubus, and their amphibian companions returned to what they might understand as normative space and consciousness. The whirling light show of cosmic destiny, hallucination, and spiritual rapture that was the deathship's transition into and voyage through the darkvoid released its hold on their minds one by one, offering in its place a post-ecstatic peace of spirit and warmth of body.

Grimlar's tears spilled out against the palms of his hands. Esshi wrapped herself around his shoulders, her usual confidence broken, her face human in its profound awe. Synod felt no pain but stood upright and proud with his new weapon, mouth ajar as he searched for visions and augurs in the swirling energies beyond the docking bay's energy field. Leftworth had removed his green and black hood to feel the light of the cosmos upon his face. Áine was on her knees, bent forward as if in rigorous prayer.

"Twin stars," Synod said. "They are angry. I think they are dying."

They appeared out of the gloam of post-transition

space, formed from the swirling mists of the cosmos.

"This is impossible," Áine said, sitting up. "What I saw is impossible."

"There are greater wonders than these, before us, Áine," Grimlar said. "We both know it to be so." The familiar smell of the wizard's weed wafted over them all. Grimlar handed the burning joint to Esshi, who took an enthusiastic puff and offered it to Áine. The knight shrugged, emotionally and physically exhausted, and shared in the smoke, as did they all.

Basking in the radiation wash of cosmic decay and the touch of the wizard's weed on their minds, they rested and enjoyed the beauty of death at system's scale. Energy pulsed and rushed about this quadrant of the deathship as solar collection panels turned toward the dying suns to collect the radiological gift of their death throes.

The frogmen prayed and sang hymns in the language of supplicants.

They all watched and sang and smoked until the stars flickered into darkness, the timescale of their death somehow accelerated, somehow beautiful and wondrous, a miracle to be witnessed by the living and the dead.

When the stars had died, truly and fully, Sir Mire and his knightly frogs led the warband away from the docking bay and the wonders beyond. The corridors of the deathship were alive. Screens previously dormant and dust-ridden pulsed with datastreams, spinning vector graphics, local star charts, engineering data. Lights pulsed a calming blue. Running lights along the floor, color coded for navigation, led them deeper inside. The atmosphere was one of life and welcome rather than the dismal, dangerous gloom of their arrival.

As they followed Sir Mire, a familiar skull appeared on screens along their path.

"There is a gate, not far now, that will lead you from this ship, if that is what you desire."

"What of you? How was your…transition?" Áine asked.

"Erotic."

"Is that good?"

"I am not purely the being with whom you first spoke," the skull said. "I am something more now, greater. This graphical representation is meant to project friendliness and familiarity to calm your animal mind."

"I see. What is the gate you mentioned?"

"We—I—have alighted the path of your armored escort. You can use the gate, or choose to remain aboard."

"Now that you are part of the ship—does that mean the ship is amiable toward us? That we are welcome?"

The screens displaying the skull whirred and a rain of pixelated distortion signaled the processing for the proper response.

"I am permitted—deigning—to tell you, Ser Kard, that your question is meaningless."

"Escape from the deathship after all, then."

"Perhaps," Grimlar said. "We do not know where a stoneway gate will take us."

"I am willing to try for it," Leftworth said.

"As am I," Synod said. "I have had my fill of terrors

and wonders, for now."

"But perhaps we will return," Esshi said, the smile on her face and curve of her eyebrows indicating that she found this all quite entertaining.

"We shall take our chances with this gate," Áine said. The skull nodded, then was subsumed by the datastream.

There were skulls aplenty built into the stoneway gate itself, piled among stone and mortared in formation, impassive smiles and black eye sockets greeting the travelers within the terminal corridor. It stood well over the height of a knight in powered armor, and wide enough to pass through two abreast. Within its arch was a flat, black plane, indistinct and swirling in subtle patterns.

The frogmen hopped excitedly to each side of the stoneway gate, forming parallel rows as honor guard for their departing guests, still and disciplined as any soldiers Áine had known. Sir Mire bowed low before her.

"Good luck to you, fighters of honor and renown. For slaying the revenant-knight, we will honor thee with a song, and would welcome your return aboard this deathship should destiny and darkvoid guide you to safe return."

Áine extended a gauntlet, taking Sir Mire's tiny hand within her own.

"Good-bye, Sir Mire. May you fare well in sojourn across this haunted fortress."

"It is our home," he said and, uncertain of the ritual, withdrew his hand. Then he stepped back to join his comrades in formation, standing rigid at attention. He croaked, and the frogmen snapped their weapons up before them in salute.

Áine looked to her comrades. Their eyes were on her. She donned her helm, her human face disappearing beneath a mask of resolute metal. She walked toward the stoneway gate, willing to face whatever it might bring, whatever it might put before them, wherever it might lead them. For she—they—had faced the travails of doomed crusade and the deep terrors of a darkvoid deathship, both.

They had endured, survived, and grown in strength.

Whatever lay before the warband was theirs to challenge and conquer.

EPILOGUE

The cold wind brought with it a taste of mountain air, invigorating as they made their rigorous journey over the dirt road that wound through deep forest. The earthy, wet smell of the land was a welcome counter to the oil, ozone, and incense of the deathship, which had been so pervasive as to not even be noticeable until they had left it behind. But this country was free of the mark of technology thus far, as not even the road they walked on hinted at the passing and impression of wheels.

They camped for one night, resting peacefully in the deep wood, and, seeing no sign of others, risked a fire. They slept under boughs laden with leaves beginning to turn their colors in the first paintbrush strokes of autumn. The stars were visible in patches through the boughs of pines and leafed trees alike, and while unfamiliar, bore no sign of darkvoid or the movement of starships. They slept deep and well, and did not dream of the future.

The next day, they found the village.

The road wound through stone ruins, first, and then through an area of low hills bearing graves whose stones were dulled by time. The trees broke ranks to reveal great fields and plains pockmarked with distant, lonely houses, and the great grey mountains, sharp and imposing, beyond. They left the road, which died here regardless, and walked through fields of corn and pumpkin vine toward the nearest cluster of buildings.

Áine Kard tuned her armor's power levels to minimal augmentation, careful to conserve its energies for whatever might lay ahead. Her sword, tall and imposing even when left magnetized on her back, felt heavier these last few miles. She did not complain. It would not have done her any good, for it was her burden to bear.

Soon they reached a new road, one wider and well kept, with stone in long stretches and the recent scat of passing horses. This led them over a stone bridge in good repair, and toward houses whose chimneys breathed smoke into the grey sky. Human forms bent low in neat rows of field, or drove beasts of burden. Children ran and tumbled, laughing. None had seen them. There was no guard to speak of, no toll, no checkpoint. Not even a bored youth playing at local militia.

Maybe they are in need of a scholar's wisdom or a knight's sword, Áine thought.

She looked to her companions. Their faces were set and hard, but weariness spoke to her from their eyes, their drooping shoulders, their slow steps. These were warriors, proud and unbroken, but tired. The warband had been shouldering their weapons—their burdens—for far too long.

Maybe these people need ronin to protect them from bandits, wolves, or the tyranny of petty lords, she thought.

Or, perhaps, they are in need of nothing at all.

The warband will continue their adventures in

Darkvoid
Deathmage

About the Author

Jonathan Raab is the author of *The Mausoleum of Gore: A Halloween TV Special*, *Project Vampire Killer*, *The Haunting of Camp Winter Falcon*, and more. He is the designer of the *Vampyrvania* and *Splatter Zone* tabletop games and edited the anthologies *Euroschlock Nightmares* and *Behold the Undead of Dracula*. His short fiction has appeared in numerous magazines and anthologies, including *The Best Horror of the Year*, Volume Fourteen. He lives in Gothic upstate New York with his wife and son.

About the Cover Artist

Lukasz Kowalczuk is a prolific Polish creator and illustrator working in comics and tabletop games. He writes, draws, and teaches workshops. His work can be found in anthologies, including *GWAR: Enormogantic Fail, FutureQuake, Everything Is Going Wrong: Comics on Punk and Mental Illness, Kayfabe: A Wrestling Anthology*, and more, and in zines and magazines including *Atomic Elbow, SLASHDANCE, WYRD Science, Strange Kids Club*, and *Unwinnable*. His art is featured in tabletop RPGs and wargames such as *Kosmosaurs, Space Weirdos*, and *Neon Lords of the Toxic Wasteland*.

About the Editor

Steve Grinstead edits books, magazine features, and exhibitions for publishers, museums, and other nonprofits. Recent titles he has edited include Jonathan Raab's previous two works, *Project Vampire Killer* and *The Mausoleum of Gore*. He is the coauthor of *Walking Into Colorado's Past: 50 Front Range History Hikes*, winner of the Colorado Book Award for Nonfiction. He lives in Denver and Salida, Colorado.